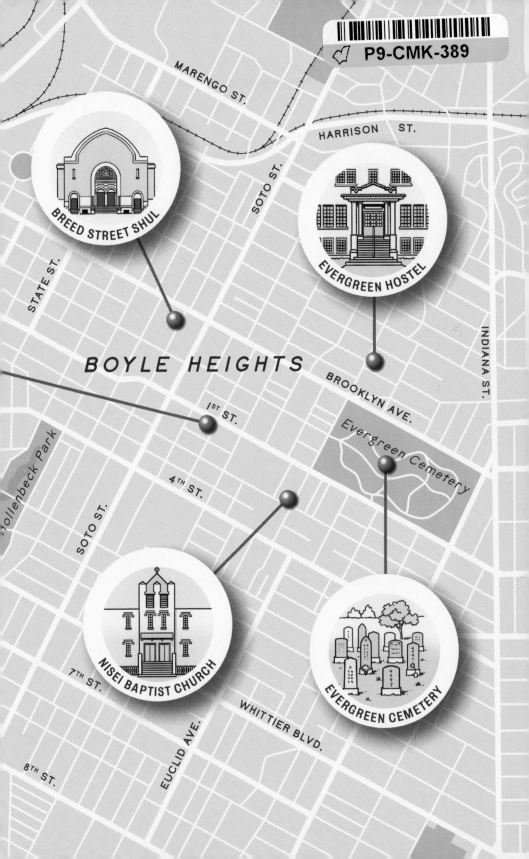

Praise for *Clark and Division*

Winner of the Mary Higgins Clark Award

Winner of The Lefty Award for Best Historical Novel

Nominated for the Agatha Award for Best Historical Novel

An Anthony Award Nominee for Best Novel

Reader's Digest 60 Best Books Written
for Women by Female Authors

A *New York Times* Best Mystery Novel of the Year

A *Parade* Magazine 101 Best Mystery Books of All Time

A *New York Times Book Review* Editors' Choice

A *Washington Post* Best Mystery and Thriller of the Year

A *South Florida Sun-Sentinel* Best Mystery Novel of the Year

A *Milwaukee Journal-Sentinel* Best Book of the Year

Barnes & Noble Best Books of the Year

Amazon Best Mysteries and Thrillers of the Year

A CrimeReads Best Crime Novel of the Year

New York Public Library Best Books of the Year

A *BookPage* Best Mystery & Thriller of the Year

An ABA Indie Next Pick

An Amazon Best of the Month for Mystery/Thriller

An Apple Best Books of the Month

Bustle's Most Anticipated Books

"Crime fiction is at its best when telling a compelling story while also analyzing the shadowy foundations of human nature. Very few writers do that better than Hirahara."

—S.A. Cosby, *The Washington Post*

"A beautifully written novel. A telling and touching story that echoes across the decades. Naomi Hirahara uses the past to inspire us to be relentless in doing the right thing, right now."

—Michael Connelly, bestselling author of the Harry Bosch series

"*Clark and Division* opened my heart and mind to specifics of the experience of Japanese Americans during the Second World War. Rich in period detail, it is page-turning historical fiction, a tender family story, and a mystery that plays on two levels: *What happened to Rose Ito?* and *At what cost are Japanese Americans finally seen as full Americans?* It's a story that moved me deeply."

—Attica Locke, *New York Times* bestselling author of *Heaven, My Home*

"Part historical fiction, part thriller, all a deeply moving family story, set in 1944 Chicago against the backdrop of the shameful treatment of Japanese Americans by the US government. Hirahara's gifted writing is a master class in how to bring a historical epoch to life."

—Sara Paretsky, bestselling author of the Chicago detective VI Warshawski series

"A heart-stopping crime novel woven inextricably into another, much larger atrocity: the treatment of Japanese Americans during World War II . . . In this immersive and resonant tale, Naomi Hirahara has given us the very best of what we hope for from historical crime fiction: a novel that is both intensely researched and deeply felt."

—Amy Stewart, *New York Times* bestselling author of the Kopp sisters novels

"One part mystery. One part historical fiction. In Naomi Hirahara's expert hands that 1+1 equation somehow equals 10, leaving you with a story that is enthralling, enlightening, and edifying."

—Jamie Ford, *New York Times* bestselling author of *Hotel on the Corner of Bitter and Sweet*

"Gripping . . . This immersive true-crime historical mystery novel takes place in Chicago in 1944, at the height of the mass incarceration of Japanese Americans." —*Ms. Magazine*

"A moving, eye-opening depiction of life after Manzanar. Naomi Hirahara has infused her mystery with a deep humanity, unearthing a piece of buried American history." —George Takei

"Beautifully written and deeply moving . . . Hirahara's novel is an accomplished and important story about a time in American history that I felt privileged bearing witness to."—*Minneapolis Star-Tribune*

"*Clark and Division* is as much about communal trauma as it is about the anguish of the Ito family, who are at the story's center. The grief of the Japanese community in Chicago infuses the atmosphere of this novel, offering a compelling, nuanced tale of loss."
—*BookPage*, **Starred Review**

"The treatment of American citizens of Japanese descent during World War II comes to life in this mystery by Hirahara . . . Hirahara does a masterly job of incorporating extensive historical research into an emotionally compelling story. Highly recommended for readers who enjoy high-quality historical fiction with well-drawn characters and an engrossing plot." —*Library Journal*, **Starred Review**

EVERGREEN

EVERGREEN

NAOMI HIRAHARA

Published by
Soho Press, Inc.
227 W 17th Street
New York, NY 10011

Library of Congress Cataloging-in-Publication Data

Names: Hirahara, Naomi, author.
Title: Evergreen / Naomi Hirahara.
Description: New York, NY : Soho Crime, [2023] | Series: The
Japantown Mysteries ; 2 | Identifiers: LCCN 2023005653

ISBN 978-1-64129-359-4
eISBN 978-1-64129-360-0

Subjects: LCSH: Japanese Americans—Fiction. | Little Tokyo (Los
Angeles, Calif.)—Fiction. | Los Angeles (Calif.)—History—20th
century—Fiction. | LCGFT: Detective and mystery fiction. | Historical
fiction. | Novels. | Classification: LCC PS3608.I76 E844 2023
DDC 813/.6—dc23/eng/20230206
LC record available at https://lccn.loc.gov/2023005653

Map by Mike Hall
Interior design by Janine Agro

Printed in the United States of America

10 9 8 7 6 5 4 3 2 1

To Gwenn

While we were gone, the military dismantled our fishing village in Terminal Island.

While we were gone, schools and cities buried our Japanese community gardens.

While we were gone, Dutch immigrants looked after our flower market in downtown Los Angeles.

While we were gone, Black defense workers from the Deep South, having no other place to live, moved into empty buildings of Little Tokyo.

While we were gone, beloved classmates mourned our absence.

While we were gone, thieves plundered our storage units.

While we were gone, Baptist churches rented our temple buildings.

While we were gone, our competitors took over our farming operations and produce markets.

While we were gone, friends wrote letters asking the government to release our Issei fathers from alien detention centers.

While we were gone, White Memorial Hospital birthed babies in our hospital in Boyle Heights.

And then, after four years, we returned.

EVERGREEN

CHAPTER 1

I had only been working at the Japanese Hospital on Fickett
Street for a month when Haruki Watanabe was brought into
an examination room. The one Issei doctor on call was treating a
patient who had been suffering from severe hypertension. It was
up to me to take Mr. Watanabe's vitals and update his medical
chart. I was only a nurse's aide, not a full-fledged nurse, but the
hospital had just reopened in spring 1946, three years after we
had been sent away, and the facility was severely understaffed.

Mr. Watanabe had sad eyes with bags that drooped down
onto his sagging cheeks. Everything about his face seemed to
be melting away. His lip was swollen and the side of his face
was beet red, inflamed from some kind of trauma. The only
sign of vigor was in his hair, still jet-black and abundant, like
a badger's coat, despite his fifty-two years.

I put the glass thermometer under his tongue, which was
thick and streaked with bacteria. His temperature was a little
higher than normal.

I gently took hold of his wrist, which was sturdier than I
expected, to take his pulse. His pulse was fast, but that was not
unusual when people came for emergency care. I spied something red on his upper arm and lifted his shirtsleeve. Bruises
the pattern and color of smashed raspberries—not fresh, but
not months old, either.

"What's happened here?"

"*Nandemonai*," he said in a low voice, as if he didn't want anyone to hear. Realizing that I was a Nisei and might not understand much Japanese, he said it in English, too. "Nothing."

I got a cotton gown out of the cupboard and left it next to him on the examination table. "Can you get dressed in this?"

"*Doushite?* I only have my head problems."

"The doctor will probably want to do a thorough checkup."

"No need," he insisted.

"Please, Watanabe-*san*," I said as firmly as I could. I had found that attaching *san* to their names usually softened the most distraught of Issei patients.

I left the examination room, closing the door behind me to give him some privacy.

Dr. Isokane appeared from around the corner. He had been in Santa Anita Assembly Center and then Manzanar, like us, and then Topaz after that, serving other Japanese Americans in bleak wartime camps. He was older than my father and should have been thinking of retirement, but instead he had dedicated himself to those who had been exiled.

"Isokane-*sensei*." I handed him Mr. Watanabe's medical chart and shared my concerns about the bruises on his arm.

The doctor didn't reveal any emotion. He was trained, after all, not to be shocked by practically anything. "Is he working?" he asked in Japanese.

He was, as a driver. Not as a gardener or janitor—no taxing physical labor. I wondered if he was a good driver. He was living with his son in an apartment in Little Tokyo.

Dr. Isokane pulled his stethoscope out of his white coat pocket and looped it around his neck, a sign that he was ready to see his patient. I excused myself to prepare for the vaccination of children at a hostel down the street.

I was gathering needles in our storage room when Dr. Iso-kane appeared from the examination room. "His mind seems fine but I wanted him to get X-rays," he told me in Japanese. "Some hearing loss, but that's not unusual for his age."

"Did you see?" I asked.

Dr. Isokane had. Apparently there were bruises all over his upper body.

"Life has been hard," he concluded.

I searched his face. Was he saying that our Issei elders were all walking around with wounded bodies from the wartime experience and beyond? Or was he making an excuse for some kind of continual abuse?

An orderly, a Nisei who had been in Jerome, Arkansas, helped me wheel Mr. Watanabe from the examination room into the X-ray room. He was dressed in a gown and clutched something so intensely that his knuckles were turning white. "What do you have there?" I asked him. I gently turned his fist to see a gold pocket watch, the second hand meticulously ticking around the dial. The old man snatched his hand back, protecting his treasure.

As the orderly strapped him onto a gurney, I asked him, "Who brought you here, Mr. Watanabe? Perhaps he can hang on to your watch."

"My son, Shinji. I'm not sure if he's still here."

"I would like to speak with him."

"*Doushite?*" Mr. Watanabe's face revealed fear more than irritation at a lowly female nurse's aide. "Job of docta, *desho?*"

This wasn't simply a case of an old man falling down the stairs, as was stated in the intake papers. I had seen my share of old-timers who had taken tumbles. Bruises, first red and inflamed, followed the pattern of their fall. Mr. Watanabe, on the other hand, resembled a human cheetah, with spots all over his upper body.

I decided not to fight him over the watch. The orderly wheeled him off to get his X-rays.

Shinji Watanabe wasn't sitting in the waiting room. The receptionist reported that he was in the hallway having a smoke.

The son's back was toward me, a halo of cigarette smoke around his head. The surge of tobacco won out over the constant odor of disinfectant that usually overwhelmed our corridors.

"Shinji Watanabe?" I said softly, almost afraid to be in the presence of someone who might have caused Mr. Watanabe harm.

The man turned. The lights were bright in the hallway, casting a yellowish tinge over his broad face. Even healthy visitors ended up looking sick when they entered the hospital building.

I stood there frozen, hearing a rush of air escape from my lips. I knew this man. Mr. Watanabe's son, Shinji, had been my husband's best man in our Chicago wedding a year and a half earlier, in November 1944.

"Babe?"

Babe dropped his stub of a cigarette onto the linoleum floor. "Oh, Aki. Hello."

"I didn't know that your real name was Shinji."

"Well, it's my legal one. Hardly anyone knows my Japanese name."

"You're back already." I waited for him to fill in the blanks.

"Yeah."

That's all Babe was going to give me? I wanted to ask him directly, *Why are you out when my Art still hasn't been discharged?* But I opted to be more discreet. "Art's due any day now."

"Yeah, I heard."

They were communicating. I felt a pang of jealousy. Why hadn't Art told me Babe was back and in Los Angeles?

"The doctor said that my old man is getting X-rays?"

I tried to regain my composure and return to my professional duties as a health provider. Of course, that was the crucial matter at hand. The well-being of Mr. Watanabe.

"They want to make sure that he doesn't have a concussion."

"He's pretty clumsy in his old age. Falls down a lot." He lowered his eyes as if he was ashamed to lie to me.

"You must be worried. Him working as a driver."

"He was a truck driver before the war. Even a midget-car racer back in Arroyo Grande."

I knew of at least one Nisei man, the son of a florist in Los Feliz, who had died in a stock car race before World War II. I didn't know why these men were so attracted to speed, enough that it might take their lives.

Babe checked his watch and I had the feeling that he was pressed for time.

"They probably will want him to spend the night. Just for observation," I explained.

Babe released his tightened lip. I could feel the conflict inside of him. He was obviously relieved that his father seemed to be okay, but was that a touch of guilt, too?

"I can call you to give you an update," I said. Seeing Babe had elicited a flood of emotions. I wiped my perspiring hands on my uniform.

"We're in the San Mark Hotel. We don't have a phone in our room, but you can leave a message with the front desk."

"Well, it was good to see you, Babe," I said, trying to convince myself it was.

"Yeah." Babe couldn't even reciprocate the lie. "I'll see you again when Art comes back."

• • •

Babe was the reason I don't have many photos of my wedding day. My fiancé, Art, had returned to Chicago in the late fall of 1944 from Camp Shelby in Mississippi with Babe, who had become his best friend in boot camp. He didn't resemble his father much aside from the healthy black hair that seemed hard to tame. He was tall for a Nisei, although not as tall as Art, with a beefy body and squinty eyes kind of like the famous slugger's. Actually, people from his hometown in Arroyo Grande called him a Japanese Babe Ruth for his pitching and hitting skills, and his athletic prowess was known throughout the Central Coast. I had never heard of Babe Watanabe before. My older sister, Rose, and I were city girls, and there was really no reason for Babe to enter my consciousness when I was growing up in Los Angeles.

Babe Watanabe's eyes were narrow but his vision was as sharp as an eagle's. Those eyes could register if a ball was coming at him curved like the letter C or straight and furious. He bought a camera in high school and when not playing ball immersed himself in snapping pictures: of the flat farmland of the valley, of his teammates, both in action and goofing around. He had to turn in his camera, as all of us did, after the bombing of Pearl Harbor. Our family weren't shutterbugs, so we weren't that inconvenienced, but I can imagine the loss had been especially painful for him.

As soon as Babe arrived in Mississippi in October 1944, he bought a camera—apparently not as fancy as the one that he'd once had—in a store in Hattiesburg. There he was in an American army uniform, and he wasn't going to let a store clerk tell him that he was too seditious to own a camera.

Art had told me all this in letters, excited that his friend had volunteered to take photos of our wedding ceremony. It was simple, at a church on the South Side that Art's aunt sometimes attended. My parents were the perfect hosts, dressed immaculately as they would have for special occasions in the old days. Only I knew of their private doubts. Pop maintained that our wedding had happened "all of a sudden," when they had known about our engagement for some months. I sensed that they had always expected to be the parents of the bride for Rose's nuptials and to skip over that to mine stirred up some unmentionable and buried sadness.

I didn't tell Art, but I wasn't impressed with Babe from our first meeting. He never looked straight at my face when I spoke to him. He also seemed to be all thumbs. I couldn't imagine him being a star baseball player because he seemed so awkward and clumsy. Art later said that he was nervous to be around a girl as pretty as me, but I figured he was just making excuses.

About five minutes after the ceremony had ended, we were posing outside the church doorway when all visual evidence of my wedding was erased forever. I wasn't sure exactly what happened, but Babe's camera, complete with a newly purchased lamp flash, crashed onto the concrete steps, bouncing a few times for good measure. Babe ran after his camera, cradling the shattered remains as if it were a hurt kitten. He then announced that the film was ruined.

I was in a state of disbelief. I could hear Mom releasing a few tsk-tsks as if this was all confirmation that our union was indeed cursed. Dropping my wedding bouquet, I fled to the ladies' room inside, tears spoiling the makeup that my Chicago Nisei friends, Louise and Chiyo, had applied. I wished that Nancy Kowalski, my friend I'd met working at the Newberry Library, was there. She was a real photographer, but my parents hadn't allowed me to invite her. No outsiders at the ceremony or reception, which meant no one who wasn't Japanese.

I dotted my lips with Red Majesty, which had been the favorite shade of my sister, Rose. "There," I imagined Nancy saying to me. "That will give you good luck."

I knew that I was being silly. Most of the people I cared the most about were at the ceremony to share these memories with me. But still, I did want some evidence that I, Aki Ito, now Nakasone, had been chosen for marriage. I was no longer that girl declined entry at a private pool party, the anonymous wallflower at high school or city college. At Manzanar, a government photographer had snapped a photo of my sister, Rose, with the Owens Valley wind tossing her hair. I would always be grateful for that glamorous image of her, despite the circumstances. I wanted a counterimage of me being happy and entering a new phase of my life.

After I came out of the powder room, Art was waiting, looking so handsome in his uniform, gold pins on his lapels and chevron stripes on the arms of his jacket. He handed me back my bouquet of white stephanotis, daisies, and yellow carnations. "Listen, we'll take pictures of the rest of our wedding day with our minds, how's that?"

"What do you mean?"

"Take a moment and snap, file it away in our brains. That way it will never go away." Art took a few steps back. I felt foolish, but went along with it, gripping my bouquet with both hands. He closed his eyes, revealing his fine line of lashes, and then opened them. "See, I just took one. Your turn."

Art could be such a romantic at times.

"Here." Art directed me to a mirror by a coat rack. "C'mon, I'm not goofing around."

I stood beside him, bouquet in my right hand as I held on to the crook of his arm with my left. In the mirror's reflection was a handsome Nisei couple. My mother and I had covered the bodice of a plain white dress with lace to make it look more bridal, while Louise had lent me her pillbox hat, which she had worn for her own wedding two weeks before. Art counted off, "Three, two, one," and we closed our eyes in unison.

"What if something happens to our brains and we forget this?" I asked him as we prepared to walk outside where our family and friends were waiting to throw grains of uncooked rice on us.

"We are only twenty-one years old. It's going to take some time before we get batty," he said. "We'll take some photos when I get back from overseas. Maybe you can even get a fancier dress."

"What's wrong with this one?"

"Nothing, nothing, darling. You should look exactly the way you do right now. We'll do it all over."

But, of course, we never did.

CHAPTER 2

That Chicago winter without Art nearly killed me. In fact, the bone-chilling cold and menacing snow threatened the mood of our whole family. My parents and I could have moved out of our stark fourth-floor apartment on LaSalle, near Clark and Division, into a proper house around Lakeview, where other Japanese were moving to. But my parents feared that putting down any kind of roots, no matter how shallow they were, would seal our future.

"We have to get out of here. *Zettaini*," Pop vowed.

I had abandoned my plans to become a cadet nurse. That training would have taken thirty months with an assignment perhaps at a military hospital. I couldn't make that commitment and be away from my parents, much less Art when he was finally honorably discharged, whenever that would be.

Many a night when my parents had fallen asleep in the bed beside me, I had stayed up late recalculating Art's points of service over and over. I added up every possible military campaign, hoping each event might be the one that would magically transport my husband back home to the United States. And with his thigh wound, wouldn't that qualify him for an immediate medical leave? But no, even when the war was officially over in both Europe and the Pacific, he, like other soldiers, couldn't automatically return to the US until he had accumulated a certain number of points for time served, battles fought, and injuries suffered. Loitering around Europe under other circumstances would be a dream, especially if Art and I were enjoying a proper honeymoon. But in Art's later letters I sensed his dark feelings of purposelessness, trapped as he was in a place that was not home.

Throughout the winter and spring of 1945, I tried to make the best of working as a nurse's aide at the Henrotin Hospital on LaSalle Street, the same place where my father worked as a janitor. Although swankier medical facilities were less welcoming toward the Japanese, the Henrotin was open to us. One of my last patients in Chicago was my father's former boss from the Los Angeles produce market, Mr. Tonai. Picked up right after Pearl Harbor, he had been separated from the rest of the family for some time in an alien detention center in Santa Fe, New Mexico, before being reunited with his wife in Manzanar. Their only son, Roy, was a couple of years older than me and had moved to Chicago a few months after my older sister, Rose, did. He carried a torch for Rose, but then all the fellows had been wild about her.

Roy joined the army while we were in Chicago. He was assigned to the 522nd Battalion, which handled artillery for Art's unit, the all-Nisei 100th/442nd Regimental Combat Team. Roy's parents eventually made it out of Manzanar and to the Windy City. All that displacement and confinement took a toll on Mr. Tonai. During the winter of 1945, he died of pneumonia. I felt so bad that Roy was overseas, risking his life traveling through the minefields of Europe, while his father passed away in a land completely foreign to him. On his deathbed, Mr. Tonai had murmured about the price of cucumbers in Long Beach and celery in Venice. I didn't have the heart to tell him that he was thousands of miles away from California.

• • •

Nisei were slowly starting to make their way back to the West Coast by the beginning of 1945. A few months earlier, Esther Takei had been released from a concentration camp in Amache, Colorado, to Pasadena, not far from where my older sister Rose and I grew up. A few years younger than me, Esther was a test case on whether our former neighbors would accept our return. I followed her progress through updates in the Japanese American Citizens League's newspaper, *Pacific Citizen*, as well as verbal reports from my friend Louise, who was from a longtime Pasadena family with lots of connections with *hakujin* rich people. A man named George Kelley organized a "Ban the Japs Committee," and rallied two hundred people at the local library. My heart grew tight as I read of the lingering antagonism toward us in Southern California.

Hakujin veterans, knowing the exploits of the 100th/442nd, were the ones who stepped forward and protected Esther. Even though I feared for Art's safety in Europe, I realized that the Nisei soldiers were changing the minds of those who once reviled us. Known as the Go for Broke boys, they fought furiously in Italy and Europe, even rescuing a Texas battalion trapped by the enemy at the expense of their own lives. While I was proud as punch, I couldn't help but wonder why our men had to die on the battlefield for all of us to get some respect.

In spite of the conflicting stories we heard about the public's reception to our return, I still entertained the thought of re-enrolling in a city college in Los Angeles and pursuing a nursing degree. I'd learned it's important to hold on to hope, no matter what happens in reality.

That winter nearly did all of us in. Pop especially was vocal about leaving for the warmth of Los Angeles. Mom was more cautious, doubtful of what our former home would still have for us. I was eager to leave Chicago, just to escape the lonely ghost of my older sister. At least back in Southern California, I could conjure up sweet images of our legs entwined on the bed or laughing over our dog's silly antics.

When it finally came time for us to depart Chicago on the last day of February 1946, packing was much simpler than when we left Los Angeles. Practically all our dishes and pans were hand-me-downs from the Quakers and Art's family on the South Side. I was more than happy to abandon our old-fashioned, leaky icebox that only held bad memories.

As we latched the last of our suitcases, Mom declared with a sense of satisfaction, "*Owari*."

Yes, it was indeed the end of our time on Clark and Division.

I still held on to hope during our train ride back to California. Traveling west instead of east, watching the sunset in front of us along the prairie, I imagined returning to our two-bedroom Spanish-style house in Tropico. In the backyard, next to a giant cedar tree, was where I had buried our dear dog, Rusty, my regular walking companion along the concrete bed of the Los Angeles River. But, like most middle- and working-class Japanese, we hadn't owned the property where we'd lived.

Mr. Tonai, who had sojourned to America from Japan before the enactment of California's alien land laws, had been among the lucky exceptions. He had secured a deed to the family residence in South Los Angeles on Thirtieth Street in the early 1900s. The Tonais had a loyal employee, Pablo Sandoval, who took care of their property during the war and even visited Manzanar a few times to bring Tonai's personal items from their South Central home. He was trusted enough to drive my father's beloved Model A from Manzanar to the Thirtieth Street house, an undertaking that gave both Pop and me some semblance of peace. Almost all had been taken away, but at least we could count on the car still being there for us, someday.

We couldn't retrieve the Model A until we had a place to live, which turned out to be a challenge. We began our search in downtown Los Angeles. Union Station was only a few blocks from Little Tokyo, which, in addition to be being called Japantown or Nihonmachi, now had a new name: Bronzeville. Blacks from the Deep South, answering the call for workers in the burgeoning defense factories in Southern California during World War II, flooded into Los Angeles looking for housing, only to find that desirable areas were as closed to them as they had been for us. Little Tokyo, now a ghost town and embarrassment to city hall, could conveniently be the home for these newcomers.

As all of the beds in area hostels were filled, we first rented a room at the most visible Little Tokyo hotel in Bronzeville, Miyako Hotel, which now had an additional neon sign, CIVIC HOTEL, announcing its new name. A room with a bath for the three of us cost $3.45 day, which was quite substantial as one day's salary for a working person could be as low as $6. Since there was not even a hot plate in the room, we had to eat at a restaurant for every meal. The hotel seemed like a center for its share of nefarious activities, with young Nisei in zoot suits skulking by the main entrance and women of all ethnicities tempting single men from their doorways.

North Clark in Chicago had been the same way, but to witness these risqué activities in our former Japantown jarred me. I had been so eager to reclaim Los Angeles, not realizing that it had changed beyond recognition. My parents, surprisingly, showed no such emotion. Since the loss of my older sister, they both seemed resigned that nothing would be quite the same.

I was determined to find a proper home for us. The Quakers and other church people had housing listings available. I also picked up our local community newspaper, the *Rafu Shimpo*, which had resumed publication in January. I knew returning to Tropico, which now had become a hoity-toity neighborhood, was out of the question, so I focused my search on Boyle Heights, a Los Angeles neighborhood next to Little Tokyo. Taking the streetcar east on First Street, I entered a crowded neighborhood of narrow hilly avenues dotted with small wood bungalows. Even before World War II, Boyle Heights was a place where people, many of them immigrants, came to rebuild their lives. I was ashamed that at one time, being a Tropico girl, I'd felt somewhat superior to the more working-class residents in Boyle Heights. Even though I always felt like an outsider in high school, I harbored some pride that I went to school with mostly *hakujin* students, as if their elevated societal status lifted mine as well. But in the end it didn't matter how much money you had or where you lived in California. All of us Nisei were sent to the same type of shoddy barracks in ten concentration camps, scattered across the US by the hand of Uncle Sam.

I found the classified listing in the *Rafu Shimpo* for the house for rent. It was on a street called Malabar and according to my AAA map, it was accessible via one of the major streets running down Boyle Heights, Evergreen. On Evergreen was Evergreen Hostel, operated by the Japanese Presbyterian Union Church, and Evergreen Cemetery, where many of our Issei were buried.

Malabar was a couple of streets north of the cemetery, which comforted me more than spooked me. And the house was walking distance from the Japanese Hospital, which was sorely in need of both nurses and nurses' aides.

The wood-framed house was worn but fairly clean. The deep porch had no signs of spider webs and corners of rooms were free of dust. The owner was a small bald Jewish man who was moving to the west side of Los Angeles, closer to the ocean breezes.

"Now that Hitler tried to wipe us out, they are lifting the housing covenants for us," the man, who was named Abe Zidle, said. "Too bad it took the gas chambers for them to see that we are also human."

He didn't identify exactly who "they" or "them" were. But I understood. "They" were the ones who called the shots, determined who could live where. Boyle Heights was among the few areas open to those who were deemed non-white, a classification that before World War II included the Jews.

"How many in your family?" he asked.

"Well, it's me and my parents. And my husband, who's still in Europe."

"A soldier."

I nodded. "Have you heard of the Go for Broke boys?"

The man's face, which had been so impish, darkened and his hooded eyes flashed. "Heard stories about US soldiers with Japanese faces opening the gates of some death camps."

From letters that Roy had sent to his father, I knew that he was referring to Roy's artillery unit. I was surprised that Mr. Zidle had heard of the 522nd's encounter with Holocaust survivors in Germany. Hardly any other Americans seemed to be aware of what our boys did there.

"I'll sell this house to you," he announced.

"Oh, we don't have that kind of money."

"Can't your husband get a loan from the GI Bill?"

"I suppose." Art wasn't even home yet. What promises could I make without his consultation?

"I'll lease it to you until your man returns. If you decide to buy, I'll count your rent payments as part of the down payment."

"Really?"

I couldn't believe my luck. I wasn't a religious person, but at times I felt that a godly presence touched our lives.

"I'll draw up the papers with my lawyer tomorrow. You can come the day after that to make it official."

I could have hugged that old man; he wasn't that much taller than me. His bare scalp shone as if it had been polished like an apple on display in a high-tone market.

Before I left his porch, I heard him call out, "I think it's awful what they did to you people."

Again, that "they." His sentiment was not lost on me. In fact, to hear it said so plainly and openly startled me so much that I couldn't respond. Tears wet my lashes and cheeks as I traipsed to Evergreen and turned south, hoping that I wouldn't run into anyone I knew from various places I had lived in the past four years.

Ever since childhood, I was known as a crybaby, but my eyes had been dry since I had last seen Art for forty-eight precious hours in November 1944. After our wedding ceremony, we had a chop suey banquet in a Chinese restaurant on Wentworth Avenue. Chicago's Chinatown wasn't like the ones in Los Angeles or San Francisco, with narrow winding streets and alleys. Instead it was wide open with expansive streets lined with pagoda towers.

Even though I was the newlywed bride, Babe had commanded Art's attention at our round table. He planted his beefy body so close to Art's thin frame that their elbows were practically touching. They shared personal jokes about basic training or full of army terms, jargon meaningless to me.

First, I was amused, and then less so. After the ceremony, we had barely another day together and I feared that Art's entire leave would be spent with this giant Babe by his side.

Before the sliced almond duck appeared at our table, a waiter seated a nattily dressed group of *hakujin* young people right beside us. Babe focused on a young woman in the party—her blond hair was rolled in a shoulder-length bob à la June Allyson. Babe was mesmerized by her—his stares were quite unbecoming and even embarrassing—but at least she provided an opportunity for me to have Art's undivided attention.

When our stomachs could no longer hold any more chow mein or fried rice, we finally dragged ourselves out the door. Art's mother, his Aunt Eunice, and his sister, Lois, surrounded him, touching his back and his face as if to give him extra protection before he was shipped out to the European front. They all had decided to say their goodbyes tonight because seeing Art off at the train station would be too much. His Issei father lagged behind, his chin on his chest, holding back any emotion. Before Art and I got into a taxi, his father bowed low, then apparently couldn't help himself and clutched at his only son.

Ruining this sweet moment was Babe, who positioned his body between me and the Nakasone men. "Aki, you're a lucky woman." Babe squeezed my elbow a little too hard. I gritted my teeth and managed a smile. I hated when people kept saying how lucky I was. Who was going to tell Art that he was the lucky one?

Traveling in the taxi to our hotel, I tried to be careful with my words, as Art was still recovering from saying farewell to his family.

"That Babe is something else," I said. I had to make some kind of commentary to release my contempt for my husband's new friend.

Art picked up my disdain. "Oh, he's okay. He's had a rough time of it with his dad and he has no siblings. In the past, his teammates were his brothers. I guess now I've become part of his family."

I turned to look out the side window so he couldn't see my grimace. For the life of me, I wasn't going to let Babe Watanabe ruin my last hours with my new husband.

After signing the lease with Mr. Zidle, I went to reclaim the Model A and some boxes we had left with Pablo Sandoval and his wife, Hortencia. Instead of going straight to pick up my parents, I found myself on my way to Tropico like old times. I drove around my and Rose's alma mater, the stately John Marshall High School, and over the Hyperion Bridge to the neighborhood where we were raised near the Glendale and Los Angeles border. I parked on our old street, across from our house, a two-bedroom Spanish-style home with a new red tile roof. I sat in the car and stared at it for a while, picturing myself sitting on the front lawn with Rusty and running after Rose through the front door.

All the yards were well maintained, adorned with bright flowers. At one time there had been a handful of Japanese families here, some whose hedges had been trimmed in the shapes of floating clouds.

A mangy dog with matted hair crossed the street, reminding me of Rusty. I wanted to pay respects to his burial site underneath a cedar tree, but that would be impossible. A *hakujin* woman appeared from the door, wiping her hands on a dish towel with a concerned look on her face. Our Model A was sorely out of fashion among the sleek new sedans that now populated Los Angeles' streets and the Arroyo Seco Parkway, the first freeway of its kind in California. I was clearly now an outsider. Before the new resident of our old home confronted me or called the police, I started the ignition and hightailed it out of there.

We were no longer the Itos of Tropico. We were the Itos (and one Nakasone) of Boyle Heights, neighbors to other Japanese Americans and Mexican families, as well as the longtime residents, the older Jews and White Russians.

I was well aware that we were in a much better position than others settling in Southern California. We had a place to live and in a matter of days, after answering an advertisement in the *Rafu Shimpo*, I had a job at the Japanese Hospital. In the beginning, I was assigned to work 7 A.M. to 3 P.M., five days a week. The hospital was organized just like the camp hospitals for nurses and aides—with three shifts throughout each twenty-four-hour period. Because I was married, I was given the early shift, even though Art was away. It was presumed that the single girls didn't have as many household responsibilities at night, an assumption that wasn't correct, but I didn't fight it because it happened to benefit my schedule.

The forecasts for Pop's work opportunities, on the other hand, were less promising.

Before the war, he was the big shot manager of the Tonais' large produce market. During the war, the Tonais had had no choice but to leave the enterprise in the care of *hakujin* trustees, who had been essentially the company's competitors. While Roy was in Chicago, the trustees' lawyer paid him a visit. *No one wants to deal with a market owned by a Japanese*, the attorney told him. *Sell it to the trustees and at least your family will get some money.*

Roy had just enlisted and felt like he had no time to even consult with my father. He signed the papers to sell the produce market. Pop learned what had happened days after Roy had left for Camp Shelby. I had feared the sale would lead my father to drink again, but instead he spent late nights scribbling away in the margins of old ledger sheets that Art's father had given him. I couldn't read the vertical lines of cursive Japanese, but from Mom I learned that he was concocting a comeback. One day we would return to Los Angeles and he would help take back the market.

After we moved into Boyle Heights, he was fully devoted to carrying out his plan. First on his list was to consult with Issei lawyers he knew. I thought that he would be better off talking to a fully credentialed Nisei attorney, but Pop insisted on speaking with his contacts even though they couldn't be recognized by the bar because of their Japanese immigrant status.

During one of his trips to downtown Los Angeles, Pop struck up a conversation with a man from the garment district, Mr. Kroner, who lived around USC and was looking for a domestic. I was shocked that my father passed that inquiry along to my mother and doubly shocked that she agreed. I thought that she had left that occupation behind when we returned to Los Angeles. Truth was, we needed money and Mom was an experienced cleaning woman because of work she'd had to take on in Chicago.

In a matter of weeks, she had been hired by a number of professors and a Jewish fraternity house near campus. I hadn't had much experience with Jewish people before the war or even in Chicago, but now I lived in a neighborhood that had once housed the largest number of Jews in the country outside of New York City. Like Mr. Zidle, many of the residents and businesses were now leaving the east side for the other end of town, but notable Jewish landmarks still remained. A few blocks from the Japanese Hospital was a grand shul on Breed Street. On Saturdays in that neighborhood, I'd see children dressed exactly the same as the Nisei ones going to church, only the Jewish boys would be wearing colorful yarmulkes.

In the evening, when I walked past the synagogue, I would look at that star that decorated its façade and think about Art in Europe, sacrificing himself to fight against those who would take a life just because of religion or ethnic background. Sometimes I would walk down a street called Chicago, just one block west of Breed Street, and wonder if Art would be able to adjust to life in Boyle Heights. Family was everything to him, and in California he would be away from his parents; kid sister, Lois; and Aunt Eunice, all living on the South Side.

His household was loud, bright, and cheery, with a parakeet, a cat, and two dogs, while our house was a bit dark, with no animals wandering at our feet at present. Our neighbors, the Fujitas, had a big German shepherd that rushed to the gate and barked ferociously whenever we went outside to take out the trash or get into Pop's car in the garage. We all were living on the edge, not fully secure in this Los Angeles that we had returned to.

The afternoon I'd treated Haruki Watanabe and confronted Babe in the hallway, I left the Japanese Hospital feeling shaken. I walked home down Evergreen and went immediately to my bedroom to change out of my uniform. We didn't have a washing machine yet and since I couldn't go to the laundromat every night, I handwashed my uniform in hot water in the bathtub a couple times a week. I had extra uniforms, but not five of them.

After I finished my laundry duties, I walked into the living room in my housedress and slippers. Mom had finished cooking and supper was already on the table. *Okazu* again, stir-fried vegetables with a bit of meat, this time pork. When I looked closely, I discovered I was mistaken. It was *buta dofu*, pork shoulder and tofu with slices of green pepper, flavored with simmering miso. I preferred the kick of *buta dofu* to plain *okazu*, a simple stir-fry which could seem tasteless without a healthy sprinkle of Ajinomoto from a red metal can that we kept on the kitchen counter.

"I saw Babe Watanabe today," I reported to my mother, who was still in her apron.

My mother's face remained blank. She had once been the main source of scuttlebutt, knowing who was who, but after the war, her gossiping skills were sorely out of practice.

"You know Babe." I took my seat facing our front window.

"He was Art's best man. The one who was supposed to take our wedding photos."

The lack of wedding photos had been a sore spot for Mom, too, and she nodded. "Oh, *sou*," she said and moved on from that unwelcome memory. "Maybe Art come home soon, too."

My thoughts exactly.

Instead of chopsticks, we chose to eat our dinner with large spoons to enjoy every drop of the sauce. It wasn't until the second spoonful that I noted my father's absence. "Where's Pop, anyway?"

"Downtown. Meeting with Tonai's old workers."

"Do you think he really can get the market back?"

"I don't know. That's your father's business."

My mother, who, before the war, had been entrenched in life at the produce market, must have sensed that Pop's odds were not good. She was a practical woman and rarely bet on a losing horse.

CHAPTER 3

The next morning, when I arrived at the hospital, I immediately checked on Mr. Watanabe. The wound on the side of his head had taken on a bluish tint, but according to the radiology department, he had no damage to the brain. I told him that I would call Shinji to relay the good news.

"No need. He knows." His words were like a door slamming shut. He obviously wanted me out of his business. I felt slightly hurt but I brushed that discomfort aside. Mr. Watanabe had escaped serious injury; that was all that mattered.

"*Mata guzu-guzu shiteiru.*" It was the familiar nagging voice of the senior nurse, Mrs. Honma, and a familiar accusation. *Dawdling and wasting time again.* Her irritated expression was also familiar to me, her lips pursed as if she had swallowed something distasteful.

I had been assigned to accompany Mrs. Honma to administer shots to children at Evergreen Hostel. Mrs. Honma was seven years older than me and a Kibei, a Nisei who had spent some time in Japan during her early years. She had studied nursing and returned to Southern California immediately before World War II. Since I was only an aide and my ability to speak Japanese was pretty miserable, she didn't think much of me. She was constantly correcting my methods, from how I disinfected the thermometers to how I wore my white cap, which often came loose on one side. Sometimes I wondered if she felt that it was part of her job to torment me. But I never gave her the satisfaction of showing any weakness. I had lost too much to let her petty grievances penetrate my heart.

I was on the lowest rung of the nursing hierarchy, even below another nursing aide, a young Mexican woman named Soledad Montiel who went by the nickname Chole. She had apple cheeks, thick lips, and big eyes adorned with naturally full eyelashes. She lived in the neighborhood, a few blocks away from me, and had worked at the hospital during World War II when White Memorial had taken it over and turned it into a maternity ward. While our medical facility was called Japanese Hospital, we turned no one away, and needed Chole's Spanish-language skills for our Mexican patients.

Because we were close in age and lacked nursing credentials, Chole and I had become fast friends. She actually had some relatives in Mexico who had Japanese blood but she herself didn't know much about the culture or language. I taught her some Japanese words and she taught me some Spanish. When she learned the meaning of *guzu-guzu*, she teased me throughout the day. "No *guzu-guzu*." She waved her finger at me as we passed each other in the hallway. Her husband, Manny, was in the marines and was serving in the occupation of Japan. How strange it was that she was sponging clean the bodies of sick Japanese immigrants while her husband was part of our country's plan to tame Japan, our former enemy.

Chole flashed me a look of sympathy as Mrs. Honma and I left with large kits filled with needles, syringes, glass flasks of vaccine, and Band-Aids. She knew that I was dreading embarking on an excursion with our senior nurse. We packed everything up in the hospital's Ford sedan, with Mrs. Honma in the driver's seat.

"No one will want to get their shots," Mrs. Honma warned me. "They remember what happened at the assembly centers."

Those earlier years of our exile were quite a madhouse. My family had gone straight to Manzanar, while others were sent to racetracks and fairgrounds. We had lined up for our inoculations, almost like cattle and sheep. Each detention center had thousands of us behind barbed wire with limited lavatory facilities. There were no walls separating the toilets, which in some assembly centers were only holes dug in the ground—quite inhumane, especially when hundreds descended on those privies at the same time. Rumors flew fast and furious. The government was poisoning us with these shots, many claimed. But often our camp-wide digestive problems could be traced to food that was left out too long before being cooked and served.

During my training as a nurse's aide at Manzanar, I realized that the inoculations were done for our safety. Living in such close quarters in confinement—if a virus spread in one of the barracks, it could easily go on to infect hundreds or maybe thousands. Our humble hospital, first located in temporary barracks, had been in no position to handle an epidemic. That would have been disastrous.

Once Mrs. Honma and I arrived at the hostel, we set up our makeshift inoculation station in one of the meeting rooms. As parents pushed their children forward, they resisted, running into the folds of their mothers' dresses or hiding behind older children.

I brought out some Hershey's chocolate candies from my pocket. These were the miniatures, which came in handy during times like these.

"A candy for a shot," I called out, and the children flocked to me, raising their hands to volunteer to be first. Mrs. Honma glared at me, disapproving of my methods. She preferred the traditional ways to spur people to action—obedience and *giri*, obligation. However, after everything we had gone through these past four years, nobody was much in a mood to obey.

As I instructed the first brave or perhaps greedy little boy to roll up his sleeve, I heard a murmur of voices. "The mayor, the mayor."

A photographer with a camera had appeared. He held a giant flash, round and silver, in his left hand as he steadied the box camera with his right. I thought first that he might be with one of the local newspapers, the *Los Angeles Times* or *Daily News*, but he seemed to answer to the mayor. I had seen the mayor in person before on the steps of city hall declaring the opening of our Nisei Week Festival in Little Tokyo. He wasn't that tall, maybe the height of the average Nisei man, with soft jowls and graying hair.

Mrs. Honma murmured something in Japanese under her breath. I couldn't catch exactly what she said, but I could tell it wasn't positive. She wasn't about to be in any photographs, especially ones with *hakujin* political leaders. I wasn't that thrilled either, but I felt trapped. I was in the middle of administering shots and couldn't retreat into the background like Mrs. Honma. Before I knew it, the flash blazed and the bulb popped. The mayor, who had apparently stood a few steps behind me, tipped his head and his men ushered him out the door of the hostel.

"Damn bastard." I heard the male voice next to me, low and guttural. I immediately felt goose bumps of recognition, even before I inhaled the whiff of pungent musky cologne that took me back to the streets of Chicago.

"Hammer! Are you living here?" I hadn't seen Hammer Ishimine since I had run into him at a church service at Chicago's Moody Bible College in 1944. The slight scar by his eye hadn't faded. His skin was darker than ever but in California he blended right in.

We had originally met near Clark and Division, but learned that our pasts had intersected before, in camp. As a young adult, Hammer had been in Manzanar at the Children's Village, the orphanage that held all Japanese American minors from the West Coast who had no parental support during World War II. I hadn't seen him in Manzanar, but apparently he remembered seeing me.

"We were in the hellhole of the Winona trailers in Burbank, but thanks to Reverend Kowta of Union Church, we were able to move over here."

Hammer's mention of "we" prompted me to take stock of the young person standing beside him. "Who's this?"

"My brother."

I stifled an exclamation of surprise. I didn't know that Hammer had a brother. I somehow assumed that he was completely alone in this world, without a single blood relative to his name.

"This is Tr—Aki," he introduced me. I knew that he had started to call me Tropico, his nickname for me. His brother's name was Daniel.

"Hello, Daniel," I said.

The brother was a few inches shorter than me, so I pegged him as being ten or eleven. He had ashy, light-colored hair which was haphazardly trimmed, probably Hammer's handiwork. His eyes were light, too, and I got the sense that he wasn't full Japanese.

Daniel barely acknowledged me and I got a distinct feeling that he was afraid of needles. He turned away when I gave him the shot and once released, didn't even accept my reward of a candy bar. He ran outside to join some other boys loitering around the gate.

"Don't take it personal," Hammer said.

"Have I ever?"

Hammer smiled, revealing his crooked eyeteeth. "You were always a good sport."

"It's good to see you."

"I've been watching out for you. I see you walking up Evergreen to the hospital."

"Why haven't you said hello?"

"I could never catch up. You walk a lot faster than in Chicago. Besides, you're a married woman, I heard."

"Yes, I'm Aki Nakasone now." Hammer had never met Art, that I knew of—Art had only ever seen Hammer in a scuffle at a dance at the Aragon in Chicago. They were from two different worlds—Art, a lifelong Chicagoan and soldier with the US Army, and Hammer, a rootless petty criminal who I'd thought had no family.

"I didn't know that you had a brother."

"You never asked."

My face flushed. Even though I had good reason to be self-involved in Chicago, I could have at least shown some interest in Hammer's life.

Mrs. Honma was giving us looks.

"I better get back to work," I told Hammer.

"Can we talk afterwards?"

"Ah, I have to pack up and take everything back to the hospital."

"Can I meet you at the cemetery then around five-thirty? The gates close by six."

My shift officially ended at three but today I'd agreed to stay until five to assist with the inoculations. Evergreen Cemetery was close by, on my way home, and most likely without gossipmongers, as burials were usually held in the mornings or weekends.

I nodded my yes, feeling surprised by a rush of excitement to be arranging a clandestine meeting with a young man like

Hammer. I quickly tamped down my feelings. I was now Aki Nakasone, emphasis on the Nakasone.

Easter was this Sunday and Evergreen Cemetery was weighed down by flowers in practically every corner. The cemetery was a little like Boyle Heights in that it was divided into sections—the grand headstones along the driving paths for better visibility and easy access; a Black section in the north dating back to the 1800s; and the Japanese section with headstones featuring names in both Nihongo and English toward the front. In contrast to the Montrose Cemetery in Chicago, the ground was not green and lush but bone-dry, tufts of grass stubbornly attempting to break through the beaten-down dirt.

I figured that Hammer wanted to meet in the Japanese section, which had a row of overturned soil. Noticing the number of gravesites for Nisei soldiers who had been killed in combat, I felt chills go up my spine and almost mouthed a prayer for my Art. I now felt ashamed for agreeing to meet Hammer in this sacred place.

I stopped to wait for Hammer by an obelisk, a 1937 memorial to Japanese pioneers by the Federation of Japanese Women's Societies of Southern California. I opened up my pocketbook to get my mind off my environment. Ever since childhood, I'd been a bit careless and untidy, stuffing unnecessary items in pockets and sometimes losing the very necessary. In the bottom of my purse, I found three bobby pins, a transfer ticket for the Red Line streetcar, and an ID card issued by the War Relocation Center. I unzipped the side pocket and there, almost like a talisman, was a high school photo of my dear sister, Rose. No matter where I was, I wanted her close to me.

At around 5:40 P.M., I finally spied Hammer coming through the cemetery gates with his trademark jaunt. In his right hand was a bouquet of lavender flowers, wrapped in newspaper. *Oh, what was I thinking?* Here I was in a cemetery, empty-handed.

Hammer came up to my side without apologizing for being late. It was a Tuesday around dinnertime and the cemetery itself would be closed in twenty minutes. No other mourners, as far as I could see, were present in the sprawling grounds.

"I should have bought some flowers." I didn't have any family members buried there, but if I bothered to look more closely at the gravestones, I knew that I would find my father's business acquaintances or family friends.

Hammer walked through the maze of headstones, all of them dated before the war, and I followed, making sure that I didn't trip over any loose dirt or rocks. "I'm seeing a girl from the flower market," he explained. "I can get the flowers that are on their last legs." In his makeshift bouquet were several stalks of tall blue lupine, which indeed were close to wilting, leaning a bit too much to one side.

He finally stopped at a small primitive-looking headstone, an unfinished square rock on top of a rectangular one. Hammer left the bouquet of lupines on the dirt as he went to fill a metal container with water.

I remained at the gravesite. The headstone read, MOMO ISHIMINE, 1903–1940.

I calculated the years to determine the connection. "Your mother?" I asked as he returned.

Hammer nodded and inserted the cylinder, dripping with water, into the hole in the ground. I knelt down next to him and helped assemble the stems in the water.

"Those flowers are sure pretty. Blue Hills?" I asked. The city of Whittier was known for the blue lavender blooms that carpeted the slopes behind residential homes.

"Yeah, the ranch is over there. My girl helps her father sell them."

It was sweet that Hammer had a steady girlfriend and I told him that.

"She's too good for me," he replied. "At least that's what her family thinks. Her father's a big shot at the flower market."

"How did you—"

"After coming back from Chicago, I got a job at the market in the stall right next to their family's. We both attended the Nisei Baptist Church and one thing led to another. When her father found out that we were spending time together outside of the market, he got me fired. I wasn't high-tone enough for him."

"That doesn't seem right," I stated.

Hammer chuckled and shook his head. "I see that you haven't changed much."

I resented his implication that I was too naive. I was a completely different woman from the one who arrived in Chicago in 1944. "Well, aren't we all starting over from scratch? Seems like every Issei and Nisei man is picking up a lawn mower and every Issei woman a broom. We can't be thinking we are better than any other Japanese."

"Some folks still do. Especially the ones who came early to America and were able to buy land before the anti-Jap laws. Also, it didn't hurt to have good *hakujin* friends that looked after your property during the war."

The old Hammer would have sneered at anyone who would put him down. I couldn't stand that this new version had seemed to lose all his fight. "Go to college then." I had told myself that I would continue my nursing studies—East Los Angeles College was the closest school to us—but I hadn't made even an effort to pick up the admission papers.

"I should. The pastor of Nisei Baptist is telling me to go to seminary."

I tried to hide my surprise. I couldn't imagine Hammer as

a minister, but perhaps I had limited vision. My sister, Rose, and I had gone to Sunday school in Glendale and I recalled the stories of Jesus selecting the most unusual men and women to spread word of his mission. "Well, if he's recommending it, maybe you should look into it."

"You really think so, Aki?"

I nodded, first ever so slightly and then definitively. If Hammer needed encouragement to better himself, I'd give it to him.

I turned the conversation back to the inoculations at the hostel. "What was it about the mayor, by the way? You really cursed him out." It wasn't a very Christian thing to do, but I wasn't going to throw that in his face.

"Don't you remember his radio speeches in 1942? How he was saying that he never wanted us back in Los Angeles? And now he's completely changed his tune." Hammer jutted out his jaw, reminding me of the fighter he had been in Chicago.

"A person can change his mind, can't he?"

"Not without owning up to what he did. Now he's first in line to welcome us with open arms. A man needs to first own up to his sins before he tries to sweep them away."

I felt convicted, as if I had done something wrong by being in those photographs.

"Listen." Hammer shifted his weight to signal a change in subject. "I need your help."

I waited expectantly. Hammer had come to my aid numerous times when I was in Chicago. For us Japanese, *okaeshi*, returning a favor, was an important value. It wasn't only motivated by obligation, but also a respect of another's previous effort to help.

"You met my brother."

"I didn't know that you even had one."

"He's my half brother. Didn't you notice that he's half-white?"

I feigned surprise out of politeness. I didn't want to confirm that I had immediately noticed something different about him.

"My mother never married his father, a *hakujin*. My father was already dead and after our mother died, Daniel's father didn't want a half-breed around. I could have made it on the streets by myself, but not with a little kid."

"You never mentioned him before."

Hammer shielded his eyes from the sun, which was starting its descent into the downtown skyline. "We were together in the Children's Village in Manzanar before I was sent to Boys Town. A friend in the village was keeping tabs on him for me. Before the war ended, Daniel got adopted by a foster family, but things didn't work out that smoothly. As soon as I could, I came back to get him."

Hammer's quest almost sounded heroic.

"I'm trying to be his legal guardian. A Nisei lawyer born in Hawaii, Elmer Yamamoto, is helping me out."

I was impressed. Hammer had changed so much since his zoot suit days in Chicago. I noticed for the first time that he was wearing a regular white button-down shirt and jeans. In fact, he looked handsome, in a wild James Cagney type of way.

"Mr. Yamamoto says that I need some letters backing up my reputation. There's not many who would write me one. But I figured you might."

"What about the pastor of Nisei Baptist? Pastor Nagano? I bet he'll vouch for you." I didn't mean to worm my way out of writing a letter but I was sincerely worried that I wouldn't be up for the task.

"It would help to get an endorsement from a woman, too."

"I'll need some instruction—" A crow flew on top of the obelisk.

"Mr. Yamamoto can give it to you."

"Well—"

Hammer knew that he had effectively worn me out. "I'll owe you one, really."

"Just tell me who to address it to and I'll get started on it." I figured that I could probably borrow the receptionist's typewriter at the hospital if I showed up before my 7 A.M. shift.

"I'll let Mr. Yamamoto know," he said. After receiving my pledge to endorse him, Hammer returned his focus to his mother's gravesite, lowering his head and murmuring something—perhaps a prayer? A bit self-conscious to witness such intimacies, I looked up and noticed a flock of seagulls flying overhead above the shaggy heads of palm trees. What were seagulls doing so far inland, away from the ocean?

After his moment with his dead mother, Hammer addressed me. "Have you thought about what you are going to do with Rose's ashes?" For him to bring up my older sister like that, as straightforward as inquiring about a living family member, made me feel unsteady. During our years in Chicago, her ashes had been safely stored in the Japanese Mausoleum at the Montrose Cemetery, due to the kindness of the Mutual Aid Society. Her remains had been next to urns of poor, long-forgotten Issei bachelors who had come through the Midwest before World War II. Once we decided to return to Los Angeles, I'd made arrangements to have her ashes released to us again. But a permanent plot seemed so final, as if the line dividing us could never be crossed again.

"Yes, we'd better buy a plot. For the whole family, I suppose."

Hammer's face immediately brightened, I assumed not because he wanted to hasten our demise. I realized then that he wanted Rose to be planted nearby, a tangible headstone marking her existence. I imagined that he would be leaving the flower market's leftover blooms at her gravesite on a regular basis.

I, on the other hand, resisted the idea of something so definitive and final. I had gotten used to Rose's ashes moving with us from place to place.

Hammer glanced at his watch. "Oh, I have to go over to the Baptist church to help Pastor Nagano clean out the storage area. You okay to walk to your house alone?"

I sighed and almost rolled my eyes. "We're not back at Clark and Division." Boyle Heights was a new neighborhood for me, but it was still Los Angeles. The city might not be exactly the same as we left it, but it was still mine, for better or worse.

CHAPTER 4

Mom brought home day-old newspapers from the house of a customer, a history professor. He subscribed to quite a few papers—the *Los Angeles Times*, the *Daily News*, and even a couple of Black newspapers, the *Los Angeles Tribune* and the *California Eagle*.

Pop read them religiously, along with the *Rafu Shimpo*, our Japanese daily in Little Tokyo, which had resumed publication in the beginning of 1946.

Every week after reading the English-language papers, he would stack the issues neatly, tie them up with twine, and drop the bundle off at the flower market for vendors to use to wrap their flowers. Like Mom, he subscribed to the value of *mottainai*, not letting anything go to waste. With the *Rafu*, he would pass them along to our neighbors, who did the same with other Issei and Nisei families on the street. It was a wonder that the *Rafu* made any money from subscriptions, the way issues were passed from one household to another.

"We are going to get the produce market back." At least once a day, Pop would make the same declaration, relaying details of a clandestine meeting he'd had with this or that returning Issei leader. He lifted up the *Rafu Shimpo*, turning to the back side, which was actually the front of the Japanese section.

My twilight conversation with Hammer remained on my mind. "I was thinking," I said, as I pulled out a pair of clean chopsticks from a long ceramic container. "Maybe we need to buy a plot at Evergreen Cemetery. A family one. So we'll be all together."

"You're a Nakasone now. You need to be with Art's family." Mom, wearing the full-length apron that she had gotten out of storage from our former Tropico neighbors, plopped a plate of some sauteed cabbage on the dining room table.

The Nakasone family plot was at Montrose Cemetery in Chicago, such a picturesque, tranquil location, but nowhere near my friends and Ito family. Just imagining that my remains would be separated from everything I knew well saddened me.

Dad was still holding on to the newspaper, and I didn't think that he was even paying any attention to our discussion about cemetery plots. "No, we should," he said. "One for us, me and Mama, and then another one."

We all knew who the extra one would be for. Even though her ashes were in a gold urn on the fireplace mantel, we couldn't say her name. We were so desperate to rebuild our lives again that we avoided thinking about how much we had lost.

For the next few days, I kept watch on the newspapers, stopping by the local grocery store or even taking the streetcar to Little Tokyo to check the papers at Dixie Liquor, also known as "the Big Corner," on the intersection of First and Los Angeles where Iwaki Drugstore once stood. No photo of me with the mayor. I breathed a sigh of relief. The big Los Angeles newspapers probably felt it wasn't worth showing what was happening in Boyle Heights. And *Rafu Shimpo* rarely published photographs in its regular issues.

I picked up some lemons at the outdoor market on East First Street, greeting the proprietor, who knew our family well from our produce market days. He kept calling me "Rose-*chan*," and I didn't have the heart to correct him. I wished that I had some extra money to pick up some *manju* from the neighboring confectionery shop, Mikawaya, but I knew that I shouldn't overdo it.

Around the corner was the jazz club, Shepp's Playhouse, entertaining defense workers fresh off their swing or graveyard shifts. Little Tokyo was still off-kilter and I was desperate to regain my balance. Ever since the bombing of Pearl Harbor, our world had changed forever.

I almost crashed into an overflowing trash can on the side-walk as I ran past the Miyako Hotel to catch the bus back to Boyle Heights. We were smashed together like sardines—Pop's favorite canned snack. I leaned toward an open window, let-ting the exhaust of sedans and trucks soak into my nostrils and hair. I was, after all, a city girl who had only experienced fresh mountain air while being in confinement in Manzanar.

I pulled the rope for my stop on Evergreen and schlepped home with my bag of lemons. I had spent too much time loitering around Little Tokyo. The sun was going down, tall palm trees swaying against a bleed of pink. As I got closer to our bungalow, the smell of sukiyaki meat wafted through our screen door. We only had sukiyaki for very special occasions. On the porch I saw a pair of shoes, brown boots covered with a thin veneer of dirt. A much larger size than what my father wore. I knew instantly whose shoes they were.

I ripped open the screen door and dropped my bag of lemons onto our area rug. Art, wearing his tan uniform, rose from his seat at the living room table. I jumped into his arms and he held me so tight that my ribs hurt.

"Darling!" His breath was warm against my ear.

We didn't dare kiss in front of my parents, but held each other long and hard, our cheeks pressed against each other. Art was freshly shaven. He smelled faintly of cologne and something else that I couldn't quite identify.

Pop looked down at his newspaper while Mom poked her head from the kitchen, a wide grin on her face. I hadn't seen her look like that since Pop had received his promotion years ago.

"You didn't tell me!" I scolded him.

"I wanted it to be a surprise."

Art looked down at the uniform that was peeking out from my overcoat. "You are looking very official."

"Well, you are, too."

When I mentioned how clean-cut he looked, he admitted that he had stopped by a barbershop in Little Tokyo. "They wouldn't accept any money from me."

"Well, that shows you how much the community values what you and the other boys did."

Art didn't look convinced, as if he needed more evidence than a barbershop's freebie.

I picked up the bag of lemons from the floor and brought them to Mom in the kitchen. "Need help?"

"No, go, go."

I led Art by the hand, like our early dating days. I pulled him through each room as if we were taking a stroll through a museum. "This is Mom and Pop's," I said as we passed the front bedroom, barely large enough to accommodate their double bed, which was covered by a quilt sewn by the wife of a produce worker. Occasionally, when I went into the bathroom late at night, I heard my parents talking in Japanese. I couldn't make out the exact words, but the beat of conversation was comforting, confirmation that some practices had returned to normal after everything we had gone through over the past four years.

"This is the bathroom." Coral ceramic tile on the floor and halfway up the walls. A gray pumice stone sat on the edge of the dingy tub. Long Japanese wash towels hung from a rod. No matter how much Mom scrubbed, brown stains remained in the toilet and around the edges of the sink. Pop promised that he would regrout the tiles but hadn't gotten around to it yet.

"And this is our bedroom." I had purposely chosen the back room for us. We didn't get the morning light through the windows, but I preferred the privacy.

He glanced at the bed and I blushed. I knew what he was thinking. He wanted to reprise the moments of passion we shared at the Hotel Roosevelt in Chicago, first before he left for Fort Shelby and then after our wedding. He opened the tiny closet, which held my two other uniforms and a couple of dresses. The long windows, wood frames in need of a fresh coat of paint, faced north and overlooked a sad backyard—a broken concrete patio and overgrown grasses and dandelions. Pop seemed to have lost all interest in gardening after the war.

"It's not much," I said apologetically.

"It's plenty," Art gratefully said. He was well aware of the housing shortage due to all the returning soldiers and defense workers who had flooded into the area.

We sat down at the dinner table in the living room. A built-in china cabinet held all the plates that we had stored in a German poinsettia farmer's barn in San Fernando during the war.

The farmer's workers and neighbors didn't know of his benevolence until a few weeks earlier, when I had gone to pick up our belongings. I drove the Model A between the glass houses of perennial poinsettias, their green leaves pruned in anticipation of Christmas. While some of our friends had arrived in Los Angeles to find their storage areas ransacked, all of our hastily packed boxes were accounted for.

I realized as I used a *shamoji* to spoon rice onto Art's *chawan* that this would be the first time for him to experience an Ito family meal, Los Angeles–style. Instead of the chipped cups and hand-me-down utensils we received from the Quakers on Clark and Division, we were eating from beautiful matching plates, indigo-blue Japanese bowls, and sparkling stemware, all intact after spending the past four years in a San Fernando barn. I felt so proud and satisfied to show my new husband that we indeed had a bit of class.

Art had been hungry, first politely taking nibbles of his suki-yaki with his chopsticks and then bringing his *chawan* full of short-grain rice up to his face and practically shoveling his meal down. Both Mom and I stifled laughter. It was the best compliment to the cook to see someone enjoying their food with such a lack of restraint. Judging from the looseness of his uniform on his frame, he had lost some weight while serving in Europe.

After Art pushed himself from the table, my mother suggested, "*Ofuro?*" and he nodded. She began to fill the tub and brought out a blue towel that would be his. He asked for an ashtray, and I was a bit surprised, because he hadn't smoked before he left for Europe. That mystery scent that I had noticed before—it had been nicotine. Pop had never developed a taste for tobacco and we Ito women were thankful not to have the stench of smoke in our clothes and linens. That would change now, one of the many adjustments that would await us as we merged our households.

Mom dug out a ceramic ashtray that we brought out for guests, and I handed Art a folded set of pajamas that I had purchased on a whim for him at the Bronzeville 5-10-25 Cents Store, right next to the greengrocer where I got the lemons. The inside of the dime store was a bit of an eyesore with a hodgepodge of goods ranging from shoes to pots and pans, but that perfectly represented our state of mind and condition. The pajamas were tan with a pattern of small brown foxes. I imagined how handsome he would look wearing them after bathing. He accepted the pajamas and ashtray and retreated into the bathroom with a copy of the *Los Angeles Times*, a box of Lucky Strikes, and matches.

Wearing a pair of rubber gloves, I began to wash the dishes in the sink. Mom joined me there to rinse them off.

"He smokes," she declared in Japanese.

"Ummm." I scrubbed our cast-iron pan of the sugary-sweet sukiyaki sauce that had collected on the bottom.

Pop said nothing at first and then excused himself to take an evening stroll. He never took walks when it was dark. Although my parents had been initially lukewarm about my marriage to Art, once the ceremony was done, they were fully on board. Divorce was scandalous—a black mark that would follow a woman throughout her life. Our future depended on the success of my marriage, and as a result, we had all eagerly awaited Art's arrival. Now that he was here, each one of us found it difficult to adjust.

After Art was in our bedroom in his fox pajamas, I took a bath. I made sure that every inch of my body was scrubbed and clean. I dressed in the same lacy lingerie that I had purchased for our honeymoon in a fancy hotel in Chicago. I tightened the belt of my bathrobe and wiped my hand against the foggy mirror. Yes, that was me, my permed waves lying limp from the steam and my cheeks more pink than usual.

When I went into the bedroom, Art was lying on the bedspread, reading the newspaper. I had imagined this reunion over and over and now it had finally come.

"I hope you won't have any problems adjusting to all of this," I told him.

"Are you kidding me? Living with a bunch of smelly soldiers is an adjustment. This is paradise." He folded the newspaper neatly and placed it on one of the side tables that we had inherited from the previous owner.

I tossed my dirty uniform and underwear in the hamper,

knowing that I'd have to wash them later, and my bra in the top drawer of our bureau. I felt strangely like I was onstage, performing for an audience of one.

"If we'd stayed in Chicago, you could have worked with James Nishimura's company." James had started General Mailing Company with other partners. I had heard through letters from my Chicago friends that it was becoming a success.

"Your parents needed to be back in Los Angeles."

"That's true. When Pop's cap froze onto his head that winter, it was the last straw."

"They are shoveling snow back home. I can handle sixty-degree weather in spring." He began giving me updates on his parents, aunt, and younger sister. All were well, as usually all was well with the Nakasone household.

I waited until he had exhausted all family news. I had to get it out now—this matter could not wait any longer. "I saw Babe recently."

"Oh, I was meaning to tell you—he got discharged early and was transferred to the Pasadena Regional Hospital from San Francisco."

"Was he wounded?" This was the first I'd heard of it.

"Ah." Art, for once, was tongue-tied. "R and R," he managed. Rest and recreation. I wasn't a fool. A soldier wasn't admitted into a hospital for recreation. Still, Art didn't budge. He wasn't going to tell me why his best man was hospitalized.

"His father, Mr. Watanabe, was brought to the Japanese Hospital. That's when I ran into Babe."

"Oh, the father's pretty old. Over fifty," Art said. "And on his own. The mother passed away a while back."

I lowered my voice so that it didn't carry through our walls to my parents' bedroom. "I think that Babe beat his father."

Art was again slow to respond. "What? Is that what the father said?"

"No. But you had to see Mr. Watanabe's body. He claimed that he fell down the stairs, but—"

"Why would Babe do such a thing?"

"I have no idea. He's two times the size of his father."

Art fiddled with the buttons on the pajamas. "You didn't say anything to anyone about this, did you?"

"Of course not. I'm not a dimwit, Art."

The pang of this difficult conversation—*Oh, why does it always revolve around Babe Watanabe?*—deflated some of my initial excitement about our reunion. Art sensed it, too. But he was never one to let conflict escalate to the point of ruin. He got up from the bed and stood close to me, close enough for me to smell the nicotine on his breath. He untied my belt and my robe fell open to reveal the lace of my honeymoon lingerie. By all signs, he had remembered this special nightgown. Pulling back the bedspread, he led me to the starched white sheets. "Let's stop talking," he said.

CHAPTER 5

I didn't notice it the first day and night. And not even the second. But on the third day that Art was with us in Boyle Heights, I noticed that a certain light in his eye had altered, almost imperceptibly. We would be talking about something totally mundane and his interest would wander. He'd ask a question that I had answered a few minutes earlier. "Art, are you listening to me?" I'd say, trying to mask my irritation.

He'd smile sheepishly and all was forgiven.

A week after his arrival, Art awoke me in the night because his leg was shaking so violently that it moved the sheets and blankets.

"Darling, darling—" I whispered. I was afraid to shock him out of his nightmare, but I didn't want him to be in so much distress in his sleep. As I gently massaged his back, he began to bellow, "No, dammit, no!" And then a stream of obscenities.

I had never heard Art use such language. It rattled me. How could I have thought that I knew the whole Art? We had only dated for a few months before we got married. He'd spent more time on the front than he had with me.

"*Daijoubu?*" my mother called from behind our closed bedroom door.

"It's nothing," I lied. I was trembling as Art stirred. He

stretched his body while his leg ceased shaking. "I think you were having a bad dream," I told him softly.

Art, his eyes half-open, nodded, and then his head fell back onto the pillow.

I took a brisk morning walk to clear my head before reporting to work at seven o'clock. I failed at convincing myself that everything was proceeding as I had imagined. Yes, Art had returned practically unblemished, aside from being skinnier and sporting a scar on his thigh. But the intimacies we were able to share in our letters had disappeared as we dealt with the everyday—his laundry, my work schedule, the filing of paperwork at Veterans Administration. I almost longed for the days in which we were separated so I could read on paper how much I was missed and adored.

Only Canter's Delicatessen and the newspaper delivery boys represented any signs of life so early in the morning. On the stretch of Brooklyn Avenue that serviced the Jewish community in Boyle Heights, men wearing white dress shirts and suspenders made their way to Canter's. The bakery goods arranged in a glass case tempted me, but I never went in. The Leaders Beauty Shop, right next door, was also a bit of a mystery until a former Manzanar acquaintance, Martha Kamei, got a job there as a manicurist. "The ladies there are a hoot," she told me when we happened to run into each other on the sidewalk. "It's more of a Jewish social club than a beauty parlor," she said. I remembered my Nisei beautician back in Chicago, Peggy, who could be counted on to provide the best accounting of Japanese American newcomers. I was convinced that more crimes could be solved there than at the police department.

As I neared the Japanese Hospital, the blare of a siren cut through my musings. A long white ambulance streaked around the corner into our driveway from Fickett Street.

I rushed into the hospital hallway, only to recognize the familiar battered face of Mr. Watanabe as he lay on the gurney. An ambulance worker was pressing the old man's stomach with a bunch of towels, which were soaked with blood.

I wanted to cry out, "What happened?" but that would have been unprofessional, even for a lowly nurse's aide like me.

"Los Angeles General was full," the ambulance driver explained. We didn't have an emergency room. White Memorial would have been a better choice. It didn't matter at this point. Mr. Watanabe needed care immediately.

Chole and an orderly were sent to prepare the operating room. Mrs. Honma shouted for me to bring clean towels and bandages, and I ran to the supply room and brought over an armful. She, Dr. Isokane, and another nurse worked quickly, discarding the bloody towels onto the ground, applying the fresh bandages and pressing down on the wound. All three of them had worked in camp hospitals and were used to being inventive with limited supplies. I wrapped Mr. Watanabe's lower body with an extra blanket to keep him warm.

He was in shock, but he was conscious. He couldn't talk but his eyes followed me while I stood at the foot of the bed.

"What is it, Mr. Watanabe?" I called out.

Dr. Isokane shooed me in Japanese to move out of the way.

I reluctantly receded into the hallway. What in the world had happened to Mr. Watanabe?

"Nurse, nurse!" A patient who was recovering from gallbladder surgery was having a difficult time of it and constantly calling out for pain remediation. Dr. Isokane didn't want to overprescribe medication, so I went into the patient's room to massage his feet and puff up his pillows. I was relieved to be kept busy, but Mr. Watanabe wasn't far from my mind. I heard two nurses in the hallway murmuring about a gunshot wound. Who could have shot Mr. Watanabe? He didn't look like he had a dime to his name. Who in the world would have benefitted from harming him?

Luckily the leading Nisei surgeon had an office on First Street in Little Tokyo, less than a mile from us, near the greengrocer who had sold me lemons. The surgeon had operated on the men who had been shot in Manzanar during a riot in December 1942. My family, including Rose, had been in camp at that time, but my parents forbade us from leaving our barracks. Later we heard that the military police had shot at least nine of us. That surgeon hadn't been able to save two men, but it didn't mean that he wasn't the best. He was one of the first to get a surgical rotation at Los Angeles General Hospital when its state-of-the-art medical facility opened in 1933.

It was about three hours before the surgeon, Dr. Isokane, and Mrs. Honma emerged from the operating room. Their surgery caps were wet with perspiration and their gowns slick with blood. The surgeon, who was known to be hale and hearty, often strutting the streets with a cigar jutting out of his mouth, looked depleted. The look of irritation on Mrs. Honma's face was replaced with exhaustion. No matter how cranky she was during day-to-day interactions, she was the nurse I would want by my side in a medical emergency.

They didn't have to say anything for the rest of us to know. Mr. Watanabe had died on the operating table.

Chole, an orderly, and our janitor were sent in to clean up the operating room while I went to see if I could be of any support to Babe. But the waiting room was empty. There was no one there for Mr. Watanabe.

CHAPTER 6

Later in the day Dr. Isokane called the San Mark Hotel, the number on Mr. Watanabe's medical file, in an attempt to contact Babe. "No one knows Shinji Watanabe," he reported.

Although Dr. Isokane could speak English, he did have a bit of an accent. He spoke in a soft, stilted tone as if he were English royalty. Maybe his accent didn't translate well over the telephone, I thought.

"I can let him know," I volunteered. "He was the best man in my wedding."

Under other circumstances, Mrs. Honma would have scolded me about speaking out of turn. But she had lost her vinegar, her eyes bloodshot and her bulky body turning in on itself.

Dr. Isokane nodded, giving me his approval to contact Babe.

Going into the receptionist's office, I promptly called the San Mark Hotel.

"I dunno no Want-a-bee or anyone by that name," said the woman who answered the phone.

"A Japanese man. They call him Babe. His father is a driver."

"No, ma'am. I have no one by that name here."

My chest rose as I let out a deep breath. Now what? I wasn't going to have Mr. Watanabe sent over to the coroner's office without first informing his only son.

I had heard about the San Mark Hotel, but I wasn't quite

sure where it was. It was notorious. There recently had been an hour-long shoot-out there involving a man who had barricaded himself in his room with a rifle. A gun battle ended with him wounding a woman and then killing himself. I wondered why Babe and his father would choose to live in such a place, but there were slim pickings for all of us Japanese Americans who had returned en masse to the West Coast to find our former homes taken over by strangers while we were behind barbed wire.

I looked up the address from Mr. Watanabe's file: 210 North San Pedro. I set out to go over there in person, bringing my purse and a sweater with me on the bus. During the ride, I tried to imagine what had existed on that block before—a cluster of doctor's offices, small restaurants, and some manufacturing outlets. As I got off at First Street and walked two blocks, it was immediately apparent that the area had markedly changed. I pulled the sweater over my bust, as if it could somehow protect me from lecherous onlookers.

The receptionist behind a caged window at the San Mark Hotel was a thin Black woman with a colorful scarf covering her hair. When she began talking, I instantly recognized her voice.

"I'm here from the Japanese Hospital," I told her. "I had called earlier about Haruki Watanabe. He had sustained wounds from a gun."

A light-skinned Black man, perhaps around my and Art's age, approached us from a dark corridor. He wore a tan tweed newsboy cap that matched the color of his face. His skin was unblemished and smooth; only something steely in his eyes revealed that he was not to be trifled with. "Room 302," he said.

"Oh, the Chinese fellow who got shot. Why didn't you say so?" The receptionist was practically scolding me for not properly describing Mr. Watanabe's tragic circumstance.

"I'll take over, Willie Mae."

The receptionist shrugged and moved out of the small booth as the man moved in. "Sorry about that. She's new." He began to sort some papers left on the scratched wooden counter and put some change in a metal cashbox. "Mighty sad to hear about Hal."

"Hal?"

"He called himself Hal Wat over here. No one knew his real last name except me. Everyone here thinks he's Chinese." The manager introduced himself as Charles Jones. From the way he spoke, I figured that he was a Californian like me.

"Hello, Mr. Jones, I'm Aki." I went to the open doorway and extended my hand. The manager first seemed to be taken aback and then quickly squeezed my hand. "Call me Charles," he said. I detected a slip of a smile on his lips.

"I'm here to speak to the son, Babe—Shinji—" I had no idea what the hotel was calling him.

"Oh, Babe moved out of here about a week ago. I don't think he was getting on with his father."

I felt weak in my knees. Could it be that my hunch was right? That Babe had hurt his own father?

"Do you know how to reach him?"

"No, I'm sorry. I know that he was tight on money." As soon as he said it, Charles closed his mouth as if he had said too much.

Why was Babe hurting for money? Hadn't he received his stipend from the government for military service?

"I'm confused," I said. "I thought that the room had been rented by Babe."

"No, the lease was under the father's name. Hal moved in three months ago. Babe only arrived a couple of weeks ago."

"Really?" I had assumed that they had come to Los Angeles together for some reason.

"You have some business with Babe?"

I stood tongue-tied. I knew I shouldn't reveal anything to the manager before contacting Babe, the next of kin, but I was at a loss to know what to do. "Uh—"

Charles's eyes widened, his right eye, either from a tic or injury, blinking faster than the left one. "Hal didn't make it," he surmised.

I shifted my weight. *Why did I volunteer to be the messenger?* I certainly wasn't equipped to be discreet.

"I'm really sorry. He was a good man," he said.

There was no sense in playing coy. I now regretted not putting on some lipstick to add color to my face. "I know that this is quite an imposition, but would I be able to look in Mr. Watanabe's apartment? There may be something that will help me locate his relatives."

"The police already took his address book."

"There may be something in Japanese that they missed. He was from Japan, after all."

Charles's brown eyes stayed on me. He then plucked a key from a grid of keys hanging from individual nails. "C'mon, let's take a look. The police didn't tell me not to let anyone in."

I followed him up the stairs, gladly bypassing the rickety elevator that reeked of urine and vomit. The hallways were dark and as I reached out to steady myself, I found that the walls were sticky with a mysterious residue. Luckily my years of living on Clark and Division in Chicago had prepared me for less-than-desirable apartment buildings.

When Charles opened the door to 302, I was relieved to see sun streaming in through two tall windows, the right one open. At least Mr. Watanabe had had some light to brighten up his living space.

A twin bed had been pushed into the corner of the room. At first because of the sunlight, I hadn't noticed the pool of blood, as long as a person's body, staining the dingy sheets and thin yellow blanket. The smell of dried blood was also not foreign to me.

Charles continued to study me. Did he think that I would faint at encountering such a terrible scene? From my white shoes and what he could see of my uniform underneath my sweater, he might guess that I was used to standing in trauma.

"Who could have done such a thing?" I said out loud. "Did he have any problems with anyone in the hotel?"

"He kept to himself in terms of the other renters in the San Mark."

"And no one saw what happened?"

"There's always something going on in this hotel."

Even now I heard a baby's cry rising over the din of two men arguing.

"People heard the gunshot. No one thought anything of it at first. Maybe a car backfiring. But then the neighbor saw Hal's door open and found him soaked in blood."

"Didn't see who shot him?"

Charles shook his head. "Probably went out the window."

I poked my head through shredded curtains. Sure enough, there was a fire escape with a series of ladders leading down to the sidewalk. The windows faced a warehouse. This area was more industrial than commercial. It would be easy for someone to disappear without being noticed.

"A lot of outsiders came by Hal's apartment." Charles volunteered this information. "Sometimes even white men."

"White men?"

"One, I think, is a doctor. He used to have an office at the Buddhist temple there on First Street. I went to him once when I got pink eye. Hodel was his name."

What was Mr. Watanabe doing with a *hakujin* doctor? There were plenty of Issei and Nisei doctors now on First Street.

"Lawyer types, too. One's a bigwig with the state attorney's office. His name is Kenny. He's been in the newspapers." Charles spoke as if that were a point of pride.

Why would Mr. Watanabe command such an audience?

"I was thinking that maybe they could be his customers." Charles crossed his arms. Even though he was thin, he had lines of sinewy muscle in his forearms.

"How odd," I said out loud. "What drivers have their customers come to their apartments?"

I took a quick turn around the small hotel room. There wasn't much to see. A tiny sink with a razor resting by the faucet. A round mirror that had been dropped, judging from the crack in its center. A metal bowl on the floor, probably for hand laundry, and two white shirts hanging from a wire strung in the corner. They were starched and pristinely washed—he must have had them professionally laundered. I sniffed a familiar scent of rice water, which was used to add stiffness to the clothes. A bamboo basket with a bunch of pressed shirts was sitting on the floor, the one anomaly of a disciplined life. Otherwise, Mr. Watanabe seemed to take care in how he presented himself to the outside world.

Before Charles could stop me, I opened the drawers to the small dresser. White underwear and T-shirts, socks and so on. I didn't see any books or letters, except for a postcard pinned to the wall near the bloody bed. It was a scene from the Colorado Street Bridge in Pasadena, a grand building in the distance.

Shouts boomed from the hallway, and Charles rushed out to see what the hubbub was. I quickly pocketed the postcard, a harmless theft, I tried to convince myself.

"Domestic dispute," Charles reported, returning to Mr. Watanabe's room and closing the door behind him. I suddenly felt vulnerable and must have telegraphed my fear because

Charles commented, "I think that you better head on home. Things can get pretty rough here when the sun goes down."

I didn't need any convincing. I was about to leave when I noticed that a black-and-white photo of a young *hakujin* woman had been pinned on the door. It was a portrait of her face; she looked coyly over her shoulder, her long hair brushing against her cheekbones. She seemed too young for an older man like Mr. Watanabe to have on display. I wonder where he got such a photo. Maybe a passenger had dropped it when she had opened her wallet to pay him for a ride? If so, keeping it was quite uncouth. Was Mr. Watanabe a *sukebe*, a Japanese term my mother used to describe nasty old men who enjoyed glancing up a woman's skirt when she climbed up a flight of stairs? Perhaps Mr. Watanabe had a dark side that led to his demise.

When I arrived home, the family was already eating. "We couldn't wait for you, Aki," Mom explained, spooning some bacon fried rice onto a plate for me.

Art had assumed my father's place at the head of the dining room table, and I wasn't sure that I liked it. Judging by his wide smile and the relaxed way he sat in the chair, I assumed that he had good news to share.

After I went to wash my hands, I took off my coat and slipped into the seat to his right, my mother's former place. "I got a part-time job," he announced. "Working at the *Rafu Shimpo*. Selling ads but writing, too."

"That's wonderful, Art."

My parents quietly picked at their rice with their chopsticks. They seemed less than enthused. I tried to quiet the doubts in my mind. Before Art's return, my mother had asked me, "What kind of work will he be able to do?" He wasn't an aggressive businessman type like Roy. He wasn't a doctor type. "He seems honest. Maybe he can work for the government?" my mother had once said. I had no idea why my mother thought honesty would be a prerequisite for being a government worker, especially with everything that we had just gone through. The government, however, would have at least offered benefits. I was sure that the salary for a part-time job at a local Japanese newspaper would be quite miserable. Even though my father valued reading his newspapers, he was less than thrilled to have family members work for them.

But I was happy for Art. Anything that would erase that occasional vacant look on his face was good for me. And newspapers were all about the news, right? Perhaps distancing himself from the recent past would restore his mental health and chase away the awful nightmares he had, night after night.

Fortunately, no one asked me about my day, and for half an hour I could concentrate entirely on the crunch of the fried bacon with the rice and green onions. Everyone finished before me, and I heard my mother fill up the bathtub while my father retreated into their bedroom.

After I washed the dishes on my own, I went into the living room, where Art was resting in Pop's easy chair. He had a pencil behind his ear while he read the newspaper.

I sat on the ottoman next to Art's stockinged feet and leaned forward. "I have something awful to tell you," I said in a low voice. "Babe's father was brought to the hospital in an ambulance. He was shot in his hotel room."

The pencil fell and rolled onto the hardwood floor.

"He didn't make it, Art."

Art went slack-jawed. He listened with rapt attention.

"Babe is nowhere to be found."

His broad shoulders sank. "It's not what you're thinking. It wasn't Babe."

"But where is he? Why would he abandon his father like this?"

Art bent down to claim his pencil. "Babe saved my life. I wouldn't be here if it hadn't been for him."

"What happened over there, Art?"

Art shook his head and returned to his reading. I noticed that his long legs were now tightly crossed, as if he was preventing an outside force from harming him.

I went to change out of my whites and hang up my sweater. I checked my sweater pocket and pulled out the postcard that I had stolen from Mr. Watanabe's room. The caption told me the illustration was of the Colorado Street Bridge in Pasadena at night. It also mentioned the Hotel Vista del Arroyo, which must be the grand building that resembled a Spanish fortress.

On the other side was a note below the postmark of January 15, 1946:

To-san,

I'm back in California. I'll visit you as soon as I can.

Shinji

CHAPTER 7

I stayed at home the next day. When I called in sick, Dr. Iso-kane understood. He was feeling pretty poorly himself.

I couldn't imagine walking into the hospital as if it was any other day. I was sure Mrs. Honma had reported for duty like always. Her parents and siblings lived in Nagasaki and when news of the atomic bombing reached Topaz War Relocation Center, Mrs. Honma had reportedly donned her nursing uniform and gone to work in the camp hospital the next morning. In that way, her constitution was a lot stronger than mine. Perhaps she protected her heart with such a tough exterior.

With Art at the newspaper office and my parents downtown, I had the whole house to myself. I couldn't remember being alone like this at home since before the war when we lived in Tropico.

I took a hot, leisurely bath, sudsing our green Palmolive soap in the Japanese towel to simulate bubbles. Getting out when my skin felt like chicken skin, I dried myself with another long Japanese towel; they required less detergent and space to clean. My cheeks flushed, I was in the middle of putting on a house-dress when I heard our pitiful doorbell release a tinny sound.

Our peephole had been painted over, so I peeked from our living room window. Two *hakujin* men, dressed in suits and felt hats. These weren't encyclopedia salesmen.

When I opened the door, they flashed their badges and identified themselves as LAPD homicide detectives. I had encountered detectives before in Chicago. It hadn't been a pleasant experience.

"Hello, we are looking for Art Nakasone," the one in a gray gabardine suit said. The other detective wore a plain black suit with a striped tie.

"Yes, he lives here. I'm his wife, Aki. What is this about?"

"Do you know a Babe Watanabe?" the striped tie asked.

"Yes." I tried to steady my voice to keep it from cracking. "He was in my wedding. He served with my husband in Company B with the 100th/442nd Regimental Combat Team in Europe." I purposely gave specifics of Art and Babe's military unit. Some *hakujin* seemed persuaded of our patriotism by mention of the 442nd.

The two detectives showed no response. They must have already known of Art's connection to Babe. I felt pressure in the pit of my stomach. Why in the world had Art been dragged into Babe's mess?

"When was the last time you saw Mr. Watanabe?"

"About three weeks ago. I work at the Japanese Hospital and he had brought his father in for a checkup." Yes, I was fibbing a bit, but I was only a nurse's aide, after all. If they wanted specifics, they could ask Dr. Isokane for details. I personally didn't feel any obligation to protect Babe, but for Art's sake, I certainly didn't want to blab and inadvertently incriminate him in some way. "My husband hasn't seen Babe since they fought together," I added.

The detectives exchanged glances. What did they know that I didn't?

"Well, we'd like to verify it with him."

"I'll tell him you stopped by."

One handed me a business card with his name, DETECTIVE

CARL MILLER, and they left in their brown Ford sedan. I wanted to tear that card up into tiny pieces and throw it in a hole in our backyard. But that wouldn't keep them from seeking a conversation with Art.

My brief Palmolive bubble bath reprieve had been ruined by the detectives' visit. I didn't like to bother Art at work at the *Rafu*, but I felt that I had no choice. I had to go through an Issei female receptionist and then Art's editor before I got him on the phone.

"What's wrong?" He could tell how upset I was from the tone of my voice.

"A couple of policemen were here at the house. They are looking for Babe."

"What did you tell them?"

"What could I? Just the truth, that I hadn't seen him for weeks. I don't like this, Art."

"Don't worry about it." Art's voice sounded breezy and casual. "We can talk about this later, okay?"

After hanging up the phone, I felt even worse than before. I paced around our small house. I could have dusted the living room and our bedroom to distract myself, but I wasn't like my mother. Cleaning and housework were the last on my list of diverting activities. I then remembered the gold watch that Mr. Watanabe had been clutching when I'd first encountered him in his hospital room. It hadn't been on his body when he died—I knew, because I had been tasked with putting all his personal belongings aside for the authorities. Could he have been killed for his watch? Maybe his death had nothing to do with Babe.

I called the number on the card. The detective wasn't available, but I asked the receptionist to have him call me back.

I opened my pocketbook and gazed at the postcard from Mr. Watanabe's room. Pasadena wasn't that far from my birthplace of Tropico, but it wasn't a place I frequented. Pasadena was for the rich, namely *hakujin*, full of fancy estates. There were some grand hotels there as well, where Issei worked pruning gardens or washing sheets. My sister and I did go to the Rose Parade once, in 1941, because one of her friends had been on the Nisei Week Court and was riding on the Japanese Community float, which had been decorated with pink cherry blossoms. It even won an award, and we all were flush with optimism, thinking that 1941 would be the best year ever in our young adulthood. How wrong we had been.

At work the next day, I assisted Dr. Isokane with an exam of an Issei patient with dangerously high blood pressure. I asked him, "Do you know the Pasadena Regional Hospital?"

"Army one? Very nice." He gave me a second look. "Not sure if they would hire a Japanese."

"Oh, no, I'm quite happy here," I assured him. Art had mentioned that Babe had been hospitalized at the Pasadena Regional Hospital before being released to Los Angeles. Perhaps somebody at that medical facility could tell me more about Babe and where he could be now.

Getting to Pasadena from Boyle Heights was a cinch. I looked up the bus line in a directory we kept by our telephone. The phone book revealed the address for the Pasadena Regional Hospital and the AAA map showed me that the hospital wasn't that far from the stop on Fair Oaks and Colorado. I put on my white nursing oxfords, even though they were embarrassingly utilitarian and dumpy. This mission required walking, and I had to put comfort before fashion.

The bus was filled with middle-aged Boyle Heights women of all races. They wore working shoes, too, black flats with rubber heels, and had their hair tied back in scarves. Some of them held paper-bag lunches. One woman even carried a bucket. They were ready to work.

After one transfer, I disembarked at the intersection of Fair Oaks and Colorado, the heart of Pasadena's downtown. Memories of the 1941 Rose Parade flooded back to me, me grabbing for Rose's hand as we navigated through the crowds standing on the sidewalk. Now that I had traveled through some midsized cities in the Midwest, Pasadena's wide streets, with their sedans and streetcar, reminded me of those communities: sedate, civilized, and definitely *hakujin*.

Grateful that I had decided on my working shoes, I discovered the walk to the Pasadena Regional Hospital was farther than I expected. I wondered if I was lost. I was in a posh neighborhood with pristine mansions. What would a military hospital be doing in a place like this?

I spotted a gardener, who I assumed was an Issei, wearing a pith helmet and unloading a lawn mower from a truck in worse shape than our Model A. "Hello!" I greeted him, shading my eyes from the May sun with my hand.

He guided his mower down two planks leading from the back of the truck to the street. The gardener seemed annoyed by my interruption; he was obviously all about work.

"Do you happen to know where the Pasadena Regional Hospital is? *Byoin?*" I added, in case he didn't understand English.

He pointed to a blue and yellow capped tower a couple of streets away.

I thought that he had perhaps misunderstood me. "Hospital. *Byoin,*" I repeated.

He glared at me as if I were an idiot. "Yeah, right there," he growled, and pushed his mower to a green expanse of grass.

I didn't take his bad temperament to heart; I was used to these kinds of characters at the produce market. These men saw no use for chitchat, and I, in turn, appreciated their no-nonsense nature.

Keeping my eye on the blue and yellow cap, I walked down a

couple of blocks, attracting the attention of a few domestics and more gardeners who were probably wondering why an Asian woman in nursing shoes was stumbling down their sidewalks. Finally, I reached a most impressive pinkish building, its tower topped with a dome of bright tiles. It looked like it could be in Spain, not in a residential neighborhood in Pasadena. I realized that it was the same building on that postcard pinned in Mr. Watanabe's room.

This was a hospital? It looked like a resort for the wealthy with a lot of leisure time. But sure enough, in the front was a sign, PASADENA REGIONAL HOSPITAL. And judging by the men in uniform walking in and out of its doors, I could safely surmise that its medical services were expressly for military veterans.

In the lobby, high windows spilled sun onto tile floors. The graceful curved archways made me feel like I was in the world of the Moors. Elaborate light fixtures which resembled ancient lanterns hung from the ceiling. I hadn't felt this overwhelmed by a building since I walked into the Newberry Library, where I had worked when we first arrived in Chicago after being released from Manzanar.

I must have looked disoriented and out of place because a young man, probably a Nisei, came to my rescue. I don't know whether it was how we styled our hair, wore our clothes, or spoke, but we shared a sense that we were both Japanese American. He approached me on a pair of crutches. "Hello, you lost?"

"This is a hospital, right?"

The man smiled, his thin eyes narrowing into crescents. "Yes, pretty high-tone digs, huh?"

I tried to think how to explain my reason for being there, but luckily he kept talking.

"I'm Harry Nakayama. I was with the Military Intelligence

Service." I accepted his handshake, which was firm and warm, and out of habit, introduced myself by my maiden name, "Aki Ito. Oh, but I'm Aki Nakasone now."

"I know some Nakasones from Hawaii—"

"May be a different family. My husband's from Chicago." The truth of the matter was I wouldn't know for sure if Art could be an extended member of this Hawaii clan. I was embarrassed that I didn't know more of Art's family's background.

We didn't bother to continue through the rabbit hole of who was related to whom. The name Nakayama was like Watanabe and Ito—the Japanese versions of Smith, Brown, or Jones.

I asked about his injury and he explained that he had been on a military ship when he took a tumble into the cargo hold. "Fell fifty feet. Can you believe that?"

I covered my mouth in both horror and sympathy. "It's a miracle that you're alive."

"Wish I could have a more heroic story to tell." He explained that he was originally from Fresno, a farming town along Highway 99 in California.

I knew a little about the MISers, who trained in Minneapolis, not far from Chicago. They were involved in covert activities in the Pacific—breaking codes and interrogating Japanese POWs.

"I think that you all did something incredibly heroic," I told him.

Harry's face colored a bit. I didn't know if he was humble or if he wasn't used to hearing compliments. Fresno folks, like my sister's former roommate, Chiyo, were more country, presenting no false front.

"My husband, Art, just got home," I said. "He was with Company B in the 442nd."

"Is he in here?"

"No, actually, I'm looking for a friend. Babe Watanabe. His Japanese name is Shinji."

"Oh, Babe? Sure. But he was discharged weeks ago."

"Yes, I realize that. Do you know him well?"

"No. He was in another ward, so I didn't talk to him much. You should probably speak to Dr. Sidney Reed. He's the supervising doctor in that ward."

"You've been so helpful. Thank you so much. I hope you get out soon."

Harry smiled back and then swung his crutches to make his way toward the door.

I checked the directory for Dr. Sidney Reed. He was listed as the head of the Psychiatric Department. My worst fears were realized. Something was wrong with Babe's head.

A *hakujin* nurse was filing a manila folder in a metal cabinet when I walked into Dr. Reed's office. She wore her red hair in a tight, sleek bun which was practically hiding underneath her starched white cap.

I saw her register my white medical shoes.

"Hello, I'm looking for Dr. Sidney Reed."

"Do you have an appointment?"

"No, I don't," I said.

The nurse was prepared to deny me a meeting so I quickly interjected, "It's about one of his former patients. Shinji Babe Watanabe."

Her lips softened a bit and then she told me to wait.

Finally a trim *hakujin* man with a pencil-thin mustache appeared in the doorway of his office. He wore a white medical coat and was holding a manila file. I had definitely caught him in the middle of work.

I apologized for arriving unexpectedly. "Babe Watanabe was the best man in our wedding. In my husband's army company. They fought together overseas. He's missing and I thought that maybe you would have clues to where he might have gone." As soon as I spit out my little speech, I realized how ridiculous I sounded. How in the world would a doctor—even a psychiatrist—know where his former patient had gone?

I don't know if it was because he had taken pity on me, but Dr. Reed ushered me into his office. He had a large window which faced the Colorado Street Bridge and the San Gabriel Mountains in the distance. How could he even concentrate on his patients with such a gorgeous landscape to gaze upon every day?

He asked me a few personal questions and I wondered if he was using his analysis skills to get into my head. When I told him that I was a nurse's aide, he asked me if I worked there at his hospital. I was puzzled by his questions. Most Southern California hospitals didn't hire Japanese women except to clean floors.

"No, I'm at the Japanese Hospital," I explained. Judging by the expression of recognition on his face, I could see he was familiar with our facility.

"Well, I can't disclose medical details of Mr. Watanabe's case. That's confidential, of course." He leaned back in his chair and I glanced at the line of cars, as small as ants from the window, moving on the bridge.

I desperately tried to think of anything that might help me figure out what was going on with Babe. "You're a psychiatrist, yes? May I ask you a general question then?"

"I'll answer to the best of my ability."

"Would a soldier going through war nerves harm himself or another person?"

"It's a possibility." Dr. Reed responded so quickly that I knew that such violence was not uncommon. A frown line appeared in between his eyebrows. "Are you telling me that Babe Watanabe has hurt someone?"

"No, no," I lied. I knew as a doctor he had a responsibility to report any patient's harmful tendencies. "I was just asking for professional reasons. Being at the hospital and all."

Dr. Reed pursed his lips and remained silent. I took it as a sign for me to leave.

"Thank you for your time," I said, abruptly rising from my chair.

"If you see Mr. Watanabe, you can tell him that he can come and see me anytime."

I nodded. As I exited, I almost crashed into his nurse. She had been eavesdropping on our conversation, but for what purpose, I wasn't sure.

As I rode on the bus back to Boyle Heights, I was so distracted that I didn't bother to look at the changing scenery through the window. I knew little about psychiatry, and to be honest, the whole field of mental health intimidated me. If a patient came to us with a broken leg, we would know to set it and put it in a plaster cast for healing. But for a malfunction in the brain . . . Those patients seemed so difficult to treat. Was Babe soft in the head? Even before experiencing combat, he'd certainly seemed emotionally needy, but at a loss as to how to make real connections. And what was the truth about Babe's relationship with his father? No matter how contentious it was, I couldn't believe that Babe would resort to shooting his own flesh and blood. I needed to grasp hold of another explanation for the violence that had ended Mr. Watanabe's life. While I unlocked the door of our Boyle Heights house, I heard the phone ringing inside. I hurried in and was able to pick up on the fifth ring.

It was Detective Miller, returning my phone call.

"Oh, detective," I said, trying to recollect why I had called him in the first place. "When Mr. Watanabe came to the hospital weeks ago, he had a gold watch. It seemed very expensive. Just wondered if the police had found it in his room."

"A gold watch, you say." I heard the turning of pages. "Well, nothing was identified as such in his room. Are you saying that it could be missing?"

"I would look for it," I told him. Stories of Issei and Nisei men being prey to robbers were circulating through the Japanese American community. A Buddhist priest, in fact, had used his martial arts training to disarm a midnight intruder. Maybe that priest could properly defend himself, but Mr. Watanabe had been weakened, recovering from injuries, and facing a firearm. He had been a sitting duck in that pitiful little bed of his.

After we finished our conversation, I returned the receiver to its cradle. The phone rang again and I half expected it to be the police asking more follow-up questions. But it wasn't.

"Hi." Art's voice was bright, reminding me of how he used to sound in Chicago. "My editor and other writers want to have dinner tonight in Little Tokyo. You up for it?"

The last thing I wanted to do was to spend time with a bunch of newspaper people. "I don't know. I'm a bit worn out."

"Chop suey," he said, knowing that would seal the deal.

We were to meet at the Far East Café, known to my parents by its Japanese name, Entoro. It was owned by a Cantonese Chinese family of cousins from Iowa, of all places. A few doors east was another chop suey house, Nikko Low, frequented by flower growers, and then San Kwo Low, farther west on First Street, up the stairs from the sidewalk. We Japanese were voracious eaters of chop suey.

When I arrived, Art's group was already seated at a table almost hidden by Far East's wooden dividers. Those dividers made the first floor feel like horse stalls, probably not appreciated by the Japanese who had been forced to live at racetracks when our exodus first began in the spring of 1942. I guessed that the dividers were there to create privacy, but they proved to be obstacles for waitstaff carrying steaming plates of noodles or hot metal pots of tea.

"This is my wife, Aki," Art said, rising to greet me.

To hear Art say "my wife" made my heart leap for a second. I hadn't heard him introduce me as his wife until now. Seated around the rectangular table were three other Nisei journalists—Henry, the *Rafu Shimpo* editor, with a long face and a reluctant smile; Mary, a columnist; and Hisaye, who wrote for a Black newspaper, the *Los Angeles Tribune*. Mary was the more stylish of the two women. Her hair was slicked back and she had on heels, while Hisaye wore spectacles on her makeup-free face. I immediately felt like I was overadorned in my Red Majesty lipstick and burgundy suit.

All three seemed friendly enough to me, but it was obvious that they shared a deep camaraderie with one another. I learned that Henry and Hisaye had both been in Poston, with Henry serving as the editor of the camp's literary journal.

"We were just trying to decide what to order," Mary said, as I took the empty seat next to Art.

"Aki will eat anything," he said, too quickly and loudly for my taste. It was true that I was a bit of a glutton, but he didn't have to reveal my weaknesses to his co-writers so soon.

Mary took charge of the menu: sweet and sour pork, chicken chow mein, almond duck, pork fried rice, and a final indulgence, *homyu*, pork patty with salted fish that only we Japanese Americans seemed to appreciate. All my favorites, but I didn't confirm my culinary passions out loud.

The clatter of plates and the smell of oyster sauce transported me to wedding and funeral luncheons before the war. "I haven't been here in so long," I declared to no one in particular.

"Hisaye, you really should read it." Mary seemed to pick up on a conversation that they had been having when I arrived.

"It's really quite remarkable. He's the Richard Wright of the West Coast."

"I want to. Been so busy. But the other reporters at the *Tribune* seem keen on it."

"Well, of course they are. It's their community's story. But we need to cross racial boundaries."

"I think Hisaye is doing that, five days a week," Henry said in a monotone voice. His expressionless face made it hard to tell if he was irritated or not. "Chester Himes lived at Mary's house while she was in camp," he commented to me. "He wrote that novel in her house."

I had no idea who Chester Himes was but nodded as if I did.

"That's not the only reason I wrote about it in my column," Mary said.

"Uh-huh," he said and then smiled broadly, revealing a line of crowded, crooked teeth. I began to warm to him. He had a deadpan humor that I very much appreciated.

I learned that Mary's column was called "New World A-Coming" (pretty formidable, if you asked me) while Henry's was "Making the Deadline." They prattled on about how the War Relocation Authority was failing us Japanese Americans by not providing adequate transitional housing from camp. And also about rumors that some *hakujin* Californians resented our return so much that they were trying to introduce a state proposition to limit our livelihoods.

When Art excused himself to go to the restroom, I felt slightly abandoned without my anchor. I wasn't a brain like these journalists. I liked to write in my diary, but I hadn't read a novel in years. Of course, a lot had happened during the past four years, but that didn't stop this group from keeping up with current events.

"Didn't someone get killed in Bronzeville yesterday?" Hisaye asked.

I finished a gulp of my now lukewarm oolong tea. "Haruki Watanabe." That piece of information I could contribute. "I work at the Japanese Hospital. He was sent there because General Hospital was too full."

The journalists gazed at me with more respect. Perhaps I had become more valuable as a potential news source. I told them about the medical staff's valiant effort to save the elder Watanabe. Henry knew more background facts about him because he was working on a story that would be going in tomorrow's paper. Art had returned to the table by this time and I was grateful that he hadn't been present for my initial mention of Babe's father. He probably wouldn't appreciate me volunteering anything related to Babe.

"Watanabe is an Issei from the Central Coast," Henry added. "His farm is part of the escheat cases that the courts may be considering."

"S-chet? What's that?" The inquiry tumbled out of my mouth before I could stop myself.

The table of journalists exchanged quick glances and I felt like a fool.

Art put his hand on mine. Normally I would have been happy as a clam to receive affection from Art, but this was different. It was as if I were a feeble old lady who was going senile. "Escheat, darling," he said, "is when the government takes back land under Nisei names because they say we skirted alien land laws." We all knew of property that had been transferred to American-born children by their Japanese immigrant parents before the war. Issei, unlike European immigrants, couldn't become naturalized citizens and the laws on the California books barred them from acquiring property. The only way Issei could buy homes and farms was if they put the title under the names of their American-born children or friends. Noticing the flush of embarrassment on my cheeks, Art added, "I've just learned of the term myself."

"Well, that's not right. They owned their farms, fair and square. It's the government's own fault for having that loophole."

The table erupted in laughter, and I couldn't understand what was so funny.

"I like your wife, Art," Mary declared. "You don't hold back, do you?" Mercifully, the waiter appeared with plates of fragrant dishes, diverting our attention from prohibitive land laws and murder. Hisaye turned the lazy Susan so everyone could claim ample spoonfuls of each dish. Yes, my mouth was watering. I hadn't eaten chop suey since my wedding reception in Chicago's Chinatown.

In the middle of our meal, a perky Nisei woman with a head full of long curls entered our eating space through the wooden dividers. "Hello, everyone! Sorry I'm late. Had to file a story at the last minute." She looked familiar and when she introduced herself as Mary Koyano, I remembered that she had served as one of the city editors of the *Manzanar Free Press*. She worked at City News Service now, alongside a Korean American woman and even a couple of Russian emigres. In addition to that work, she contributed a column to the *Rafu Shimpo* called "Snafu." I didn't bother to say that I also had been in Manzanar. We'd traveled in different circles; while I'd been passing out coats in the Supply Department, she was assigning news stories and regularly interacting with the WRA director.

With the addition of this other Mary, the conversation became even more lively, especially among the women. It was difficult for me to follow, so I kept rotating the lazy Susan, helping myself to seconds and even thirds. Henry was quietly eating while Art chewed thoughtfully, his gaze moving from one dynamic woman to another. I was definitely feeling quite insecure. Maybe if we hadn't rushed to get married, Art could have found a woman who was more his intellectual equal.

"Now, have you read Chester Himes's *If He Hollers Let Him Go?*" the first Mary asked the second.

"No, I haven't. Should I?"

"Guess you didn't get a chance to read Mary's column," Henry said dryly.

The first Mary swatted Henry's upper arm. "It's a masterpiece, I'm telling you. It will educate us Nisei about Jim Crow America." Mary wiped *homyu* grease from her lips. "How about you, Art? Have you heard of Himes?"

"No, I haven't," Art admitted, "but I'm quite familiar with Richard Wright's work. I'm from the South Side of Chicago."

The women all turned to him. They peppered him with questions. *How was it to grow up there? So you weren't in camp? How did you feel when all of us Nisei in camps invaded Chicago?* When Mary Koyano learned that Art had served with the 442nd, more questions followed. As it turned out, Hisaye's own brother, Johnny, had been killed in combat in Italy. Hisaye, while small in stature and more soft-spoken, seemed to command deep respect. When she shared a story about a Black family being burned to death in their home in Fontana, a rural town with a steel mill near the San Bernardino Mountains, our whole party became hushed. The authorities claimed the arson was not racially motivated, but Hisaye feared differently.

As the conversation continued, I felt as though my whole body was diminishing. I wasn't part of this world, one of these people who could elegantly string together words and make deep observations. I excused myself to go to the restroom, but nobody, not even Art, seemed to notice.

Remembering the way to the ladies' room from childhood visits, I made my way toward the back of the restaurant. As I stepped aside to allow a busboy to pass by with a tub of dirty dishes, I noticed a corner table with a familiar patron—the San Mark Hotel manager, Charles Jones, still wearing his cap.

I walked over to say hello. "You eat chop suey?" I asked.

Charles held a forkful of chicken chow mein in front of his mouth. "Doesn't everyone?" After chewing, he wiped his face with a napkin. "You here on your own?"

"No, I'm with my husband and his friends." I pointed to the stall in which Art was holding court in front of the rest of the newspaper crowd. "That's him, talking." I felt a rush of pride seeing him sitting back in his wooden chair, looking so handsome in his tan suit.

Charles took a sip of his water, his eyes still on Art.

"Where are you from, anyway?" I asked.

"San Francisco."

"I thought so. You don't sound like a Southerner like the other newcomers to Los Angeles." By newcomers here, I meant specifically Black people from the Deep South, an inference that Charles immediately received.

"My people are from Mississippi, but I could never understand them either," he said.

I was relieved that I hadn't offended him. Mr. Uyeda had a whole crew of workers from Louisiana and Arkansas at his Bronzeville 5-10-25 Cents Store, but I had to admit that it was difficult for me to follow their speech.

"I was in the service and heard there was a lot of work here in Los Angeles. They weren't lying, but housing is as bad here as San Francisco for Black folks."

I wanted to ask more about his family life, whether he had a wife and children, but I knew that those questions might be too intrusive.

"My husband was in the army, too," I said, trying to forge more of a safe connection.

"Looks like a decent fellow."

"He is."

After going to the ladies' room, I found myself lingering in the back of the restaurant. I enjoyed speaking to Charles more than the newspaper people. He, on the other hand, gave me a side-eye as if he was surprised to see me back at his side.

"You haven't seen Babe Watanabe since we spoke, have you?"

Charles shook his head. "But I've seen your fellow before."

I let his statement sink in before responding. Ceramic dishes clattered from the kitchen. "You have? Well, he just started working at the Japanese newspaper."

"He came by the San Mark."

I frowned. "What? When?"

"About a week ago. He and Babe were outside, sharing a smoke."

That's impossible, I thought. Art had never revealed that he had seen Babe since arriving in California.

I must have worn my doubt on my face because he added, "I remembered him because he was wearing his uniform."

Before I could ask more questions, I spotted the first Mary walking our way.

"Well, I better go," I told Charles in a rush. He seemed perfectly happy to attend to the last bit of his noodles. I gave Mary a smile as we passed each other.

By the time Mary returned to our table, the waiter was taking away all our dirty plates. She gave me a curious look. "Who's that you were talking to?"

"Oh, just someone I've met in my hospital work," I murmured, piling my teacup on my plate, which was stained with mustard and *shoyu*. I felt her eyes still on me. These reporters made me feel uncomfortable, as if they had a sixth sense to figure out when someone was lying.

When the check arrived, the first Mary tried to dive for it, but the sure and steady Henry had it firmly in his grip. There was much tussling over who was going to pay as going Dutch was a foreign concept for us Nisei. Art even put some effort into it, arguing that since he had just joined the ranks of the Japanese local newspapers, he should foot the bill, which, based on his meager salary, absolutely made no sense to me. I was thankful Henry hung on to it, claiming that he would get the *Rafu Shimpo* to reimburse him for our meal. Even I knew that wasn't going to happen. He struggled to his feet and made it over to the cashier at the front, Art following. I noticed that there were salty dried plums, one of his favorite snacks, for sale in a glass case. I knew that we would be coming home with a package.

I was waiting outside for Art by the Far East storefront window when a fashionable Nisei couple walked past the restaurant. I did a double take when I spotted the man's streak of jet-black hair. There had been so many other incidents in which I thought I recognized someone from my past—in Tropico, Manzanar, and even Chicago—and it had turned out to be a stranger. But I wasn't wrong tonight. I knew exactly who that was.

"Roy!" I called out.

I had heard from my mother that Roy Tonai had gotten married after returning to Chicago from military service. His engagement back in February had been quite a shocker. Besides being besotted with my glamorous sister, Roy was quite the ladies' man, leaving a series of broken hearts in his wake. Of all the beauties who had come through his life, he had gotten hitched to wholesome Chiyo, originally from Fresno. Hanging on to Roy's arm, she was now looking quite sharp and sophisticated in her permed bob and floral-pattern suit.

"Congratulations! I heard from my parents."

Chiyo's face shone, her cheeks dewy and pink.

"I didn't even realize you two were seeing each other," I said. Chiyo had stood beside me at Union Station in Chicago to see Roy off for basic training. At that time, I thought that Roy considered both of us as his little sisters. What had changed while Roy had been at war to elevate Chiyo to wife status?

"She won me over with her letters. She wrote pages every week while I was in Europe." Roy gave Chiyo's hand a squeeze as I felt a bit ashamed, wishing I had been as enthusiastic in my correspondence to Art. Work at the Henrotin Hospital in Chicago had kept me so busy that sometimes I only had time to mail postcards or send off a paragraph or two of encouragement.

"We arrived yesterday," Roy said. It was just like him to be out and about in his hometown. He wasn't going to waste any time by shutting himself inside. He was a big shot's son who had now become a big shot himself. "We moved in with Pablo and his wife in the house on Thirtieth Street. Mom will be on her way soon from Chicago."

"The crowded living situation is just temporary," Chiyo interrupted. I got the sense that she was probably itching to be the main woman of her household, but how could Roy kick out his faithful produce worker without finding another option for the Sandovals? We had heard stories of Issei and Nisei returning to ransacked homes, or homes that had been taken over by human vultures capitalizing on our inability to keep up with our property taxes.

"I'm getting the produce market back," he announced.

"Yes, Pop said that he's been working on something for you."

"Roy's going to hire some fancy *kuichi* lawyer to—"

"Chiyo, I told you that you're not supposed to call them that," Roy chided her. "Jewish. Or you don't have to mention anything at all."

Ku was "nine" in Japanese and *ichi* was "one." Nine plus one was ten, or *jyu* in Japanese. Jew. It was a disrespectful play on words. No Jewish person would want to be called a *kuichi*.

I knew that Chiyo didn't mean any harm, but if she was going to be the next queen of the produce market, she would have to become more enlightened and cosmopolitan.

There was an awkward lull in our conversation, which was broken by Art joining our circle. "Art!" Chiyo seemed genuinely delighted to see him, while Roy was more distant. Chiyo had been around Art more frequently at Chicago dances and parties.

"Art, you remember Roy Tonai. Pop worked for him and his family."

Art, lean and tall like a birch tree, towered over Roy, who had gained more muscle on his chest and arms while in the army.

"Weren't you with the 522?" Art asked.

"Yeah, I was part of the communications unit. We went into Germany at the end of the war."

Art offered us each a salty plum from the package he had purchased from Far East. We all declined, but that didn't prevent him from popping one into his mouth.

"It's good that we ran into you two. Joey and Louise are going to be in town in a month," Chiyo announced.

"Oh, really?" I hadn't heard anything, but Chiyo and Louise had been roommates in Chicago, along with my late sister Rose. It made sense that they would keep in close touch.

According to Chiyo, the Suzuki newlyweds would be staying with Louise's relatives in Pasadena. During their visit, our old Chicago group was planning to meet in Little Tokyo in mid-May. "We're going to the Finale Club. Have you been?"

I shook my head. There had been no reason for me to socialize in a jazz club without Art.

"Joey heard that Charlie Parker played there."

"There's going to be a Nisei dance," Roy said. "Just like the old days." Roy was always open to having fun.

"You have to come, Aki," Chiyo added.

I was going to say that we would definitely be there when I caught Art's stare. He seemed less than enthused. "I'll get back to you on that," I told her.

We then excused ourselves and let the Tonai newlyweds have their night on the town in Little Tokyo.

In the privacy of our bedroom, I grilled Art about his lack of interest in the Finale Club. "What was that all about, with Roy and Chiyo? You didn't seem to want to spend any time with them."

Art, dressed in his fox pajamas, let out a sigh as if he didn't want to get into the details. "I ran into Roy in France."

"You did? You never told me." I winced as I pulled my brush through a tangle in my hair.

"I saw him with a French girl."

"He probably was just being friendly. You know how Roy likes to talk." I hung up my robe in the closet and joined Art in our bed.

"They weren't talking, believe me."

"Well, maybe Chiyo and Roy weren't promised to each other yet."

"No, you had already written to me that Chiyo was engaged to Roy and how surprised you were." Art picked up the clock from the nightstand to make sure the alarm was set on time.

"Well, it's none of our business, anyway." I readjusted my pillows as I liked to sleep with my head propped up.

"If you say so."

"You just don't want to go to the dance."

Even though he was more than a passable dancer, Art preferred talking in small, intimate groups, whereas I enjoyed blowing off steam and losing myself doing the jitterbug to the blast and screech of live horns. When it came right down to it, I was annoyed by his reticence to socialize with my friends. After all, hadn't I spent my evening around his brainy Nisei work buddies, hearing all about politics and this writer Chester Himes?

Throughout our late-night exchange, I had been skirting around what was giving me knots in my stomach. "Have you seen Babe since you've been in LA?" I finally inquired.

"No, I told you. Why do you ask?"

"Because that Negro man at the Far East said that he saw you outside of the San Mark with him."

"He probably thinks all of us Japanese look alike."

No, Charles didn't strike me as a person who lumped us Asians altogether. He was from San Francisco, after all, the home of a big population of Chinese, Filipinos, and Japanese. Besides, he rented rooms to various people in Little Tokyo. He could probably tell one Japanese from another. In this case, I believed Charles, a practical stranger, over my own husband.

"But he said that he saw you in your uniform. That must have been the day you arrived."

"Let's not talk about Babe anymore, okay?" Art said. I wasn't sure if he meant that moment or anymore, ever. I pushed away Charles's comment, but it remained in the dark edges of my mind.

That night, Art and I made love, more passionately than we ever had. He kissed me in places that I had thought were dirty and too private for even a husband to explore. Afterwards, long after he had fallen asleep, I couldn't help but wonder if he had learned those sex techniques from a French woman he himself had encountered while serving overseas. Once a person had tasted such forbidden fruit, wouldn't he always be on the hunt for more?

CHAPTER 8

Once his feet were firmly on the ground in his hometown, Roy threw himself into his mission to regain his family's produce enterprise. In downtown Los Angeles, there were two produce entities that housed various smaller markets, City Market and the more *hakujin*-controlled organization near the Southern Pacific railroad tracks. Tonai's stall had been in City Market, but now it was under a different name and ownership due to the malfeasance of the trustees, who before the war had been friendly competitors.

To address this fraud, Roy called for an emergency meeting that Art, Pop, and I were attending. We drove through the eastern edge of Little Tokyo, or at least what remained of our Japanese town, and then south through the garment district. The area around the produce market had become an informal Chinatown to accommodate all the Chinese produce workers and small farmers who had stalls in the market.

"Trustees, they lie. They cheat," Pop kept repeating in English to Art.

We were able to find an open spot on San Julian Street and walked to a new chop suey house Pop was raving about. These days, our diet seemed to include a lot of Cantonese food, but none of us was complaining.

Pop had made arrangements for the former produce workers

to meet in one of the Chinese restaurant's banquet rooms. I was worried who was paying; even with Mom's, Art's, and my combined incomes, we didn't have much extra after the end of the month. Most of the chairs were occupied and it was a bit of a reunion for my father's former co-workers. Only a handful of them had been in Manzanar; the rest had been in one of nine other camps or maybe even the harsher, more restrictive confinement centers reserved for Issei leaders like the late Mr. Tonai. I noticed more gray hair, ravaged faces, and dead eyes. The men had aged tremendously in four scant years.

There was one bright spot in the room. At the head table sat Chiyo, wearing another splendid outfit, this one canary yellow. When she spotted me, instead of waving madly as she would have done during our years in Chicago, she dipped her head like a coy geisha. It struck me as odd, but then as I watched the old-timers approach and bow to Roy, it occurred to me that Roy and Chiyo had stepped in as the next line of Tonai royalty. I didn't know how calculated it was, but I was impressed now in Roy's choice of Chiyo. No longer was he the hotheaded bachelor. He had a dependable and wholesome woman at his side to rein him in when required.

As we took our seats in the far side of the room, I noticed how few women were in attendance. Roy's mother was in ill health; according to Mom, she had fallen into a deep depression after her husband's death.

"Thank you all for coming," Roy said. "It's good to be here, back in Los Angeles. I want to provide you with the latest news about Tonai Produce. I've secured legal representation, the best in the county. The issue, however, is that before I could even file a lawsuit, the trustees sued me."

"Damn them!" one worker, who had been imprisoned in Tule Lake, piped up.

"Sonafugun," boomed the low voice of a former celery grower from Venice, a seaside town by Santa Monica.

More jeers and cursing followed and I feared that a mini-riot would ensue.

Roy, now standing, lowered his raised hands as if he were Jesus calming the troubled waters. The trustees claimed that the Tonais were supposed to hand over equipment according to the terms of agreement. The group had taken full advantage of Roy when he was a few days away from reporting for military duty, while his father was in the Santa Fe Department of Justice detention center. How could Roy have made an informed decision without any legal representation when he signed the papers under duress?

"Traitors."

"*Inu*," an Issei senior spat out, almost dislodging his dentures.

"Yeah, they are dogs!" His son, hunkered in the chair next to him, provided the translation.

"Rest assured, I'm going to get the market back. For all of us."

The men cheered, Art scribbled in his notebook, and Pop's body was so taut that I thought he was shaking, as if a bolt of electricity had gone through him. All those years of being confined, having our lives dismantled, of being forced to move to cities we had never known before, had taken their toll. All that rage and repression was unleashed like supernatural beings waiting to terrorize an evildoer. I felt a rush of energy, too, and welcomed its release, yet a small part of me feared that Roy would not be able to deliver what he was promising.

On the drive home, Pop sat like our old golden retriever, Rusty, used to in the back seat, popping his head out the window. My father was a pendulum of emotions. When he was down, he fell so deep that he could barely be retrieved. And when he was high, he transformed into someone much younger. In his present mood, I could picture him as a child running up the hills of Kagoshima, hoisting a paper kite in the air.

The next meeting was going to be held in the Japanese-operated flower market on Wall Street in a few weeks.

"It's going to take time, Pop," I said.

"Those son-of-a-bitches," my father cursed. "They are not going to get away with it."

I sat quietly in the passenger seat, clutching my pocketbook. I knew that he wasn't just talking about the produce market. I couldn't bear to say out loud what I felt: *Pop, they already have*.

CHAPTER 9

In our old house in Tropico, we had an upright piano, a sign that we Itos were as cultured as the next middle-class Japanese family in Southern California. Rose and I took lessons from an Issei woman, Mrs. Yasutake, who railed against my terrible posture and pressed a little too hard on my fingers when I failed to hit the right key. Both of us quickly lost interest in playing. Our parents weren't especially musical and it was unfair of her to browbeat us into artistic submission. Besides, I think Pop was getting weary of hearing my half-hearted, off-rhythm melodies when he was trying to relax after a hard day at the produce market.

Even though Rose and I abandoned the piano, it still remained in our living room. Mom displayed family photos on top and crocheted a doily for the seat, which we used for young guests at holiday get-togethers. At random times, perhaps to break up a stretch of boredom, I propped up the keylid and attempted to reprise a song that Mrs. Yasutake had tried to teach me. What resulted was a terrible mishmash of wrong notes that convinced me that I was right to abandon the instrument.

Thinking of that piano reminded me of my lack of ability to succeed at much of anything. After the meeting about the produce market, I more than ever did not feel in control of my own destiny. It was as if people like my father, fueled by revenge, had found their purpose, but I was only discovering my limitations and weaknesses. Art always seemed to have a work obligation that would prevent him from going out on the town with me. Our communication was awful, one wrong note leading to a crescendo of other off-key melodies. I'd watch happy young Nisei and Black couples walking through Little Tokyo and wonder what was wrong with us.

I missed talking to Rose, lying side by side in one of our beds as we occasionally had as children. Speaking little truths, not completely every detail—often I was unaware of the depth of my feelings—then silence. We had our own Morse code that we could decipher. Rose would probably have told me not to worry so much about Art and our young marriage. *Men can be so maddening at times.* And that our broken family would eventually heal, that Manzanar and Clark and Division would be tiny dots in our rearview mirrors.

Since I couldn't speak to Rose, who else could I go to? I wished that I had some kind of access to her closest friend in Chicago, Tomi. Tomi was one of the most beautiful Nisei women I had ever seen up close. Porcelain skin, not a stray freckle or blemish visible, bright eyes with naturally long lashes. Inside, she was extremely fragile, haunted by demons in her past. I'd never forget saying goodbye to her as her train left Chicago's Union Station, and her gifting me a page from Rose's diary.

Tomi knew Rose's deepest secrets, even those she had been unable to share with me. Tomi had gone to Detroit, disappearing into thin air. I called the operator in Detroit a number of times to see if there were any listings for a Tomi Kawamura, but there was nothing. Maybe she had gotten married and changed her name. Perhaps the last thing she wanted was someone like me dredging up pain from the past.

I hid my blue funk from everyone close to me, but it was Chole who noticed that something was amiss. "You all right, *guzu-guzu* girl?" she'd ask when we passed each other in the hospital corridor. I'd nod, but as soon as I was a few steps away from her, I blinked back tears.

I was wrapping bandages in our supply closet when the receptionist popped her head in with a message. "A Negro man is waiting for you. He's outside."

I frowned. Other than my parents and Art, I never had any visitors at the hospital. I walked down the corridor toward the front door. When I went outside, the afternoon light blinded me for a moment before I could focus on who was waiting for me at the foot of the steps.

"Oh, Charles." I realized that I had forgotten his last name.

"Excuse me for the intrusion." Charles had removed his cap, revealing short groomed waves parted to the side. "But I remember that you wanted to know if I heard anything about Babe."

"Yes," I said tentatively, remembering the agreement I had made with Art not to talk about him.

"He's over in Burbank."

"Burbank." I had never been in Burbank in my life. There was no reason to, really. No Japanese vegetable growers out there, at least none that I had heard of.

"I guess that there is some temporary housing over there for the Japanese. He's in one of them."

"How did you—"

"A friend of his came to pick up his camera that I was holding for him."

"A friend? Was he Japanese? Did you get his name?"

"He was Japanese and he wasn't one to talk much."

"Oh, thank you, Charles." I turned to head back to the hospital, then remembered that I wanted to check that it was my Art who Charles had seen in uniform talking to Babe. When I looked back in his direction, he was gone.

. . .

I knew that if I told Art that I wanted to go by the Burbank housing projects he would either discourage me or go himself without me. The *Rafu Shimpo* was regularly printing stories about how wretched the Winona trailers were. Burbank authorities from the beginning vehemently opposed the influx of Japanese Americans into their city and the War Relocation Authority yanked families and children from one temporary housing complex to another. After being closed a few months for cleaning, Winona trailer camp reopened with no electricity or basic amenities.

Art was definitely harboring a secret about Babe and I was determined to pull it out—with or without his help. And I couldn't forget that look that Mr. Watanabe gave me before Dr. Isokane shooed me away. He had wanted to tell me something, I was convinced of it. I thought back to my sister, Rose, and fierce anger shot through my body. Would either Rose or Mr. Watanabe have met their tragic ends if we hadn't been removed from our homes? Our unsettled time in the camps and afterward had exposed us to the dangers of life on the margins and deprived us of our jobs and the financial security that might have protected us. The senior Watanabe should have been racing his stock cars by the dunes of Guadalupe, not rotting in a bachelor hotel after four years of being locked up in Gila River on an Arizona Indian reservation.

I couldn't continue to attend to my business, pretending that all was well. Who in the world could help me negotiate the housing projects in Burbank and locate Babe? I could only think of one person who had lived in Winona. I first went to Evergreen Hostel, walking through the open chain-link gate. A couple of boys, maybe around ten, were squatting on the concrete in front of the stairs playing marbles.

The sun practically shined a spotlight on the light-colored hair of one of the youngsters. "You're Hammer's brother, aren't you? Daniel," I said, interrupting their game.

He gave me a sharp look as if to say, *Yeah, lady, what about it?*

I tried to ignore his surly attitude. "I'm looking for Hammer. Do you know where he is?"

Daniel shook his head. His companion, a skinny Nisei boy in an oversized striped T-shirt, said, "He's over at the church. The Baptist one past the cemetery. He's helping Pastor Nagano."

Daniel scowled at his marble competitor. "Willy, c'mon, your turn."

Luckily, the Baptist church in Boyle Heights was only several blocks away on Evergreen and Second. A corner building with a three-story tower and cornices above long windows, it resembled a tiny fort. A Mexican congregation had been worshipping in the church when we had first arrived in Boyle Heights, but now the Nisei had completely taken over.

I stood in the doorway of the first floor for a minute, marveling at the sight of Hammer distributing hymnals throughout the folding chairs arranged in rows.

"Hello," I finally said.

Hammer straightened up and squinted toward the doorway. When he saw that it was me, he grinned. "Hi. I suppose you're not here early for the Bible study."

"No." I wasn't necessarily against religion, but I was wary of its practice. I stepped into the room, which was illuminated by the natural light streaming through the windows, and we exchanged a few niceties before I went straight into my request. "I want to go to the Japanese housing camps in Burbank on Saturday and I wondered if you would go with me."

"Why do you want to go there?" Hammer looked genuinely concerned. He unloaded his armful of black hymnals atop one of the folding chairs.

"I'm trying to find Babe Watanabe. Do you know him?"

Hammer paused, in deep thought. "Didn't he play baseball on the Central Coast?"

"He was Art's best man. They were in the same company together during the war. His father was the one who got killed in the San Mark Hotel."

"Oh, I heard about that. Didn't know that was his father."

"There are a lot of Watanabes around," I said, and we both nodded. There was no reason to sugarcoat this. "Babe's missing and the police are after him."

The mention of the police got Hammer's attention. He was a former juvenile delinquent and wasn't too keen on law enforcement.

"Are you saying he killed his own father?"

"I don't know. Art says it's impossible."

"Why you getting involved, Aki?" Hammer was warning me to be careful. He had seen me like this in Chicago, when casting around had gotten me into plenty of trouble.

"I saw Mr. Watanabe when he died. No one was there for him. His body is going to end up in the potter's field at Evergreen."

That seemed to shake Hammer, who apparently valued rituals more than I had realized.

"Shouldn't you be asking Art to go with you?"

I knew that it didn't look good. I didn't want to say out loud that I suspected that my own husband was keeping information away from me.

"I just need to talk to Babe."

CHAPTER 10

We could have easily taken the streetcar from downtown Los Angeles to the Burbank station at Orange Grove and Glenoaks, but then how would we get to the trailer park and other spots we needed to go? I made an excuse that I needed the Model A to see Hisako Hamamoto, an old friend from Manzanar, and surprisingly my father relented, no questions asked. Pop himself was taking the Pacific Electric to meetings at the produce market every day and he had been thinking that the Model A required a drive.

Even though Hammer wanted to take his turn in the driver's seat of the car, I wouldn't let him. The Model A had been Pop's prized possession and its temporary loss to the War Relocation Authority in Manzanar had been particularly painful. He had purchased it in the 1930s, so it was completely outdated. I felt self-conscious driving a jalopy next to fleets of Ford sedans on the freeway. It was a matter of time before we would be cited for operating an unsafe and outmoded car.

Yet it was our only vehicle and I knew enough to look after it. If I let Hammer take the wheel and something went wrong, I would have Pop's ire to deal with, not to mention I'd have to explain to Art why I was with Hammer in the first place.

Airplanes departing from or flying into Lockheed airport zoomed above us.

"Damn planes," Hammer murmured. "Couldn't think straight with all that noise when we stayed in the trailers."

There was certainly an energetic pulse to Burbank as I drove up the 99. A couple of movie studios, including Disney, had moved into town. Hammer had heard that Disney, in fact, had camouflaged the airport during World War II to keep it hidden from enemy gunfire, presumably Japanese. And now thousands of us Japanese Americans were living in trailers across from the airport.

Hammer had asked around about Babe since our last encounter. One of his old friends from the streets, Ken Kanehara, was known to socialize with Babe in Skid Row. I didn't ask for details because I knew what kind of activities occurred in that area. Ken and his father lived in a housing project on Magnolia and Lomita in Burbank, a few miles southeast of the other camp near the airport.

When I pulled the Model A up by the curb, I was instantly transported back four years ago, when we first arrived at Manzanar. Lines of barracks covered in black tar paper were assembled on a corner parcel. The drainage wasn't good at that intersection and still water had accumulated, attracting its share of mosquitos.

As I slowly got out of the car, my head spun and my stomach fell. "This is awful."

"You're telling me. And you haven't gone inside yet."

We walked past two long barracks before Hammer stopped at the third. He told me that there were once over a hundred people here but now they were getting moved over to Winona.

He knocked on the door, a familiar haunting, hollow sound. An Issei man opened the door, a short-sleeve shirt hanging from his skeletal frame.

"Ishimine-*san*," the middle-aged man greeted him.

"*Hai, konnichiwa.*"

I had never heard Hammer speak any Japanese and I was surprised that his accent was somewhat decent. Apparently, though, his vocabulary was limited to *yes* and *hello*. The man was introduced to me as Mr. Kanehara. I responded by introducing myself as Aki Ito and then correcting myself. "Nakasone. I'm Nakasone," I said and bowed.

Mr. Kanehara invited us into his barracks. I couldn't help but shudder as we entered. A room, about twelve by twenty. Mattresses on top of iron cots shoved in the corners. A stove. This was as forlorn and miserable as our original living situation in Manzanar.

The father apologized that there was no place to sit.

"No, no, we don't mind," we both assured him.

I hadn't noticed that Hammer had brought a paper bag with him. "Please," he said, offering the bag to the senior Kanehara with two hands.

Mr. Kanehara first refused, saying that he had nothing to give back. Like settling the bill at Far East, this exchange went back and forth for a few minutes. I was impressed that Hammer, despite being on his own since childhood, understood how to be Japanese when appropriate.

Hammer, of course, would come out the victor. Mr. Kanehara opened the bag and recognizing its contents, smiled widely, revealing big gaps in the top row of his teeth. "Maaaah," he sighed and explained that he hadn't had Japanese confections in four years.

As he was opening the box from Mikawaya, the door burst open. A short but muscular man in his twenties entered. Although there was no family resemblance, he was Mr. Kanehara's son, Ken, Hammer's friend.

Politeness went out the window. The two Nisei even dispensed with any greeting.

"What do you need?" Ken had a cigarette behind each ear;

he reminded me of Hammer when I'd first encountered him on Clark and Division in 1944.

"We are looking for someone. Babe Watanabe," Hammer said.

"Who's we?"

Hammer motioned toward me. In the very cramped space, Ken gave me the once-over, two times. He was wearing a sleeveless white T-shirt and he smelled as if he hadn't recently taken a shower. I tried my best not to shrink away.

"You don't seem his type."

I had no idea what that meant.

I stood as straight as I could manage. "Well, I'm Aki. I work over at the Japanese Hospital in Boyle Heights."

"The Japanese Hospital." Ken's face immediately softened. "My mother got help over there before the war."

"Then you know it, right?"

Ken waited. His father had retreated to his bed and was devouring one of the *manju* that Hammer had brought. He had bitten into his confection so forcefully that red bean paste had squirted onto his shirt and sweet rice flour coated his lips.

"Babe was my husband's best man," I explained. "I was there at the hospital when his father died. I want to make sure that Mr. Watanabe's body doesn't end up in a potter's field."

That plea, which had worked on Hammer, held no water for Ken. Hammer, to his credit, kept pushing. "Were you the one who picked up their belongings from the hotel they were staying at in Little Tokyo?"

Finally, a response. "Yeah, I did him a favor. He claimed that police were all over the San Mark and he didn't feel safe."

"But why? Is it because he did something wrong?" I blurted out.

Ken sneered at me and I felt my heart leap. "He wouldn't have killed his old man, if that's what you're getting at."

"Well, then, who did?"

"Go over to Skid Row and ask around. There's plenty of killers over there. But you may not come out alive."

I frowned. Ken wasn't making any sense.

Hammer, apparently fearing that our conversation was going south, intervened. "Do you know something or not?"

"Nothing will come out from you nosing around. Not with the police and whoever else is trying to pin the murder on Babe. We Japs don't have a fighting chance."

I wasn't sure what he was saying was true. I remembered the Jewish attorneys that Roy was going to hire. "There are some lawyers out there who are helping us."

"Hah, you think we can be saved by lawyers? Isn't that what put us in camps in the first place? The law. Supreme Court no help, either."

"Look," Hammer broke in, "who knows about all that right now. But Aki is on Babe's side. She wants to help him."

I hoped that Ken didn't detect a flush of guilt on my cheeks. Truth was, I was more than ready to send Babe down the river, if that was where he belonged.

Ken exhaled a long breath. I suspected that because he wanted us to disappear from the barracks, he finally relented. "He was at the Winona. At least that's where I delivered his belongings."

Now that we had our lead, we piled out of the barracks, leaving Mr. Kanehara to a postconfectionary afternoon nap.

Once in the Model A, Hammer slumped in the front seat. "I was hoping that he wasn't at Winona."

"Why's that?" I asked, starting the ignition.

"You'll see."

Sounds of planes taking off and landing at Lockheed rang in our ears as we approached the Winona location. From a distance, the rows of trailers looked like a vacation spot for tourists to enjoy the Burbank sun. But as we stepped onto the grounds, the mirage disappeared. Flies circled overflowing trash bins; the outdoor heat intensified the smell of rotting food, feces, and urine. I had read the sewer had not been connected during the expansion of the trailer park. I thought that I was immune to revolting smells because of my hospital work, but I was wrong.

Next to lines of laundry flapping in the hot breeze, children and Issei men gathered around a makeshift outdoor soup kitchen. A large vat of what looked like rice porridge was almost empty.

It didn't take much to shock me these days, but I was indeed upset. Boyle Heights surely wasn't Beverly Hills, but gazing upon this site made me realize how fortunate my family and I were.

As we walked through the trailers, I spotted a dustup from the corner of my eye. Two adolescent boys, probably no older than Hammer's brother, were furiously fighting, tearing at each other's faces with their small fists.

Seeking to prevent any further injury, I ran into the middle of the altercation. "Stop, boys!" I called out. I pushed one boy's forehead away with my left hand, pressing my back into the other fighting boy's body. They were both so shocked, or perhaps even relieved, that a woman had intervened that they both dropped their fists and relaxed their hands.

"Hey, lady, whaddaya doing?" a male voice rang out.

"Dammit." Another one.

I'd reacted so quickly that I hadn't noticed a circle of men squatting around them as if they were watching a sumo match. Some coins anchored a stack of wrinkled dollar bills from flying away in the wind.

Hammer, his chest heaving up and down, caught up with me, holding up his arms as if he were an umpire calling a baseball game. "She didn't know, okay? She's from the Japanese Hospital in Boyle Heights."

The men studied me. Their glances were not lecherous but curious. I felt as though I was a rare bird who had come to rest in a troubled land.

Like at the barracks on Magnolia, *hospital* seemed to be the magic word, at least to calm them for a bit. Some of them who knew Hammer gathered around him and engaged him in conversation. I wondered if Hammer participated in this horrendous game of betting on Nisei boys like they were Christian gladiators in Rome.

One of the young spectators stood in front of me. "Are you here to see Shiz?"

"I'm looking for Babe Watanabe," I said. "Who's Shiz?"

"My little sister. She's had a fever for a few days now. Breathing hard, too."

Looking into the concerned eyes of Shiz's brother, I put my mission on the back burner. The brother, whose name was Jerry, wore coveralls that were way too short for him and a pair of worn-out tennis shoes that were missing their laces. I practically ran to keep up with him until we reached one of the trailers. It was dark in there, and I was told that there had been no electricity these past few days. In a corner lying in a small bed was dear Shiz, whose face I could barely make out in the dim light. Pressing my palms against her forehead to check for fever, I suppressed a gasp. She was burning hot. Being so close to her, I could feel her tiny chest heave for air. Her mother sat with her on the sagging mattress.

"You really need to take your daughter to the doctor," I told her.

The woman had hollowed-out cheeks and I wondered how old she was. It was obvious that war and camp—not to mention care of her young children—had taken their toll on her. Other Issei women were like my mother, strong like oaks or sequoias, able to withstand the battering of disappointment and loss. But after working at the Japanese Hospital, I knew the other side. Women whose resilience had become so thin that they snapped like twigs when stepped on one too many times. I wondered if there was a husband to support her.

I asked Jerry for a towel and he could only produce foul-smelling rags. I was able to locate an old handkerchief in my sweater and asked where I could find a water faucet. Jerry went out of the trailer with me and pointed to a group lavatory, a plain concrete structure. In the ladies' room, I encountered a huge hole in the floor and gingerly walked past it to reach one of the dingy sinks. *What in the world is this place?* I was ashamed to think that we had abandoned our poorest and weakest people here while I stuffed my face with endless plates of chop suey.

I returned to the trailer and sent Jerry to find Hammer. I attempted to cool the girl's forehead with my moist handkerchief while her mother quietly cried beside me. I didn't know if they were tears of relief or shame, or maybe of both.

In a few minutes, Hammer appeared in the doorway of the trailer. "I was able to convince them not to string you up because you ruined their game. What's happening here?" Hammer glanced at Shiz's feverish cheeks and prostrate body.

"We have to take her to the hospital."

Hammer didn't hesitate. He bundled the girl up in the thin blanket and carried her outside. The sun revealed the shabby and stained state of the blanket and the girl's swollen eyelids, probably inflamed from the heat of her fever. The mother followed after us down the metal stairs of the trailer.

"I have room for you, too," I told her.

"But my other children," she said in Japanese.

Jerry was now standing in front of us with a girl who looked about six.

"I can take care of them, Iida-*san*." An Issei woman stepped forward from the small crowd that had formed around the Iida family trailer.

More tears. I wondered how long Mrs. Iida had bottled up her anguish to protect her children. Those feelings were fully on display now and all of us couldn't help but be affected. Like a mourning party, these residents of the Winona trailer followed us to Pop's Model A. I directed Mrs. Iida into the back seat and Hammer laid her daughter across her lap.

I went to the driver's side door and took a final glance at the trailer park. The two boys were still fighting, kicking dust from below.

None of us said much during the drive back to Boyle Heights. I rolled down my window to make sure that fresh air was traveling through the car. Dr. Isokane was old enough to have witnessed the influenza pandemic of 1918. He had told the medical staff that he had seen people literally collapsing on the streets of Los Angeles and dying. I wasn't sure what kind of sickness Shiz had, but I wanted to be cautious for all of our sakes.

I had barely shut off the ignition in the driveway of the hospital when Hammer hopped out of the passenger's seat. He lifted Shiz up from the back seat and carried her into the building while the mother, taking quick steps and clutching a handkerchief, followed close behind. There were no open parking spots along Fickett Street so I had to make a U-turn and cross First.

When I returned to the hospital, Chole was taking Shiz's temperature in one of the examination rooms. She gestured toward the mother. "I think she's sick, too."

"Good you brought her in, Nakasone-*san*." Dr. Isokane was there despite the fact that I knew he had been on for seven days straight. There just weren't enough doctors in Los Angeles to serve our people.

Mrs. Honma nodded in agreement. For the first time I received the senior nurse's lukewarm approval.

I then remembered Hammer and ran into the waiting room. He had already left the hospital and was about a half block away on First.

"Thank you for coming with me . . . and everything else." I was indebted to Hammer today and wasn't shy about expressing my appreciation.

My words didn't seem to sink in. His thoughts were still on the sick girl. "She looked bad. I hope she gets better."

"She will. She has the best doctor and nurses in Los Angeles, I tell you that."

"I guess we didn't get a chance to ask about Babe in Winona," Hammer said.

In the rush to help Shiz and her mother, I had completely forgotten why we had gone over there in the first place. "Oh, maybe it wasn't meant to be," I said. "At least for today."

Hammer nodded. We were both emotionally spent.

I remembered the reference letter that I still needed to deliver to him. "By the way, what should I say in the letter that I'm writing for you?"

"I'll follow up with the lawyer and let you know." He pushed back a loose strand of hair that had fallen over his forehead. "Well, I have to prepare for our Bible study tonight."

I offered to drive him, but he opted to walk. At the stoplight, I watched his determined gait as he proceeded east. We Japanese often branded people as being good or bad; the wrongdoings of the "bad" people produced *haji*, an indelible mark of shame that followed them their entire lives and even after death. *Haji* had been a gray cloud over Hammer in Chicago, but in Los Angeles, it seemed to have lifted and dissipated.

• • •

I hoped that when I arrived home, no one would be there, but I found Art settled in Pop's easy chair with newspapers in his lap.

"You by yourself?" I asked.

"Yeah, your father went to a Kagoshima Kenjinkai meeting at San Kwo Low. How was Hisako?"

My face burned a little for lying to Art. I had told him that I was driving down to San Pedro to visit my friend, a former Terminal Islander who now had a barbershop with her husband. "Oh, fine," I said, making a point to rush into the bedroom to change into my housedress.

This was supposed to have been a white lie, but now with the hospitalization of Shiz and her mother, it had become a big fib. Could the story that I had been at the Winona trailer park get back to Art?

Mom had not yet returned from work, so I went into the refrigerator to see what I could make for dinner. There were fresh eggs from a family friend who was working in a chicken ranch in Riverside. We had no chicken, though, so I couldn't make *oyako donburi*, *oya* meaning parent (chicken) and *ko* child (egg). But I still could make a meatless version with onions, bonito shavings, *shoyu*, and sake. I boiled the fish shavings in water before adding the onions and flavoring. I wasn't the best cook but I had improved during my time in Chicago.

"*Oogoto!*" Terrible! I heard Mom exclaim from the front door as I poured beaten eggs into the sauce. I went into the living room to see what was the matter.

She stomped into the house, almost forgetting to take off her shoes. After a couple of steps on our hardwood floors, she pulled them off and then stuck her hosed feet into her slippers which were lined up by the door. She attempted to place her purse on the dining room chair but she missed and it fell to the floor.

"What happened?" I asked, wiping my hands on my apron.

"There was a fire at my customer's. The college house. I had to talk to the police."

My mother didn't fully understand the concept of a men's fraternity, so she kept referring to it as the college house.

"A fire? You mean it wasn't an accident?"

"*Jujika*," my mother said in Japanese. I'd only heard the word *jujika* in Sunday school when I was a child. Christian cross.

Art's brow furrowed. He got out his reporter's notebook and sat next to her at the dining room table as I went to check on the egg concoction. I placed the egg on three *chawan* bowls topped with rice, and boiled some water for tea. After the kettle screeched, I carefully poured the boiling water into our ceramic teapot, whose metal strainer I had filled with loose green tea leaves. I overheard Mom's recitation of that day's traumatic events as I set three handleless Japanese teacups on a lacquer wooden tray.

"You don't think it's serious, do you?" I asked Art as we sat down for our meal. "Surely it must be a prank staged by some children."

"Some prank. A pretty despicable one. For someone to even think of it reveals evil intent."

I remembered then the story that Hisaye told of the Black family that was burned to death in Fontana. We had gone through so much to finally get to this place, back in Los Angeles and free, our activities not restricted because of our ethnicity or race. I didn't want to face a world in which we had to be constantly watchful for signs like burning crosses to prompt us to act before things got worse. For the first time, I wondered if Haruki Watanabe had been shot in cold blood, not at the hands of a shell-shocked son, but by someone who wanted to eliminate him from the earth merely because he was Japanese.

CHAPTER 11

Dr. Isokane often said that children have youth on their side and that was the case with Shiz Iida, who had been diagnosed with a severe case of pneumonia. With the administration of sulfa drugs, she seemed to come to life in a couple of days—the swelling around her eyes subsided and her skin color returned to a normal shade, revealing a spray of freckles on her cheeks. As she felt better, she jumped down from her hospital bed to walk barefoot down the halls.

Her mother, on the other hand, took a turn for the worse. In the hospital, Mrs. Iida apparently felt that she could release the multiple responsibilities that had weighed upon her at Winona, allowing her sickness to take full control of her body. Not only was she also found to have advanced pneumonia, but her right lung was collapsing. Dr. Isokane consulted with a Nisei doctor, formerly of Terminal Island, who was now pursuing a residency in thoracic medicine in a sanatorium in Missouri. The networks among these Nisei doctors, further forged throughout the ten camps, inspired me. While our souls were depleted, at least our bodies had been girded up by these dedicated health providers.

Of course, only so much could be done for a woman like Mrs. Iida, who had neglected her health for so long. At least once a day, I would find Shiz standing beside her mother's bed, staring into her closed eyes. Mrs. Iida didn't have much energy to interact with her daughter, even after a procedure in which excess air was removed from the chest cavity with a giant needle.

Hammer came every day, bringing used children's books and toys, including a worn Raggedy Ann doll that I thought was too juvenile for Shiz. Yet the nine-year-old clutched it as if it were human, perhaps a surrogate for her own siblings back at Winona.

"Is the mother going to make it?" Hammer whispered to me. I couldn't answer. I hoped that he was praying for her because it seemed that only a miracle could spare her life.

After a few days, the neighbor at Winona brought the two other Iida children to see Shiz and their mother. Children who weren't patients were usually not allowed to visit, but Dr. Isokane made an exception, which Nurse Honma at least tolerated.

Chole lent Mrs. Iida her lipstick and even smeared a bit on her emaciated cheeks to make her look less like an apparition. Shiz had pretty much recovered, but Chole and I didn't want to release her back to Winona. Whenever Dr. Isokane and Mrs. Honma came around to do their rounds, we instructed Shiz to pretend that she was the sleeping princess, Briar Rose, in one of the books that Hammer had brought. She delighted in the subterfuge, which she viewed as a game.

All bets were off now that Jerry and Yoko were here. They climbed into Shiz's bed with her and within a few minutes the trio were intertwined like pups. The young Iidas remained that way until I coaxed them out of the bed with honey and butter sandwiches that I made in the hospital kitchen.

We sat at the picnic table in the back where Chole and I took our breaks. Based on the way they devoured their humble sandwiches, I ascertained that they were not well-fed.

"Do you eat at school?"

The two siblings ignored my question, instead concentrating on chewing and drinking milk I had poured into paper cups.

Their reaction concerned me and I pried harder. "You have been going to school, yes?"

"We ride the bus now," Yoko responded, a milk mustache dripping from her upper lip. "Jerry was a bad boy yesterday."

Jerry recoiled, his eyes bugging out at his younger sister's revelation.

"What, you didn't go to school?"

Jerry gnawed at the remaining crust of his sandwich. I waited until there was nothing left in his hands and gently pressed my hands into his shoulders. "What do you do when you don't go to school?" I asked.

"I was trying to make some money."

My mind immediately went to day labor on farms, bunching up asparagus or spinach.

"Jerry says he went to a *kitanai* place," Yoko piped up. It was strange for me to hear Japanese coming out of her mouth for the first time. And *kitanai*, of all words. Dirty. Their lives probably were spent in all sorts of *kitanai* places, the Winona trailer camp for one; what made this location dirtier than the trailers?

"Babe Watanabe was there!" Jerry blurted out as a defense.

I felt as though my head had been immersed in ice water. "Babe. What does he have to do with you? Did he take you there?"

Jerry shook his head and covered his face in embarrassment. His filthy hands were clasped and I silently chided myself for not having them vigorously wash before eating.

"You can tell me, Jerry. You're not in trouble."

"You won't tell my mother?"

Tears almost leaked from my eyes. I looked away for a moment and composed myself. "No. Now tell me where you went."

"A *hakujin* man comes by our trailers after the fathers have left for work," Jerry said.

"Oh, the giant," Yoko commented, attempting to rub the sticky honey off her fingers. After moistening my handkerchief with some water I had poured into a cup, I handed it to her for proper cleaning.

"Who is this man?"

"His name is Ox," said Jerry.

Obviously not his given name. "Do you know what his full name is?"

Jerry shook his head. "He's always looking for boys to help him. To collect pieces of paper and deliver money."

Before going to Chicago, I wouldn't have been able to guess what Jerry was talking about. But after spending time in the red-light district on North Clark, I had lost much of my innocence. This Ox was recruiting young boys to run numbers for a gambling operation, probably by organized crime.

"Where did he take you? Where was this *kitanai* place?"

"Not far from Japanese Town."

It must have been in Skid Row, I figured. The streets of Skid Row abutted the southern border of Little Tokyo.

"A movie theater. It smelled like *shikko* in there." Jerry glanced at his little sister and whispered in my ear. "In the movies, the women weren't wearing any clothes."

A nudie show? How could this Ox expose young Nisei boys to such depravity? I felt my blood boil.

"Babe was in the theatre, too."

I almost hated to ask Jerry what Babe was doing there, but I had to. "Was he there watching the movie?"

"No, he was Ox's friend. They were talking about money. Babe didn't see me at first. And then when he did, he was upset that Ox had taken me there."

Thank goodness for that, I thought. At least Babe hadn't aided and abetted the delinquency of the Iida boy.

"Babe took me home on the streetcar. He was plenty mad at me. He told me that I cost him a lot of money that day. He also said that I needed to keep my mouth shut."

"Don't worry. You did the right thing by telling me what happened. And no more going to that *kitanai* place, okay?"

Jerry nodded and I took the wet handkerchief and cleaned off his hands.

In a couple of hours, it was time for them and their guardian to get on the streetcar back to Burbank.

Before I left for home that day, Hammer came by to make a happy announcement. "The Union Church minister has found room at Evergreen Hostel for the family."

Chole and I both clasped hands. We had completely fallen in love with the Iidas and would have done anything to improve their lot.

"Everyone. Even the kids back at Winona."

It was good news, but I was loath to reveal it to Mrs. Iida and Shiz too soon. I convinced Hammer to keep it under wraps for now. Disappointment after disappointment had hit us since we'd been released from camp, and I especially didn't want the children to get too hardened by the loss of hope.

It was five, so I left the hospital with Hammer, who was still walking on air about this new development. "The hostel's going to be a bit cramped. And all the kids will have to sleep head to toe in two beds pushed together. But it will be better than Winona."

"That's for sure," I said.

I slowed my pace, signaling that I had something serious that I wanted to discuss. I told him about Jerry's experience with Ox and the running of numbers.

Hammer wasn't surprised to hear about the encounter.

"There's a gang that's trying to recruit young boys into their operation. Gambling, drugs, you name it."

"That's awful. But to go into Winona?"

"There's a growing operation in Burbank. Their base was in Skid Row for the longest time."

I couldn't think of two more disparate communities, Skid Row and Burbank, home of Disney Studios.

"The talk is those gangs are from Chicago."

I widened my eyes and Hammer nodded. Clark and Division had followed us to Los Angeles.

Once we reached Evergreen, we lingered before going in different directions. "Heard that Tonai's old group is going to be meeting at the flower market tonight," Hammer said.

"Oh, that's right." I had completely forgotten.

"Will you be there?"

I hadn't thought about it. But I supposed that I needed to drive Pop, as we didn't trust him on his own at night. "I guess I will."

"My girl's father hired me back. Part-time. Pastor Nagano put in a good word for me."

I was relieved that Hammer's life was stabilizing. I, on the other hand, felt that I might be sinking back to the darkness that had fallen upon me in 1944.

The flower market had been on Wall Street as long as I remembered. There were actually two—the first one, referred to by insiders as the Japanese flower market, and the one across the way, which was called the American market. As a child, I had accompanied my parents to the Japanese market to buy flowers for wedding arrangements for friends or distant relatives. I had looked forward to these early-morning outings because they inevitably meant that we would be stopping in the Flower Market Café for pancakes.

There were, unfortunately, no pancakes this evening. The flower market, in fact, was a ghost town with its cavernous halls and empty buckets. Around two in the morning, the flower market would come alive with chrysanthemums and ranunculus arriving in panel trucks and pickups. Flowermen and women would fill up their vehicles with preordered blooms while florists from wealthy neighborhoods like Pasadena, Bel Air, and Hollywood came by in person to select only the finest for impressive arrangements. Even now, in spite of the tobacco smoke from the assembled produce workers' countless cigarettes and pipes, the faint fragrance of flowers lingered.

My father sat in the front row, while I chose to stand in back, my calves grazing a large cart that was used to transport flowers. Two *hakujin* and a Nisei man—who were later introduced as Tonai's lawyers—sat up at the front table with Roy. I searched the crowd for Chiyo but she wasn't there. I felt a bit self-conscious as I was practically the only woman in attendance, but I also relished the time being invisible. Sometimes being ignored was a relief.

The lawyers explained that they were going to countersue the trustees, but to tell you the truth, I didn't know what good that would do. Time had marched on and our former customers probably had gotten quite comfortable ordering their tomatoes, lettuce, and cantaloupes from someone other than Roy's father, Pop, and other Issei and Nisei workers of Tonai's. Tonai Produce even had a new name now, America's T. Who wouldn't prefer America's T to the operation that had thrived before the war?

The speakers were now fielding questions, and I was feeling quite drained. My nostrils twitched with a pungent smell of cologne. I turned and there was Hammer.

"No Art?" he asked.

"He went to a reception," I told him. I was actually getting weary of Art's nights out on newspaper business. Ever since joining the *Rafu Shimpo*, he had become almost a gadabout, rubbing elbows with various Issei, Nisei, and even *hakujin* leaders. Back in Chicago, he was part of such a niche population of Japanese Americans, only four hundred in all of the city before the war. Los Angeles's vastness, in terms of both geography and numbers, captivated him. No longer was he part of an obscure ethnic clan. We Japanese in California had once ruled farming and the fishing industry; even though we had been exiled for four years, our legacy still remained somewhat intact, at least in some old-timers' minds. I thought that Art secretly enjoyed being a small player in at least a formerly influential ethnic community.

Hammer and I stood there in silence, respectful of the mind-numbing comments from people in the audience. No one seemed to actually be asking questions but instead releasing long complaints of their personal trials and tribulations. I couldn't blame them. There weren't many places where we could congregate together and *monku, monku, monku*.

I heard a click-clacking and turned to see an older man with a cane approaching Hammer. After exchanging a few words with him, Hammer introduced me. "Aki, this is my lawyer, Mr. Yamamoto."

Mr. Yamamoto was short with a toothbrush mustache in the fashion of the unspeakable Nazi leader, now dead, thankfully. I had thought that most Issei had abandoned that style, but this man obviously followed the beat of his own drum.

"Ah, Yamamoto-*san*, I'm Aki Nakasone." I bowed and he waved for me to stop.

"I'm not from Japan. Hawaii. I'm Nisei like you. You can call me Elmer."

"Oh." I blinked and recalled that Hammer had previously mentioned that his lawyer was a Nisei. With his thinning hair,

Elmer looked like he was maybe in his forties, a little too young for a typical Issei and too old for a Nisei. It made sense that he was from Hawaii, as Japanese immigrants first settled on these islands before eventually making their way to the mainland.

"She's the one who will be writing me a reference letter," Hammer explained.

Elmer looked me over from the top of my head—there were probably unruly flyaways because I didn't have time to properly style my hair—to my scuffed loafers. I wasn't the best candidate to testify to a person's character, but I was who Hammer had.

Hammer was called away to wheel the giant cart behind us to another part of the market, and I found myself alone with Mr. Yamamoto.

"What goes into a letter like that?" I asked him.

"Characteristics that you admire in a person." He balanced his weight forward with the help of his cane. "Any real-life scenarios that attest to his ability to take care of a child."

I bit the inside of my lip. This was going to be harder than I thought, but Hammer's recent actions at the Winona trailer park certainly provided some concrete examples.

"When you are finished with it, you can mail it to me. Or if you are in the area, drop it off at my office." From a thin leather case tucked inside his suit jacket, he extracted a business card.

ELMER YAMAMOTO, ESQ. SAN PEDRO FIRM BUILDING.

I noted the North San Pedro Street address, which would put his office a block away from First Street.

"It's right next to Union Church," he said. "I'm on the second floor."

I could picture the towering Union Church, one long block south of the San Mark. It was three stories high, made of red brick and dressed up with four columns and a huge cross on top.

"Your office isn't far from the San Mark."

"You know the San Mark?" Elmer, leaning on his cane, frowned.

"There was recently a shooting at the San Mark."

"The Haruki Watanabe case."

"Did you know him?"

"No, I didn't," he said without hesitation. I narrowed my eyes to focus on his. He had said Mr. Watanabe's full name so automatically, as if he was well acquainted with him.

"Do you know his son, Shinji? Babe?"

"I can't answer that. Excuse me." He tottered off, using his cane to scale away like a hermit crab. I didn't know what he had done to his leg, but it didn't seem to handicap him much.

How odd, I thought. Did my questions about Babe scare him away?

Shortly thereafter, the meeting concluded. Sweat glistening on his forehead, Hammer rejoined me. "Where did Mr. Yamamoto go?"

I shrugged in response. "Maybe he had another appointment? Before he left, he told me what you need in that reference letter."

"Hope you won't have to make up a pack of lies."

"No," I responded with confidence.

Pop by now had had his fill with post-meeting socializing and gestured for us to go. Like most Issei fathers, he disliked Hammer and, in fact, had come to blows with him in Chicago. Now back in Los Angeles, they seemed to have entered an unspoken and delicate détente, only made possible by completely ignoring each other.

I said my quick goodbye, forgetting to ask Hammer whether he was going to the Finale Club the following weekend for the Nisei dance. Selfishly I hoped that he wouldn't be there. It was easier for me to have my life neatly divided, like the compartments of a fancy bento box. Hammer in one corner. My hospital work in another. Art occupied the space for the main dish, but how would he feel about the secrets that I was keeping from him? And why didn't I feel that he was being completely honest about seeing Babe in Little Tokyo?

Since Art was away from home so much, I went to the newspaper office on Saturdays to maintain some sort of tenuous connection. I knew that the English section staff would be busy pecking at their typewriters and the Japanese editorial staff writing their stories by hand on stationery lined with small boxes for each *kanji* character. In the back were the English-language typesetters with their huge Linotype machines; meanwhile the Japanese typesetters would pick out lead type arranged on never-ending wooden shelves. It was quite a production. When the pressman started up his humongous machine, the editorial section could finally rest.

On the night of our Finale Club gathering, I came by with a dozen freshly baked blueberry muffins for the English section. As the staff gratefully snatched them up, Art had to step out to interview someone about an upcoming event, leaving me alone with the editor Henry. I noticed Art's unattended typewriter.

"Could I use this typewriter?"

"Of course, be my guest." Henry handed me a couple of sheets of paper. "You have aspirations to be a reporter like Art?"

"Oh, far from it. There's just, ah, a business letter that I have to compose and we haven't had time to buy a typewriter yet." It was a bit of a white lie. Although Henry knew the paltry sum of money that Art was earning, I still didn't want to say that we couldn't afford any big purchases right now.

I bit the edge of the nail on my thumb before I started to peck the keys.

```
To Whom It May Concern:
I am writing you regarding Hammer
```

I paused. *Gosh darn it.* I didn't want to crumple the paper that Henry had given me. *This will be my rough draft,* I decided.

```
Hammer Hajimu Ishimine. I have known Mr.
Ishimine since we met in Chicago, where
we both had relocated from Manzanar War
Relocation Center in May 1944.
```

I could see him standing in front of Rose's apartment, wearing that ridiculous zoot suit. Memories of Rose then shot through my body and I couldn't go any farther. I released the roller and pulled out my uncompleted letter. I wanted to throw it in the trash, but that would be disrespectful to Art's employer. *Mottainai*—waste nothing.

I abruptly rose from Art's work chair. "Please tell Art that I'll meet him at home."

Henry insisted I take the half-baked letter home in a manila folder. I rode on the streetcar feeling so inferior to the Marys and Hisayes of the Nisei literary world. Here they were making commentary on significant social matters on a daily basis and I couldn't even adequately compose one business letter.

That evening, Art was more upbeat about going to the Finale Club than I was. He had purchased a couple new ties from Bronzeville 5-10-25 Cents Store and took turns holding them in front of his white dress shirt. "The one with the blue stripe or the one with the floating maroon squares?" he asked.

"What does it matter? It's just Chiyo and Louise. Married women." I said it in such a snooty way that Art gave me a second look. "Well, I'm just saying." That familiar well of insecurity was rising inside of me. What I really feared was the smarty-pants Marys appearing and sucking up all of Art's attention.

We decided to take the bus instead of driving or riding on the streetcar. The bus was the most direct and convenient—there was always a bus traveling up and down First Street at all hours of the night. Getting off first in Little Tokyo, Art reached for my hand to help me down the steps onto the sidewalk. We kept holding hands as we strolled past streetlights, dark storefronts closed for the night, and an occasional neon sign. The faint beat of a drum echoed from the west, while teenage Nisei boys ran together in packs and Black couples, dressed to the nines in fancy hats, walked toward Shepp's Playhouse across the street.

I felt a renewed lightness, the excitement I'd felt when Art and I would go out when we were single in Chicago. No matter how painful other aspects of my life might be, Art could certainly lift me up. Maybe this reunion with our Chicago friends was precisely what we needed.

We went down an alley and I felt like I was back in Chicago, traveling up North Clark Street. After climbing up the stairs, we entered a low room, full of people already, their voices bouncing off of the walls and the ceiling, the sheer number of bodies increasing the club's temperature. Art immediately took off his suit jacket while I pulled off my sweater. This was promising to be one hot evening.

Roy and Chiyo had already staked out seats in the back. As the space was so small, most of the floor was reserved for dancing. The stage was in the corner, a padded vinyl folding screen in the back to amplify the audio and the spotlights strewn above. This wasn't the Aragon in Chicago, but it was more than adequate for Bronzeville.

Chiyo was outfitted in the most gorgeous persimmon-colored

silk dress. I wondered how she found the time to do all that shopping. I felt like an ugly duckling in a simple frock, one that my Chicago friends had seen me in numerous times. I could have worn one of Rose's cocktail dresses but I hadn't been in the mood to don her clothing for months.

Roy, who was used to playing host no matter the setting, handed us drinks. They were his favorite, gin and tonics. I usually avoided hard liquor as it made my face a terrible reddish color, but I nonetheless took a big swallow. I anticipated that I might need liquid courage tonight. Art's drink of choice was a god-awful liquor called Malört. When he couldn't get this wormwood-flavored drink, he was most content with beer, but he too accepted his free drink without complaint.

I heard a familiar voice shout out, "The gang is all here!" It was Joey Suzuki, his large eyes accentuated by his wire-rimmed glasses, a new style statement. Louise was right behind him, looking like the complete fashion plate that she was, in a mustard dress that buttoned up the front. I had been at the Aragon in Chicago when Joey had asked Louise to dance for the first time. Who would have known that first meeting would lead to marriage?

Joey was a talker, great at parties but a little exhausting in long stretches, at least for me. Shortly after he enlisted, he'd learned during a routine military physical exam that his astigmatism would prevent him from being a soldier. He continued working at the Olivet Institute, keeping Nisei teenagers out of trouble and on the basketball court.

Placing our drinks on the floor, we rose and gave them hugs and handshakes. I hadn't realized how much I missed the happy couple. They really were the gold standard of what we all aspired to be.

"I won't be doing too much dancing. We're having a baby!"

Louise announced. Another round of hugs and handshakes. Roy went off to order more drinks while Chiyo and Louise, the former roommates, sat together, their foreheads almost touching as they shared secrets, presumably about the little Suzuki to come.

Feeling like the third girlfriend wheel, I surveyed the other Nisei men and women crowding into the already-tight room. I thought I spotted at least one of the two Marys and shot a glance at Art. He was too preoccupied, having a discussion with Joey about Ted Williams, a star baseball player from San Diego who had returned from military service to play for the Boston Red Sox.

If Tomi had been there, at least I would have had someone to talk to.

"Has anyone heard from Tomi?" I called down the row.

"No, isn't she still in Detroit?" Louise said.

"I think that she wanted to forget about us," Chiyo remarked. She did have updates on others I had known in Chicago. Ike had married Kathryn and was in a surgical residency in Cleveland. Harriet Saito had caused quite a scandal by running off with the WRA community analyst, Douglas Reilly, and moving to New York City, where he and his ex-wife were from.

"Can you imagine running into your husband's ex-wife on the streets of Manhattan?" Louise said.

"Who says they are married?" Roy interjected and took a gulp of his drink. "Maybe they are smart and just shacking up."

Color instantly drained from Chiyo's face.

There was an awkward moment of silence and then Joey offered, "The Chicago police still haven't nabbed a suspect in the Suzanne Degnan case."

Louise rubbed her tummy. "I'm sure no one wants to hear about that."

She was right. *Ugh, what a thing for Joey to mention during our reunion.* We had still been living at Clark and Division when a six-year-old girl disappeared from her own bed in the middle of the night. The whole city had been obsessed with her whereabouts. Later the police extracted parts of her body from Chicago's sewer system.

Just in the nick of time, the saxophonist, Lucky Thompson, and a singer and drummer took their places on the corner stage. The crowd erupted in applause. When the rhythm of the drum sounded, Joey swayed back and forth and snapped his fingers. Out of all of us, he was the most enthusiastic dancer, albeit not the most graceful.

Louise rolled her eyes. "Will someone please dance with my husband?"

Roy nudged Chiyo. "Go take him off Louise's hands. She looks desperate."

A faint frown line appeared on Chiyo's forehead before she dutifully rose to accompany Joey onto the dance floor.

Lucky Thompson's saxophone wailed from the corner throughout the crowded room and soon everyone was stepping and swinging their hips. I couldn't help but tap the heels of my shoes on the hardwood. It was going to take some coaxing to get Art on the floor.

Roy had left his seat to approach us. He leaned into Art's ear. "Hey, can I dance with your wife?"

Art looked uncertain, but he still nodded. "Sure."

"Let's go." Roy pulled me up to my feet and before long we were in the center of the dancing mass, bumping into backs and elbows. Heat shot through my body, and I felt all my worries temporarily evaporate. Joey bounced up and down like a pogo stick while Chiyo, flustered by his erratic moves, danced out of step with the music. Too quickly, the song ended, with Lucky wiping his wet lips with a handkerchief.

"You still have it, Aki." Roy bent forward, hands on his

thighs, to catch his breath. I didn't know if it was my physical work at the hospital, but I wasn't tired at all. "It's so good to be with you again," he said.

I grinned. Roy and I had known each other since Tropico. It was comforting not to have to explain life at the produce market or Manzanar. Or what a blazing flame of life my sister had been. We had both worshipped the same flame; now that it was extinguished, Roy and I still had our shared memories.

"When I get the produce market back, maybe Art would be interested in joining the team of directors."

"Ah." I attempted to tug surreptitiously at my slipping stockings. "I'm not sure. He's working for the *Rafu Shimpo*."

"There's no money in newspapering, you know."

"We'll make do," I told him. I resented that he should repeat my mother's and my private concerns.

When we returned to our seats, Art was in the middle of an earnest conversation with Louise. She was from a long-established family in Pasadena but had fully embraced the Windy City after being released from Gila River detention center in Arizona.

"Don't you miss Chicago?" she asked, rubbing her belly, which was barely extended. My own stomach looked like that after a New Year's meal with too much mochi.

"I miss my family, that's for sure," Art said. He squeezed my hand. "But I'm with my new family."

"Awww, don't be such a sap, Nakasone." Roy tried to make a joke but none of us, not even Chiyo, were laughing. Sometimes Roy's mean streak reared its head during the most awkward moments.

"Ohmygosh," Chiyo blurted out. "Is that Hammer Ishimine?"

Hammer was maneuvering his way through the crowd alongside a young Nisei woman—most likely the flower market girl he had talked about. She had a smooth face, reminding me of Tomi's beautiful complexion, and thin eyes that literally twinkled, giving her an air of amusement.

Roy downed his drink. He was no fan of Hammer, a dislike that had begun during Hammer's short stint in the produce market, so brief that I had never encountered him. It continued at Clark and Division, and boomeranged back to Little Tokyo. "The bastard," he said. "He never served."

"I think he has a bum heart." It made sense that Joey, who had received a medical leave himself, would come to Hammer's defense.

"No, it's not his health. Morally unfit to serve."

I remembered that there had been some ruckus about Hammer stealing supplies at Manzanar and being sent to Boys Town in Nebraska. Roy might be right about that.

"I have no idea why Haru would spend so much time with that loser." Liquid flew from Roy's lips as he spoke. I wasn't sure if it was sweat, mucous, or a little of both.

Art fingered the rim of his glass and stayed quiet. He wasn't the type to bad-mouth anyone, and he didn't know Hammer from Adam.

I prayed that Hammer wouldn't come to our table and cause trouble. To be honest, I was selfishly most worried about myself. What if he mentioned that we had gone to Burbank together? I had told a bold-faced lie to Art, and that would cast doubt on my integrity. I had done it all for him and our marriage, though, hadn't I? To protect him from the quicksand enveloping Babe.

"Heard that this neighborhood is called Bronzeville, just like Chicago." Joey attempted to change the subject.

"Yeah, the Negroes took over Little Tokyo but we'll get it back," Roy replied.

I couldn't meet Art's eyes. I knew that my friends' feelings about interracial issues were plain prehistoric compared to those of his journalists' circle, who dreamed of an integrated "new world a-coming," the name of the first Mary's column.

I wished that Art and I could escape to the dance floor and move like nobody's business, leaving words and rumors behind. I was tired of attempting to make sense of the world because honestly, there was no sense to be made. Why had all of us Nisei been taken from our homes when the second-generation German Americans and Italian Americans had been free as birds throughout the war? Why had our parents had to give up the businesses they had built from scratch, only to have usurpers take what wasn't theirs? Why was I considered some kind of enemy of America when I had never set foot in Japan and couldn't even speak Japanese that well?

Allowing the live music to soak into my skin, I was transfixed by the moving body parts on the dance floor. The Finale Club's drinks were not strong, yet my cheeks burned. I feared that I looked like a red-faced demon.

Just as my thoughts were about to descend into darkness, Hammer's girl, fresh as a daisy in a white top and yellow skirt, stood in front of us. "Roy, you're back. It's so good to see you."

I saw Chiyo's body stiffen. I carefully observed the newcomer's demeanor. She was genuinely happy to see Roy, which meant that they probably had never been an item.

"Oh, I'm Haru." She held her hand out to Chiyo, who accepted with hesitation, signaling her suspicion of her husband's past relationship with this cheerful woman. Haru went down the line, greeting everyone enthusiastically, while Hammer stood back, not out of politeness but probably self-preservation. Roy and Hammer had come to blows at a dance two years ago and neither one of them seemed enthused to go another round, especially in their hometown.

When Haru arrived in front of us, I murmured my name,

hoping that the screech of Lucky Thompson's saxophone would mask my identity. But unfortunately that didn't happen.

"Aki!" She bent down to give me a quick embrace. "Hammer has told me so much about you. Good thing you two took that girl and her mother from the Winona trailer park to the hospital. My aunt works there and says that you probably saved their lives."

"Your aunt?"

"She's the head nurse. Naoko Honma."

I was speechless. There could be no biological connection between this sweet-looking woman and the senior nurse who intimidated me five days a week.

Hammer tugged on the back of Haru's shirt and she excused herself, saying, "This is our song!" The tune that was filling the room was bluesy, with funny lyrics like "I know that I'm not good lookin'."

I was going to ask Art if he knew the name of it, but from his stone-faced expression, I understood that my deceit had been revealed. I felt especially vulnerable after being exposed in front of my old Chicago friends. I wanted them to view me and Art like the Suzukis, an impossibly happy couple who were optimistic about their future.

"You want to go?" I asked, and he nodded.

We made our rounds again, this time saying goodbye to the gang and promising to stay in touch. "You better tell us when you have your baby, Louise," I told her.

"Thank goodness it will be in the fall when the weather will be mild," she replied. Joey practically beamed, already anticipating his role as a proud father. Having devoted hours to rehabilitate wayward youth, he was well prepared to nurture his own biological family.

Once we were outside, the cool air stung my flushed cheeks. Art's fingers didn't caress mine as they had when we were going up the stairs. His mood had definitely shifted and I feared the reason. The towering obelisk of city hall loomed only blocks away, adding to my sense of dread.

Art went straight to what was bothering him as we walked to the bus stop. "So what was that girl, Haru, talking about back at the club? You and that Hammer were at the Winona trailer camp?"

"Ah, well." I could have told Art the whole truth, but I didn't want him to know that I was chasing down Babe. He definitely wouldn't have liked that. "I got called to go to Winona. I didn't want to worry you."

"And why Hammer? What does he have to do with your hospital duties?"

"He works with the Baptist church and wanted to help. We went through a lot together in Chicago."

"What do you mean by that?"

"Well, I met him when we first arrived on Clark and Division. Everything was so confused then. We had just learned that Rose had passed away. He and Rose had been friends."

A frown line appeared on Art's otherwise smooth forehead. "Oh, I didn't know that. I never knew your sister, but it seems strange that she'd be friends with someone like Hammer."

No, you never knew Rose, I thought. Now I felt anger rise inside of me. *How can you come to any conclusions about my sister?*

Hammer had been there for Rose when she needed the most help. But I had never told Art the complete story about Rose. The situation was so shocking that I had buried it deep. I wanted to keep my sister's struggles private and sacred. Throughout our courtship, Art had been my one ray of sunshine. I hadn't wanted to tarnish that gold sheen with my sordid troubles. Art, however, was now my husband. He probably had a right to hear it all.

I'd do it someday, I pledged to myself, *but not tonight.*

We got into the bus, which was full of men worn out from drink or work. We rode in silence.

After we disembarked in Boyle Heights, we trekked to our house on Malabar Street. At some point, Art decided to iron out the night's tension. "Great news about Louise," he said.

"What? About having a baby?"

"Of course. What else could it be?"

"Well, I guess it's good news for them. They seem happy about it."

"How about us?"

"I'm not ready for that, Art."

"What are we waiting for?"

"I want to go back to school, too."

"You do?"

"I want to become a nurse, like a real nurse." I told him about pulling out of the cadet nursing program because I didn't want to abandon my parents in Chicago.

"You never mentioned that to me."

"How could I? You were gone."

"You could have written about it in a letter."

I felt heat rise up to my collar. I had been trying to spare him any stress or worry, didn't he realize that? "If I had joined, I might still be in some far-flung place today," I said. What would that have meant for our marriage?

"How long does it take to be a nurse?"

"Three years. But I may be able to shorten that a bit, with the training I got in Manzanar. And the on-the-job training I did at Henrotin and now the Japanese Hospital."

We walked past the locked iron-rod gates of Evergreen Cemetery. One side of the gate was connected to a concrete archway that looked downright menacing at night. It wouldn't surprise me if bats slept in there.

"Wow, three years is a long time."

"But I can make good money. Good enough to support both of us. Because you working for the *Rafu Shimpo* is going to send us to the poorhouse."

The minute I said what I did, I wished I could take it back. Art's face fell, and I knew that in one cruel comment, I had denigrated the only activity that gave him confidence and connection to his new home.

That night Art stayed on his side of the bed and I on mine. I had a fitful time as I tried to release my guilt about the multiple lies I had told my husband in the first real weeks of our marriage. I must have finally fallen asleep around three. When the sun reached our north-facing window, I stirred, finding myself alone in bed. Art had already gone to cover some kind of Sunday event and hadn't even left me a note to tell me when to expect him home.

Dear Tomi,

I'm not sure why I'm writing this to you as I don't think you'll ever receive this letter. But last night, I saw Louise and Joey from Chicago and it made me think of you. I wonder whether you are still in Detroit or maybe moved back to San Francisco.

Art and I got married in Chicago before he was deployed to Europe with the Go for Broke boys. He came home with only a scrape on his thigh. He was one of the lucky ones, I guess.

CHAPTER 12

Fresh with my thoughts about Tomi Kawamura, who had probably been my sister's closest friend in Chicago, I had begun writing her a note. Try as I might, I couldn't go any farther than two paragraphs. After claiming that Art and I were a married team, I felt like such a fraud. I had no idea about what I was doing or what I really expected out of marriage. Mom had married my father sight unseen except for a black-and-white photograph. She didn't know anything about romantic love, the kind we Nisei were obsessed with. Obligation for her was a virtue, not a bother. If I shared my frustrations and insecurities with her, she'd think that I was being silly, emotional Aki. "*Ochitsukinasai*," she would tell me. Get a grip on yourself. You're an adult woman, after all. You made this decision to marry Art Nakasone and now you need to deal with it.

The more I tried to settle down my emotions, the more they seemed to bubble up to the surface like boiling rice gruel in a covered pot. A couple days after we had gone to the Finale Club, I was sitting with Chole outside at a picnic table behind the hospital. I was finishing the last bit of my egg-salad sandwich when I felt this pressing weight on my chest and throat. I tried to swallow but coughed up half-chewed bread and a smear of mashed boiled eggs into my handkerchief.

"Oh my goodness, were you choking?" Chole, ever the

nurturer, rested her hand on my back. She had me take some sips of still-warm coffee from her thermos.

Tears starting running down my face. Just to experience such a simple caring act released a dam of emotions that I had been repressing since my reunion with Art.

Chole listened sympathetically. She assured me what I was feeling was common. "Nobody tells us about the problems that newlyweds have in combining two separate lives."

She explained that she and her family had first come to Boyle Heights from Mexico when she had started grade school, and then the US government forced them out during the Depression. "We had jobs in Los Angeles; there was no need to send us back," she said. I had never heard about Mexicans being removed from their homes in California. It sure sounded like what Japanese Americans experienced during World War II.

"When we were kicked out of America, the two governments promised us land and resources back in Mexico. We got neither." A rare flash of anger appeared on Chole's face. "Luckily my sister's in-laws came to our rescue and we moved to Mexico City from a smaller village."

Living next door in Mexico City was Manny's extended family. "He was visiting them one spring. That's when we started dating." Chole and Manny fell in love while taking walks underneath blossoming jacaranda trees, which Chole's family benefactors, horticulturalists and Japanese immigrants, had brought to the city. I remembered as a child being entranced by a few of those lavender flowering trees near Tropico. "I adore those purple blossoms," I said, drying my eyes with a handkerchief.

"See, you need to look around for beauty. Have fun. What do you do for fun?"

Dancing would have been on that list, and also spending

time with Art. Other than those activities, there wasn't much. Before the war, I had spent a lot of time walking my dog, Rusty.

"Maybe you need a hobby. I like to embroider."

I smiled weakly. Chole had showed me her beautiful stitching in the past. In fact, she had given me some tea towels embroidered with Mexican designs, which had immediately brightened our dark kitchen. "I'm hopeless with a sharp needle," I told her.

"I don't know about that. I saw you help Dr. Isokane with some stitches on that little boy the other day." One of the hostel children had taken a tumble on a discarded tire when playing hide-and-seek outside and cut his chin open. While the interior of the hostel was clean and pristine, former residents abandoned unwanted or broken items, even a Model A, in the back outdoors.

"That's different," I told her. Whenever I encountered a real emergency involving another person, all my external doubts fell away.

Chole's talk with me did have a positive effect. Before I had been wobbling back and forth, moved by my emotions but not moving forward. I resolved that I couldn't sit around and be a crybaby. I asked the receptionist if I could use her typewriter during her midday break and managed to complete Hammer's reference letter by the time she returned.

After work, I took a bus into Little Tokyo to deliver the letter to Hammer's attorney. Mom was working late at the Jewish fraternity house, Pop was at a produce market meeting, and Art was covering another story about a Japanese American organization restarting after the war. I'd be rattling around the rooms of our bungalow on Malabar alone if I stayed home, anyway. I pulled out Elmer Yamamoto's business card from my purse. The San Pedro Firm Building on San Pedro Street, right next to Union Church. It was easy to find—a three-story brick building with storefronts on the bottom floor.

The glass door was locked. I stood outside the building, considering my next move, when a graying Issei woman pushed the door open. She had a purse and paper bag with handles hanging off her forearm. She was obviously on her way out.

"*Konnichiwa.*" She greeted me as if she knew me and held the door wide so I could get through. Being an unthreatening-looking Nisei woman could be advantageous at times like this.

I went up the staircase, searching for a room that could be an office. On the second floor, I walked past an open residential room, a tiny studio with hardwood floors and a Murphy bed that was pulled down from the wall.

On the west side of the building facing San Pedro Street were two offices. Affixed to the door of the north office was a handwritten sign—ELMER S. YAMAMOTO, ESQ.

I balled up my fist and rapped the door with as much authority as I could muster.

"Come in," Elmer's refined voice emanated from within.

I walked into the corner office. Out the side window I could look into the courtyard of Union Church. The humble office was immaculate. I wondered if it was because of a lack of clients.

"Mrs. Nakasone," he addressed me.

I was surprised. How did he remember my name from that brief meeting in the flower market? And how did he know I was a missus? Because of hospital work, I left my ring at home during the week for safekeeping. I had been forced to sell the ring once to a pawnshop on Clark Street in Chicago and wasn't about to be careless with Art's family heirloom again.

"You have a good memory," I told him.

"People have mentioned you before," he said. He walked forward, balancing some weight on his cane. "And I also met your sister once."

I felt my stomach churn.

"It was at a JACL meeting. I think in San Pedro."

"I was there," I told him. Rose had pushed me to attend a special conference sponsored by the Japanese American Citizens League, a Nisei group committed to showing that we were as American as anyone else. I wasn't one to join groups and listen to speeches, but before World War II Rose had been all about waving the flag.

I pulled out Hammer's reference letter, which I had folded in threes into an envelope. That envelope had gotten smushed a little in my bag and I attempted to straighten the corners. "Here." I held it out to him. "Hajimu Ishimine's letter to get guardianship of his brother." I waited until he positioned himself behind his neat desk. He slowly took out a pair of reading glasses from his vest pocket and after perching them on his nose he finally accepted the wrinkled envelope from me. His movements were so deliberate, as if he were acting in a kabuki play. It made me nervous to be in his presence.

I couldn't bear to watch his facial expressions as he read my prose. It had never seemed to be the right moment to ask Art to check over my letter. Besides, I had revealed too much about my recent activities—going to the Winona trailer camp and rendering assistance to the Iida family. As much as I hated to pigeonhole my new husband, he had been raised with a silver spoon in his mouth—in terms of domestic stability, if not financial riches. Art hadn't experienced being ripped away from his home. Hammer and his brother had gone through it multiple times and we understood each other's experiences in a way Art could never fully comprehend.

I retreated to the back of Elmer's office. A framed diploma on his office wall revealed that he had received a law degree from Loyola University in Los Angeles in 1928. He must have been one of the first Japanese Americans to actually be able to practice law in the US.

"Very good," he finally pronounced. "This will help him greatly. I like how you mentioned that you are the wife of a veteran. That will carry weight with the judge."

My face flushed. I felt shame about using Art's status that way—especially without his knowledge. But my position as a mere nurse's aide would mean nothing in a court of law. I specialized in transporting bedpans and changing sheets. I was close to the lowest rung of the working woman.

"Would you like some tea before you go?"

I nodded. I was never one to turn down another person's hospitality.

Again, the making of tea was a measured process. Elmer had a hot plate on a table by his desk. He poured water from a glass carafe into a metal coffeepot and placed the pot on the hot plate coils, which eventually glowed orange. On a rack next to the table were copies of JACL's *Pacific Citizen*, neatly folded.

"Are you still active with the JACL?" I asked him as we waited for the boiling of the water.

"I was when I was in Poston. We had a legal team there. We were trying to conceive of a strategy to legally challenge the internment."

That had obviously been a failed effort.

"I'm not that involved now." Elmer presented two Western teacups with matching saucers on his desk. "The JACL has become more involved in public policy. A state politician is introducing legislation to support escheat cases against Japanese Americans."

That strange word again, *escheat*. After I'd first heard it at the Far East Café from the *Rafu Shimpo* journalists, I'd looked it up in a fat dictionary Art kept in the living room. It was spelled pretty much how it sounded. Definition: the reversion of property to the state. In our situation, the "cheat" part of the word seemed perfectly apt.

"You told me that you never met Haruki Watanabe. But maybe his son came to you? To solve their escheat problem?"

He filled a teapot with boiling water. "I had heard that you were clever," he said.

I was stunned into silence. No one had ever said that to me before. I had made middling grades at John Marshall High School and never was part of the egghead crowd.

He poured the steeped tea into the cup in front of me. It was black tea, which I appreciated. I enjoyed green tea, but I felt more grown-up sipping black English tea in a law office. "I don't have any cream or sugar," he apologized.

I shook my head. Drinking it black was most appropriate. This wasn't a garden party.

"You know there's something called attorney-client privilege," he said. He picked up the teacup, holding the saucer underneath it, and took a gentlemanly slurp. "I can tell you that my representation is nothing related to his father's murder."

"Do you know where Babe is?"

Elmer shook his head. "I gave him a one-time consultation. He never returned for anything more."

"And you won't tell me what that consultation was about."

Again, that enigmatic smile.

"How much would it be to hire you? To find out what happened to Mr. Watanabe." I blurted out the request before even thinking clearly. No authorities had come forward to try to find out what happened to my sister, Rose, in Chicago. Mr. Watanabe needed someone to advocate for him and if it wasn't Babe, maybe Art and I needed to step in.

Elmer adjusted the sleeves of his suit jacket. "You don't need a lawyer. You need a private investigator."

"Do you know of one?"

Elmer chuckled. "This is Los Angeles. There are PIs on every corner, especially in downtown."

"No, I mean a Nisei." I needed an investigator with a Japanese American face.

"I do have a man who helps me out. He's a bit unconventional. Served in the war doing covert activity. But that was in the Pacific. He's bilingual and I don't think that you need that."

"I'd appreciate his name and contact information."

"He's right in Little Tokyo. On the second floor of the Kawasaki building on First Street. He goes by Key Wakida. The business is called Wakida Insurance Services. It's right next to a beauty shop."

"Insurance?"

"A sideline. Until the private investigation gets more lucrative." Elmer turned on his desk lamp and scratched the address on a piece of paper with a fountain pen. "But I have to warn you that he has irregular hours. He's more of a night owl."

Gray twilight spilled through Elmer's windows. I glanced at my watch. It was already past six-thirty. I had promised Mom I would start dinner. I had to go home.

On the bus, there were no empty seats. I clutched the hand-hold above to steady myself through the short ride. Could I do something so audacious as hire a Nisei private investigator? If Babe was indeed involved in his father's shooting, I could push Art to cut off any associations with him. PIs were the realm of Humphrey Bogart and Dick Powell movies. In them, the actors wore fedora hats and always got the girl at the end. I was no femme fatale or Girl Friday. I was a married woman. I had no business even entertaining the possibility of hiring this Key Wakida. Besides, how much would a PI cost? I had been saving extra money to buy a used wringer washing machine. I was about five dollars away from my goal. To use those funds for a PI instead didn't make any sense. I pushed the idea out of my head.

When I arrived at the Malabar house, Pop was already seated at the dining room table, his arms crossed. "Is Art home?" I asked, searching for his loafers among family shoes by the door as I changed into my house shoes.

"Art not coming. *Shigoto.*"

Work? Again? I surveyed the refrigerator. Not enough time to make rice. Lifting the door of the bread box revealed a half loaf of bread. Thank goodness.

"Sandwiches okay?" I asked.

"*Shoganai,*" he replied, obviously disappointed.

Well, with Art at work, that was one less sandwich I had to make. Liverwurst with a side of *tsukemono*—an unconventional combination, but as it turned out, the spreadable German sausage was enhanced by the tang of Japanese pickled cabbage. Pop, who relished meals more than he ever had before, was mollified for tonight.

Mom came home right when Pop had finished. Surprisingly she made no complaint about my humble offering. Her hip had been giving her problems and now she walked with a staggered limp. She was in more pain than she let on. She took a couple of bites of her sandwich and excused herself to take a hot bath, her only relief after a long day.

I washed the dishes, hearing the dog next door howl at people walking home from work. It was past dusk and I wondered what event was occupying Art's time.

I was taking my Palmolive bubble bath a couple of hours later when the frame of our small house shook as the front door opened and closed. I heard the familiar squeaks of our hardwood floor, Art's heavy footsteps. But the steps were irregular as they came down the narrow hallway. He walked past the closed door of the bathroom without even saying hello.

I got out of the bathtub and pulled up the stopper before quickly drying myself with the long Japanese towel. In the steamed mirror, my pink face looked strangely gaunt. I had been hoping to lose some weight, but I found that a thinner face didn't do me any favors. After tightening the belt around my bathrobe, I stood in the bedroom doorway and watched Art roughly pull off his white long-sleeve shirt. He failed to unfasten a middle button, causing it to pop off and roll to the floor.

"You're drunk," I declared.

Art abruptly turned, his mouth slightly ajar. "Hello, s-s-s-sweetheart." His speech was uncharacteristically slurred.

I entered the room and shut the door behind me. "You're drunk," I repeated. Pop himself used to have a drinking problem, which had worsened in Manzanar and our early months in Chicago. Not until he almost killed a man did he walk away from booze forever—or at least we hoped he had.

I couldn't believe Art was coming home under the influence. A streak of anger shot through my body.

"I'm a full-fledged reporter now," he announced.

His declaration, so full of boyish joy, sounded pitiful to me. "So is that where you were? Galivanting with your newspaper friends? I suppose Mary was there." I hated how I sounded. Like a jealous shrew.

Art furrowed his eyebrows. "No, Henry and I ran into somebody who was in Company B. Went over for tacos and beer at Carioca. Kenji Nomura. He's from Honolulu. Can't use his left arm anymore. But he makes do. Visiting relatives in LA. Remember I wrote about him? He taught us all Hawaiian pidgin. Like 'don't fall on your okole,' you know, your rear end?" Art broke out in a smile, but I refused to abandon my anger and resentment. "Aki, what's going on?" He grabbed my shoulders so he could look straight in my eyes. His breath stunk of beer and cigarettes.

I turned my head away. "You need to brush your teeth. You smell awful. No woman would want to go to bed with you."

Art looked wounded and I immediately regretted my cruel words. Before I could manage an apology, he stumbled out the door into the hallway. The bathroom door swung shut.

I picked up the loose button from the floor and put it on the top of the dresser. I meant to sew it back on the next day but when I finally got around to it, the button was lost.

CHAPTER 13

The next few days were torturous. Art and I were extra polite to each other in front of my parents but in the privacy of our bedroom, an invisible wall had been erected between us. I replayed our last interaction—a fight over his late night with an army buddy. I had blown it out of proportion, but I knew that our problems went beyond one argument.

"Art seems to be gone a lot." Even Mom, despite her nightly exhaustion from physical labor, seemed to notice the growing gulf between Art and me.

"*Shigoto*," I said.

"Ah, *shigoto*." She said it in such a knowing way, like work may be an excuse for overdrinking or dalliances. My father didn't have affairs but we knew plenty of Issei men who had. I was always shocked to learn of the mistresses, who sometimes were physically unremarkable or quite plain. "Maybe you need to learn to cook better," she added.

I resented her insinuation, that our happiness as a couple rested on my mastery in the kitchen. My marriage wasn't arranged, a transaction between families; it would be based on communication and romance—red roses, kisses, the holding of hands in public, love notes. I was desperate to forge a different kind of marital relationship even though I had no clue how to sustain it.

On Saturday morning, as my mother could have predicted, I was alone again in the house on Malabar Street. Before I could go into the kitchen to have my morning coffee, three *hakujin* men knocked at the door. They identified themselves as detectives, but only one of them wore a uniform and sported a badge. The other two were in ill-fitting suits that seemed too formal to wear in spring. The fabric around their elbows and knees had lost its sheen, as if the men were called to do physical labor on a regular basis. I supposed that detectives would have to get on all fours to examine fallen bodies or crouch in tight crime scene spaces.

They didn't ask who I was but got right to the point of why they were there. "We're looking for Babe Watanabe."

"He's not here," I told them. "I have no idea where he is."

"But he hangs out here," the husky man in plain clothes asserted. His right ear was a bit mangled, as if an animal had chewed through it. Behind him stood a thinner man with pale skin. He was freckled everywhere, including his neck and the back of his hands.

"No, he's never been in our home. How did you get that impression?" I wasn't sure that Babe even knew where we lived.

"Your husband is Art Naka-sony?" the big man continued. I supposed that he was the spokesman out of the bunch. The freckle-faced man couldn't look me in the eye for some reason.

"They were in the same company in the army. That's about all."

"You wouldn't happen to know where he's living now?"

My heart pounded as I shook my head.

"Are you working together with Detective Morgan?" I asked. The detective's name was actually Carl Miller, I remembered even as I was saying it. I let my error stand, thinking it might be good to dangle it out there as a test.

"Ah, he's in a different department." The uniformed officer spoke up from the back.

I focused on the patch sewn on the upper arm of his uniform. It read "Burbank." Why would the Burbank Police be involved in investigating a murder that occurred in downtown Los Angeles? Unless Babe had committed some other crimes within Burbank city boundaries, which could have been possible.

"Well, we'll come by again. In case you hear from Babe." They left in a hurry before I could even ask for a business card or phone number.

I observed them drive away in a black sedan that was newer and shinier than the one the first LAPD detectives had been driving. Across the street stood one of our Issei neighbors, a woman who worked as a cleaning lady, mostly for households within Boyle Heights. She was beating a braided rug with the bristles of a broom but her eyes were on me, as if she wanted to make it clear that I was being watched.

In response, I flashed her a huge smile, which almost caused her to drop her broom. She murmured something in Japanese and turned back into her house. Giant crows cawed from telephone poles, reflecting my mood. I was weary from swallowing my feelings and couldn't stand being isolated in my house. I decided to take one of my walks around the neighborhood.

My first sidewalk encounter was Kilroy, our neighbor's German shepherd, who was always making a racket. I was so used to seeing him confined to the backyard that I almost didn't recognize him on a rare walk with one of the Fujita boys. I girded myself for an explosion of barks, but Kilroy approached me cautiously on his leash. He smelled my shoes. I extended my closed fist and he licked it enthusiastically.

"He likes you." The Fujita boy, who was about eleven, was honestly impressed. I was astounded, too, because the dog had showed me no such kindness or gentleness before. Kilroy had been so aggressive behind the chain-link fence because he wanted to be free.

"I like dogs," I said, realizing this was the first time I had ever engaged in a conversation with any of the Fujita children. There were at least four who lived next door; I wasn't sure if they were all from one family.

"But you don't have one?"

"I did." I couldn't believe that it had been four years since Rusty had died. My eyes were getting wet with tears. Was I that fragile?

"Maybe you can get another one?"

I nodded but realistically didn't see that happening. There was too much imbalance and uncertainty within the walls of the Malabar house. A dog could be the one addition that threatened its complete collapse.

Separating myself from Kilroy, I continued down Evergreen toward the hostel, which was a few blocks away. It was a three-story structure with a series of long multipaneled windows and foliage shading the impressive doorway. The hostel certainly looked more welcoming than most buildings in Los Angeles.

I wasn't planning to stop by to see Hammer; it was barely nine o'clock in the morning. But there he was, standing in the sun with a push broom in his hands. "Morning." I felt guilty that I was so happy to see him.

"*Ohayo*," Hammer called out, purposely pronouncing the good morning greeting more like "Ohio." He opened the gate to invite me to chat longer. "You up and about early," he said.

"That's the Ito way," I replied, temporarily forgetting again that I was now a Nakasone. "You were never a morning person in Chicago."

Hammer shrugged. "I guess I've changed. Or at least had to change." He leaned on his broom. "Sorry if Haru spilled the beans about going over to Winona. I thought Art knew."

I swallowed. "It wasn't your fault." I was more embarrassed that both Hammer and Haru had probably realized that my marriage was on the rocks. I then recalled my recent trip to see Elmer Yamamoto. "Oh, I wanted to let you know, I turned in my reference letter to your lawyer."

"Yeah, he showed it to me. You made me out to be a saint." Hammer, like me, found it difficult to take compliments, especially those documented on paper.

"What happens now?"

"Mr. Yamamoto has filed all the papers. I have to wait until the hearing, which is at the end of the month."

A strong wind had blown through Boyle Heights at night, resulting in a bunch of stray fallen palm fronds. From the looks of the pile on the grass, Hammer had been hard at work clearing the grounds. "When did you get to be the janitor of this place?" I asked.

"I told Reverend Kowta that I'd help out if he was able to take in the Iida family."

"You didn't tell me that was the deal."

"I made the offer on my own."

"How many jobs do you have, anyway?" Hammer had not been known for being a hard worker and I was impressed that he had taken on so much here at Evergreen.

"That's not the end of it. I may get my own route."

"You mean gardening route?" I couldn't picture the former zoot-suiter in work boots and a pith helmet pushing a lawn mower from one front yard to another. Some old-time Japanese gardeners sold their lists of customers, or their routes, to those just starting out. "But you'll need a truck."

"Someone left a car at the hostel."

"You mean that jalopy in the back?" That Model A was older than ours. And if I remembered correctly, it was missing a windshield and even an engine cover.

"Me and another guy in the hostel have been fixing it up. We've been going to the junkyard for spare parts. I think that we can get it running soon."

"I can't picture you a gardener," I said.

"Neither can I," Hammer easily admitted. "But when I thought about it, it makes sense. I'll be my own boss. If a customer gives me a hard time, I'll just quit. Making money will depend on how hard I decide to work."

"What does Haru think of this?"

"She'd prefer me to work at the flower market. But I'd just be under the thumb of another guy."

"Like her father."

"Maybe. You know that's not my style."

"Does Haru know . . . everything in your past? I mean, everything." I didn't even know all the particulars but I suspected that Hammer had secrets. In Chicago, he had spent a lot of time with a fellow we called Manju. Manju, a stick-up man, was now in the slammer for a couple of robberies near Clark and Division.

"She does."

"Weren't you scared to tell her? To maybe lose her?"

"Well, then, she wouldn't be worth keeping. It wouldn't be fair to her either." He rubbed the scar above his eye.

His confidence blew through me. I couldn't imagine having that kind of mindset. If I could manage it, though, how free I would feel.

"I think Art is keeping things from me." I felt naked saying those words out loud on the sidewalk along Evergreen.

Hammer's face didn't reveal his concern, but his voice did. "He seems to be a stand-up guy."

"I know that he wouldn't have an affair," I said, almost trying to convince myself of it. I certainly feared that he could form an emotional or intellectual bond to another woman.

Who knows what kind of attachments he had made in Europe? "Something awful happened during the war. He won't tell me what, or even admit to me that something happened. Only his army buddy seems to know."

Hammer lifted his head to gaze beyond the telephone poles lining Evergreen. In that moment his resemblance to his half brother was undeniable. "Pastor Nagano has had a lot of late-night phone calls with some fellows who were part of the 442nd. A lot of them can't sleep. Nightmares of explosions going off, machine gun fire coming at them in the darkness."

Just to hear that other Nisei veterans were plagued with bad dreams made me feel less alone. "I wonder if Art would talk to him."

"You can mention it. You can come by a service some Sunday."

I grinned. "This is probably to your grand plan. To get me to come to church."

Hammer laughed. "I know better than to pull something over on you, Aki."

I had gone once to a church service in Chicago. Truth be told, I wasn't that impressed by the minister's sermon. But I had to admit there was something about the choral singing that touched me deeply. "Are you still singing in the choir?"

Hammer nodded. "Haru, too. That's how we got to know each other better."

"Well, if you ever have a concert, let me know. I'll be there for sure." Children spilled out from the hostel door, released from breakfast, according to Hammer. Some of them grabbed the fallen fronds that Hammer had meticulously gathered together.

"Hey, hey, watch it. I'm trying to clean up around here," Hammer called out to them.

I stifled a giggle and raised my hand to say goodbye.

. . .

At home, I went to the kitchen to make something to eat. Next to the stove, I spied a note in Art's graceful handwriting with its long loops. *Rafu got a delivery of lead bars for the linotype machine, so they need my help to move it. I'll be home for lunch.*

Instead of throwing away the note, I kept it folded in my apron pocket. This was a sign of better communication between the two of us.

I was plating tuna fish sandwiches when Art returned home, a bit sweaty, the sleeves of his shirt rolled up to his elbows. He was surprised when I suggested that we eat our lunch on the porch but went along with it. Back in his home on the South Side of Chicago, we'd often lounged in the Nakasones' screened-off porch in the evening. Our conversations at that time had no particular direction; nuggets of our pasts had emerged organically, sparkling gems that we held on to when we were separated. I sought to capture a bit of that sweet intimacy in Boyle Heights.

We started off with regular everyday pleasantries. I pretended to be interested when he discussed how the typesetting machine worked.

I told him about my conversation with Chole, and what I had learned about her family. "She actually has distant Japanese relatives in Mexico. Her sister's in-laws. Made me feel better because her Japanese pronunciation is so much better than mine."

"Well, aren't Spanish and Japanese based on the same vowel system anyway?"

"Just don't ask me to roll my Rs."

We both laughed a little too loudly at my weak attempt at humor.

I wiped a few crumbs away from the edges of my mouth with my cloth napkin. I knew that I couldn't postpone it any longer. "Listen, three *hakujin* men came by here this morning."

Art became very still. "Police?"

"I'm not sure. They said that they were police but they didn't give me their names or business cards." I had been so startled by their visit that I hadn't been in the frame of mind to ask them to appropriately identify themselves. "And two of them didn't even look like officers. Their suits seemed a bit inappropriate. Cheap quality, you know, the ones that are shiny when new?"

Art's face, which was already much paler than mine, seemed to lose its color. "Listen, don't open the door to random strangers anymore," he said.

"They weren't salesmen going around the neighborhood. They knew our address. And your name."

"Crime has gone up recently. Haven't you seen those articles in the paper?"

Art was treating me as if I were a nincompoop. Was this the way that I was going to have to communicate with him now—through required reading of newspaper articles instead of in-person conversations? "Anyway, I wouldn't be opening the door in the first place if I wasn't home alone so much," I declared. I couldn't contain my unhappiness at being neglected any longer. "I didn't imagine marriage was going to be like this. I thought we'd be together. We spent more time together when we were dating and living in separate houses."

Art gestured with his long, elegant arms. "I'm trying to make a life for us, Aki. Isn't it enough that I moved from the only city that I've known to be with you and your family?"

I felt blindsided. This was the first I had even heard of Art having any apprehensions about coming to Los Angeles. "I didn't know it was such a sacrifice. I thought that you wanted to experience the West Coast."

"It hasn't been easy for me. Quite the opposite." He stood up abruptly, causing the plate balanced on his lap to overturn. The tuna fish sandwich fell onto the ground. "Aw, shit."

I felt hot tears fill my eyes. I had leftover tuna stored in the refrigerator and could have easily made him another sandwich, but I felt that all my efforts to improve our marriage only backfired. "Why don't you free yourself from Babe? You know that he probably killed his father."

Art's face darkened with anger. "You know that's not true."

"I know no such thing. I've heard from another person that Babe physically abused his father. What if things went too far that morning?"

"Stay out of it, Aki." I had never heard Art sound so menacing. "You know nothing."

That's the point! I wanted to scream. *You tell me nothing.* "Why are you so protective of Babe? What happened during the war? You yell out in the middle of the night. And don't say that you can't remember. It's like you care more about him than me, your own wife." I hadn't meant for all that to tumble out as harshly as it had. Art stood stunned for a moment. I did, too. When I finally knelt down to retrieve the remains of the sandwich, he headed down our walkway.

"Hey, where are you going?" I called out. By this time, our raised voices had apparently awakened Kilroy because he was back at the fence, gnashing his teeth and making an awful racket.

Art didn't turn around. I watched as his erect body turned the corner and proceeded west on Malabar.

"When will you be home?" I yelled.

Of course, I did not receive an answer. Furious, I tossed the ruined sandwich over our neighbor's fence and enjoyed a short break from the barking.

I nearly shattered a drinking glass as I deposited the dirty dishes into the sink. My attempt at a leisurely fun picnic on the porch had been a failure. I was so tired of being the dutiful wife. If Art wasn't going to tell me things, I'd have to find out on my own.

Since Elmer had mentioned the Kawasaki building on First Street, I thought that there would be a name etched on its facade. Instead, the building was practically as narrow as a doorway with no outside identifying signage. I held on to the wooden banister for dear life as I climbed up the steep staircase. The beauty shop on the second floor faced the street and sunlight hit the glass pane on the door. Someone had painted the business name in both English and Japanese. Walk-ins were accepted, but based on the darkened window, the beautician was closed for the day.

Across the way in the tight hallway was another office whose sign read simply INSURANCE. I felt strangely self-conscious. What in the world was I doing? I was having second thoughts and was contemplating leaving when the door rattled open.

Standing in front of me was the strangest-looking Nisei man I had seen in Los Angeles.

He had waxed the tips of his mustache upward like a lion tamer in a circus. Instead of a suit, he wore a khaki safari jacket. I wasn't sure what kind of covert operative he could be as his presence would be immediately noticed in any room he stepped into.

"Are you Mr. Wakida?" I asked.

"Yes, but call me Key."

I wondered what his given name was.

"I was sent here by Elmer Yamamoto."

"Come in, come in." He waved for me to enter, but I was a bit reluctant. I wasn't sure if there was another soul in the whole building at this late-afternoon hour. Key Wakida's office, unlike Elmer Yamamoto's, was a complete wreck. There were a couple of metal file cabinets strangely standing in the middle of the room. Odd paintings of European landscapes hung crooked on the walls. It was almost as if the detective was seeking visual clashes in his working space to provide inspiration.

"Elmer." Key stomped through his office in a pair of old military boots. "He doesn't look like it, but he's a tough bird. You know that his neighbors shot at him and his family when they first moved into Orange County after being released from Poston?"

"No, Mr. Yamamoto said nothing about that. Is that how he got injured?" I had assumed Elmer Yamamoto limped because of age-related frailty, but obviously there was much more to him. I considered how I should never come to any conclusions based on appearances.

"Oh, his legs? No, I think that he was roughhousing in Kauai when he was a boy. Injury never healed right." Key leaned against his desk, which was crowded with sepia-colored medicine bottles; tools, including a handsaw and wrench; and a pair of binoculars. A giant blue glass bottle of milk of magnesia was treacherously close to the edge. "So how can I help you?"

I searched for a place to sit. Key moved a crumpled coat from a wooden chair in the corner, where a typewriter sat on a small table.

"You got marital problems?" he asked.

"Why do you say that?" I was taken aback by Key's assumptions, especially since he had hit a sore spot.

"You're not wearing a ring."

"I'm a nurse's aide at the Japanese Hospital. I can't be wearing rings when I'm working." Why was I justifying my marriage to this investigator? I cleared my throat. "I'm here about—" I hesitated a moment because it did sound a bit melodramatic. "A murder."

Key looped his thumbs in the flaps of his jacket. I had captured his attention.

"You know about the killing of Haruki Watanabe?"

"The San Mark. Such a volatile place. There's some kind of incident in that hotel every day."

"Well, Mr. Watanabe's son was my husband's best man. They were in Company B in the 442nd."

"I've heard of Babe Watanabe." Key said Babe's name without any inflection. I contemplated what he had heard.

"I want to know who killed Mr. Watanabe." I swallowed. "Specifically if Babe did it. And if he did, I need proof to convince my husband of his guilt." The minute I made that admission, I felt ashamed. I weakly added without any conviction, "I really want the truth."

"Well, that's the million-dollar question," Key responded.

Hearing "million dollars" brought to mind financial considerations. "So how much do you charge?" I asked.

"How much are you willing to pay?"

I hadn't given payment much thought. "I'm not sure," I said. "I could spare ten dollars." I hated to dip into my Maytag washer fund, but I could surely postpone the convenience of clean clothes for Art to forsake his dangerous military buddy.

"What do you want me to investigate with your ten dollars?" Key asked. "That's about a half day's work."

I was shocked that private investigators made so much money. I made barely ten dollars for two days of work. "Solid proof that Babe did it."

Key tugged at his vest. "That type of work may cost you extra."

"I don't have any more extra money." The chaos of the detective's office had started to give me a headache.

"So no witnesses, huh?"

"Apparently not. At least none that want to volunteer any information."

"Well, it's the San Mark, after all." Key seemed familiar with the type of people who stayed at that low-income hotel. "Not sure if I can do all you want in half a day. Where can I find Babe?"

"That's partially why I want to hire you. His friend, Ken Kanehara, who's in the Magnolia barracks in Burbank, may know."

"What does Babe do for a living?"

I recalled Jerry's experience in the *kitanai* place. "Maybe something illegal. He's gotten connected with gangsters in Skid Row."

"What did the father do?"

"He was a driver."

"He had his own car?"

"Oh," I said. I never had considered whether Mr. Watanabe had his own vehicle. "I'm not sure."

"I'll check car registration records. I have sources in the police department. Old military connections. I'll start with them. They may give us all the information you need."

I nodded. Just to learn what the police knew would be helpful. "I don't have the cash on me."

"I'll take your word. You're a type of woman who is true to her word," he said.

I blushed. That was the kindest thing that a stranger had said to me since I'd returned to Los Angeles.

When I got home to the Malabar house, everyone else was already there. In front of my parents, Art acted as if nothing was wrong, but I could feel the growing distance between us. When we went to bed, he didn't try to have sex, and I noticed he wasn't wearing the fox pajamas. Instead he had on striped cotton pajamas, crisp and new. I asked myself where he had purchased them and why my gift of pajamas was not enough for him.

I was still in a state of disbelief that I had contacted the private investigator. A part of me was astonished that I had resorted to extreme measures to get answers about my husband's best man. Another part was impressed that I had actually taken action, even investing my precious savings to elicit help. I wasn't just spinning in an inner tube in the rapids, wondering what my fate would be. If I drowned, at least I had shown some initiative in attempting to solve my problems.

I kept thinking about Mr. Watanabe's tiny, miserable room, with the pristine hanging shirts. Since he seemed to be quite meticulous with his clothing, why had he left a basket of ironed shirts on the floor? Maybe there had been a witness who was delivering those pressed shirts.

The next Monday after work, I stopped by the San Mark. I was disappointed to see that instead of Charles, the same thin woman receptionist was behind the caged window.

"Can I help you?" the woman asked. This time, her hair was uncovered, revealing smooth bangs and shoulder-length curls.

"Yes. I'm Aki Ito, I mean Nakasone. I spoke to you the other day."

"Oh, yes, Charles's acquaintance. I'm Willie Mae."

"Regarding the man who was shot, I was wondering if you were aware of him receiving any laundry deliveries."

Willie Mae straightened some check-in cards by the receptionist window. "There was a Chinese girl. I'd see her a few times, but after Mr. Wat died, she doesn't come round anymore."

It had probably been an Issei laundry woman, not a Chinese one. And I doubted that the laundry woman was a girl—more likely a full-grown woman. Wherever Willie Mae had come from, she wasn't used to living among Japanese Americans. My annoyance must have shown on my face because she asked, "Did I speak out of turn?"

"Oh, Mr. Wat was actually Mr. Watanabe. He was Japanese. And the woman who brought the laundry was probably Japanese as well."

"My apologies. My husband and I came from New Orleans last fall. We don't run into too many Orientals there."

"No, I understand," I told her. My experience in California had been limited to *hakujin* students in school and then my parents' mostly Japanese world. Chicago had actually provided opportunities for me to have more Black friends.

Willie Mae fanned herself with a registration card. "Finding someplace to live has been something awful," she said. "Can't wait to move out of here. My husband and I are sharing our room with two other people, practically strangers."

I had never encountered anyone from New Orleans like Willie Mae, and my heart opened up to her. We both seemed like pawns on a chessboard, a master player pushing us here and there with some larger strategy, unknown to us, in mind.

The elevator next to the receptionist cage screeched open. It didn't have a proper elevator door, only a metal accordion gate. Charles emerged, clutching a screwdriver and an oilcan.

"You got it working?" Willie Mae asked.

"It's on its last legs. The owners have to do something."

"Handy as hell, this man," Willie Mae commented to me. "He's our Mr. Fix-It."

I pondered what Charles had done in the past. His mechanical abilities seemed to surpass the needs of the San Mark Hotel.

"Oh, Aki." Charles squinted at me.

"She was asking about the Japanese laundry woman that used to bring the Japanese man his laundry." Willie Mae seemed proud to have included "Japanese" two times.

Charles seemed less than amused. He didn't comment immediately and went into the booth to store the oilcan and screwdriver. He waited until Willie Mae left the reception area before he spoke to me. "That laundry woman kept to herself, but Hal mentioned they had both been locked up in a camp in Arizona near Phoenix. I wasn't sure if she could speak English. I think that she may have been scared of me. I'd see her walking around Bronzeville with her big basket of laundry. I'd say 'howdy do,' but she'd pretend that she couldn't understand me." He seemed to harbor some resentment. "Why do you want to talk to her? You're not looking into Hal's murder, are you? Because the police are on top of that now."

"Of course not," I lied. I wanted to ask him about whether Mr. Watanabe had left his car at the San Mark, but figured that I had lost my opportunity.

"I don't believe you." Charles somehow could see right through me. "You know what they call a woman who doesn't know her place."

"No, I don't."

"A dead woman."

Charles's warning shook me but I didn't let him know it. I smiled as pleasantly as I could and told him to have a nice day.

I was still committed to identifying this Japanese laundry woman. Who in Little Tokyo would know? Convinced that I needed to target places where women frequented, I went into a store that specialized in baby clothes. They gave me a couple names of laundrywomen and phone numbers, but both were located in Boyle Heights. I couldn't imagine that either one of them would travel to Little Tokyo to deliver laundry, but I was open to being proved wrong. Before starting to prepare dinner, I called them to ask whether they knew Haruki Watanabe. Neither one of them had heard of him.

Dinner was a quiet one with me and my parents. Art and

Henry had gone off to a meeting held by the Nisei Veterans to identify Gold Star mothers for Memorial Day services. I grilled mackerel, Pop's favorite but loathed by Art for its pungent fishy smell, and served it with grated daikon and *shoyu*. We didn't bother to engage in small talk at the table, which was a relief for all three of us.

Later, when we were wiping the dishes, I asked my mother, "Have you heard about someone who washes clothes in Japantown?"

"You don't have time to wash your own clothes?" She implied that I was thinking that I was a queen, too proud to clean my and my husband's undergarments and shirts.

"No, it's not that." I sighed. I couldn't come up with a good reason.

After my parents retired early to their bedroom, I racked my brain, trying to remember who I knew in Los Angeles who had been in Gila River. Who had been sent to that camp, located on an Indian reservation in Arizona? People from Pasadena. The coastal farming towns like Santa Maria and Guadalupe, the region where the Watanabes had lived. And the heart of grape and peach cultivation. Fresno.

Chiyo! Chiyo was from Fresno and had been in Gila River—just like Louise. Chiyo enjoyed keeping tabs on people in Chicago, so I suspected that the same would hold true about her fellow inmates in Gila River.

Before Art arrived home, I carefully dialed the phone number I had written in my phone book. I had made a fresh entry for *Tonai, Roy and Chiyo*, underneath all the various addresses that I'd had for Roy in the past.

"Hallo." The female voice didn't belong to Chiyo or her mother. Then it dawned on me that the Sandovals were still living in the South Los Angeles house.

"Hello, Hortencia? It's Aki Nakasone, Gitaro Ito's daughter."

"Oh, Missus Aki. You doing okay? I wished we could have talked more when you came to pick up your father's car."

I wholeheartedly agreed and then asked to speak to Chiyo.

"Missus Chiyo!" she bellowed, not bothering to cover the receiver.

"Hello." Chiyo's voice, a bit irritated, came on.

"Chiyo, it's Aki."

"Oh, Aki." Her formality evaporated.

"Listen, I'm trying to find a laundry woman who works in Japantown here. She used to be in Gila River."

"Well, Gila River was such a big camp."

I'd realized it would be like searching for a needle in a haystack. But I had to try.

"What's her name?"

"That's it. I have no idea," I admitted. I felt so foolish I was ready to end the call.

"Wait a minute." Chiyo's society mind was at work. "I do know someone. She used to belong to my mother's Fujinkai group at the temple. Her name is Senzaki. She doesn't have a phone yet but I have her address."

I waited through a moment of silence. Chiyo was probably searching through her address book.

She finally came back on, giving me an address and room number of a low-income hotel on First Street.

"Thanks a bunch, Chiyo."

"What—" Before she could ask me why I needed to find out about the laundry woman, I abruptly hung up the phone. The less she knew, for my sake and hers, the better.

I decided to stop by Mrs. Senzaki's room early, before I was to report to duty at the hospital. Before the war, the Ito household had been early risers. The produce market had required Pop to get up before dawn to take orders from the East Coast for California cantaloupes, celery, and cucumbers. When the drink took over Pop's nights in Manzanar, he stopped being a morning man. But these days, free from alcohol and brimming with hope, he was regularly up before sunrise again. As a result, my parents didn't bat an eye when I walked into the living room fully dressed at six o'clock. Art, meanwhile, was still softly snoring on his side of the bed.

As I left our house for the streetcar stop, the Fujita dog blasted me with his barks. In the distance, a rooster crowed, probably from one of the Mexican blocks. In Boyle Heights, you could identify the ethnicity of a house's residents based on smells and sounds, not to mention how they landscaped their front yards.

When I stepped into the streetcar, I thought about Tomi, who had grown up in San Francisco. I had gone to the Northern California city once with my parents and Rose for a produce-related convention. I was charmed by the cable cars, how they were able to climb the city's hilly slopes and how you could watch the ocean flash by in between tall buildings.

Smelling coffee and fried shrimp from the neighboring Nisei Grill, I approached the laundry woman's building. Through a narrow glass door, an Issei man exited, dressed formally in wool pants, a sweater vest, and tie. Spotting my white uniform under my sweater, he opened the door wide for me, even bowing a little, holding his fedora on his head with his other hand. If all these Issei knew that I had come under covert circumstances, they probably would have never let me in.

Once I reached the second floor, my nose led me to Mrs. Senzaki's quarters. The scent of fresh steamed rice wafted from the first room, the door ajar. A Japanese woman was bent over an ironing board, her salt-and-pepper hair pinned away from her face. She was obviously applying rice starch to the white shirts she was ironing—a trick my own mother had used before we began to buy commercial starch.

I had alerted her to my presence because she stopped ironing and looked up. Her face was round without many wrinkles, even though she was probably about my mother's age.

"Pick up?" she asked me.

"Ah, no. *Ohayou gozaimasu.*" I wished her a good morning. "My name is Aki Nakasone. I work at the Japanese Hospital."

Mrs. Senzaki at first seemed concerned, as if I was there to deliver some bad news.

"Haruki Watanabe was my patient." Saying "my patient" was a little over the top, but I knew I had to justify why I was invading her home and privacy. "His son was the best man in my wedding."

Before I could ask if she knew him, Mrs. Senzaki wiped her hands on her full-length apron and gestured for me to enter. "Come in, come in." She walked around the ironing board to firmly close the door behind me.

Stiff white shirts hung on hangers from two rows of clotheslines stretched in front of the windows facing First Street. Mrs. Senzaki specialized in an old-fashioned style that perhaps Issei were used to. Art preferred his own shirts to be softer with less starch applied.

The laundry woman sat me down at a small table and insisted that I drink some instant coffee with her, even though I was a stranger who had interrupted her work morning.

We made chitchat about what camps we had lived in.

"We lived in Gila River. Canal." Mrs. Senzaki shared with me information that I already knew.

I had heard enough about Gila River from people who had come later to Chicago. It was actually made up of two camps, Camp 1, Canal, and Camp 2, Butte. Canal was the smaller one, with five thousand inmates, half the size of Butte, so people really got to know each other.

"Did you meet Mr. Watanabe and his son, Babe, in Canal?"

I asked. Based on her reaction to Haruki Watanabe's name, I assumed that she was acquainted with the elder Watanabe in some way.

"Watanabe-*san* and Shin-*chan*, good family friends." To refer to Babe as *chan* meant that Mrs. Senzaki thought of him as a son. I couldn't picture anyone feeling remotely maternal about him.

"You know about Mr. Watanabe—"

"So *kawaisou*." She honestly seemed devastated about his demise. "He was my regular customer."

"At the San Mark?"

"Yes. I told him to move out of such an *abunai* place. I thought something bad would happen to him. He didn't listen to me. *Ganko*," Mrs. Senzaki declared. Mr. Watanabe definitely could be classified as stubborn but then most Issei men were. Their hard heads enabled them to survive the harsh circumstances they had encountered in this country.

"And Babe—Shinji—you know him well, too?"

"Of course, he's *yuushuu*." She praised his baseball skills, saying that he had been a star at Gila River. She and the other Issei women in camp were all worried when he was drafted in 1944.

My heart beat faster as I recalled when Art had received his draft papers in Chicago. I had already felt that my world was falling apart without Rose, and then Art had been taken from me.

"How is Shinji? I mean, what kind of person is he?"

Mrs. Senzaki screwed her face up in a frown. "Your friend, too, *deshou*?"

"My husband knows him. They fought together."

"War changed him," she said before gulping down the rest of her coffee.

"What do you mean?"

"One time I delivered Watanabe-*san*'s laundry. Early in the morning. Shin-*chan* seemed possessed by an *oni*." The laundry woman's hands began to shake and she grasped hold of her empty coffee cup to steady herself. "When I walked in, he woke up, like he had been in a trance. Then he ran out."

I remained silent, not wanting to break her reverie. Finally, I asked, "Did he harm his father?"

Mrs. Senzaki wouldn't respond directly. "He's a good boy," she murmured.

A stout young woman with a round face and thin eyes appeared from a side room. Her hair was cut unattractively in a *chawan* bowl cut. "Oh, Et-*chan*—" Mrs. Senzaki spoke out. "This is Aki. She's a friend of the Watanabes. My daughter, Etsuko."

"Hello," I greeted her. She, in turn, barely acknowledged me as she filled a mug with tap water from the kitchen sink and disappeared to the room behind the side door.

"Young people," her mother said in Japanese. "I can't keep up with her moods."

I nodded and then realized that I fell into the same age category.

"When's the last time you saw Haruki-*san*?"

Mrs. Senzaki stared blankly in thought. "I had laundry to deliver to him. But I didn't go. Maybe if I was there, he would not be dead."

I felt my stomach sink. I was hoping that Mrs. Senzaki had been the witness I needed to put to rest this mystery.

"No, you can't take that kind of responsibility." I pushed away my half-empty coffee cup and got ready to leave.

"Please don't mention anything about what I said." Mrs. Senzaki obviously regretted her moment of disclosure about Babe's mental state.

"Don't worry. Have you seen Babe recently?"

Mrs. Senzaki shook her head. "You? You see Shin-*chan* soon?" she asked me.

"I hope to. I'm looking for him. You wouldn't know where he might be?"

"No," said the laundry woman, who then searched through one of her drawers. She brought out a rolled piece of off-white fabric. At first I thought it might be a bandage but as she unfurled it, I saw that it was a belt made out of maybe a large rice bag. It was adorned with rows of embroidered red Xs.

"*Senninbari*. You know?" she asked me.

I was somewhat familiar but I didn't know what it was called.

Sensing my ignorance, Mrs. Senzaki explained that kamikaze pilots wore such belts. I did know that in camp women sewed them to protect young Nisei soldiers from harm on the front lines. According to the laundry woman, *senninbari* literally meant a "thousand-person stitch," and was supposed to keep the wearer safe through the spirit of the women who contributed to it. "My friend make stitch and pass to another woman. We keep going." I wasn't sure if there were a thousand stitches, but there certainly were hundreds. "Soldier wear around stomach. It was to keep Shin-*chan* alive," she explained.

"I'm sure it was appreciated."

"I wasn't able to give it to him. I was the last to receive it and was late to his farewell party. He was already on the bus, gone."

"But he came back, safe and sound. All the good wishes and the prayers—that was enough."

Mrs. Senzaki was obviously guilt-ridden. I hoped she didn't think that his psychological problems had anything to do with him not wearing the protective belt.

"You should give it to him now," I told her.

"No, no. He won't accept it from me."

We both became quiet. I took in a deep breath of the rice starch, which was simmering on a hot plate in a tiny kitchen-ette.

"I better go or I'll be late for work. Thank you so much for talking to me. And thank you for the coffee," I said.

"*Nandemonai.*" Mrs. Senzaki shrugged off the small bit of hospitality. "But please, take this." She held out the stitched belt.

I didn't know why Babe would need the good-luck charm after wartime, but I stuffed it into my handbag nonetheless.

As I walked down the stairs, I felt a sense of accomplishment, but also dread. Babe was obviously a tortured soul and if he wasn't in Art's circle, I might have felt pity for him. But many Nisei servicemen on the front lines had probably gone through hell; that didn't mean they turned on their own fathers.

A bit dazed and lost in my thoughts, I stood at the intersec-tion of First and San Pedro. My mother always warned me to be aware when I walked around by myself in Little Tokyo. With great force, the purse in my hands was snatched away. Running away with it was a Black man in a worn green tweed jacket.

"Hey, you—" I shouted.

For a moment, my body failed to move. It was my mother's old purse, one she was ready to throw away. I only had about two dollars and some change in that purse. But the *senninbari*, the treasure that I had agreed to present to Babe, was in there. Not only that, in the zipped compartment was Rose's photo. I should have put it in a safe place in the Boyle Heights house. Placed it underneath the floorboards in our closet. I couldn't bear to be separated from a part of my older sister. It wasn't like she was a talisman. Or even an angel. More like a memory of who I was. An Ito sister.

My rubber soles finally hit the pavement. I was thankful to be wearing my work shoes instead of silly heels. I pumped my muscular legs; Roy had always referred to them meanly as *daikon ashi*, white-radish legs, but they were certainly serving their purpose now.

When the thief reached the San Pedro Firm Building, he ran across the street, almost getting run over by a pickup truck in the process. Car horns blasted once for him and another time for me as I continued pursuit. I didn't know if he was an older man, or sickly, but somehow I was able to keep pace.

He burst through the door of a former residential hotel and I followed. I didn't know what was there before, but it could have been the foyer at one time. The stale room was dark, the windows covered with blankets, but I sensed the presence of people.

"A man stole my purse!" I shouted, not knowing if anyone would respond to my declaration.

I heard hard heels against the wood floors following the thief. I took some gulps of air, feeling quite winded from the chase. Aside from my long walks, I didn't engage in any physical exercise that made my heart race like that.

On the floor was the *senninbari*, looking like a white snake that had overeaten. The thief had probably dropped it thinking the fabric had no financial value. He was definitely right.

I stooped to pick up the *senninbari*. As I rose, my head brushed against a line of laundry that hung in the middle of the room, reminding me of our days back in Manzanar. The foyer seemed to be transformed into living quarters. I took a few steps forward and encountered a Black family of six sunken on a bare mattress, staring at me, the trespasser in their home. There were three little ones, no more than five years old, and the mother with a baby suckling at her breast. A matriarch, probably the mother's mother, based on their resemblance, sat on one end of the sagging mattress. "Have yourself a sit." She gestured to a rocking chair beside the bed, the only sign of domestic life, which seemed so out of place from the shambles of the room.

"Yes, sit yourself down." The mother covered her bare breast with a sheer towel. I felt so self-conscious invading their privacy that I silently did what I was asked to do.

Out of nervousness, I rocked back and forth in the chair, the loose planks of the hardwood floor creaking underneath. A putrid smell entered my nostrils. This room wasn't sanitary for this family with a baby to live in.

"He ran off but I got your purse." A Black man appeared holding up my purse as if he had caught a coveted fish.

I immediately leapt out of the rocking chair, the *senninbari* falling to the floor. "Oh, thank you so much." I opened the purse to make sure that Rose's photo was still intact in the side pocket. It was.

"Thank you." My coin purse with my two dollars was missing. "I have nothing to give you as a reward."

"No, ma'am, that's not necessary," the man, probably the father of these children, replied.

I didn't know why, but I bowed to them, like my Issei parents would do. I felt ridiculous immediately afterwards.

"You're forgetting something." The older woman interrupted as I attempted to find my way out.

The *senninbari*, of course. It was as if I really didn't want it in my possession. I stuffed it back in my purse.

"Well, have a good day," I called out, pushing my way out the door.

On the bus ride home to Boyle Heights, I hugged the purse against my chest and reevaluated the events surrounding the theft. I was shocked to see the abysmal state of housing for this one family. Was this the best our city could offer newcomers from the South who were working for our nation's defense industry? Issei and Nisei wanted to reclaim Little Tokyo as ours, because it had been ours for decades. But the world had shifted and maybe we needed to reevaluate the shift. Should Bronzeville be part of this consideration? Even though these workers had only lived in what was once Japantown for three, four years, was it now their home as much as ours?

When I got home after my shift at work, I immediately dumped out the *senninbari* from my swollen purse. Soiled by being dragged on the hotel-room floor, the cotton belt would have to be hand-washed. I had considered showing Chole, the master stitcher, the *senninbari* but decided against it because I knew women in Japan made them for kamikaze pilots. I didn't want her to get the wrong idea.

I knelt down to the floor of our bedroom closet. I removed four loose boards and took out a metal bento box that I had brought from Chicago. Once open, the box revealed a small gun resting on balled-up pages of the *Chicago Tribune*. I took out Rose's photo from the side pocket of my purse, kissed it, and then set it on top of the gun.

My parents knew about the gun but never mentioned it. A topic so taboo or shameful was one we chose to avoid talking about at all costs. The gun had been Rose's major purchase in Chicago, and I couldn't bear to let it go. I had packed it in my luggage when we'd left Chicago to return to Los Angeles.

When I was getting ready to meet Key Wakida to get his report, I considered putting the gun in a new purse that I'd bought in a shop on Brooklyn Avenue in Boyle Heights. The encounter with the thief had rattled me, reminding me of Babe's own nefarious connections. I shook off my fears. What was I thinking about? If I brought it with me, I probably would end up accidentally shooting the private investigator.

I wore my purse—without the gun—across my body like

a newspaper boy. I certainly lacked the style and pizzazz of a made-over Chiyo Tonai, but at this point, I didn't care.

Key and I got right to the point as soon as I walked into his office. It was a Saturday morning and I could tell that he was definitely not a morning person. Even the tips of his mustache seemed to droop downward.

"It doesn't look good for your Babe," he said from his oak desk. He slurped his coffee from a white ceramic mug I recognized from the Nisei Grill.

"What do you mean?" I felt so divided. I wanted evidence to implicate Babe yet a part of me also wanted him to be innocent.

"The police have his gun. It was left at the crime scene. It matches the bullet that killed his father."

I could imagine the sound of that bullet rolling around in a metal basin that Chole carried from the operating room. Obviously that bullet had been submitted to the police as evidence in the murder of Mr. Watanabe.

"How in the world do they know the gun is his?"

"It's an unusual one. A Singer."

"You mean like the sewing machine company?"

Key nodded. "The army commissioned Singer to make .45 pistols, believe it or not. I guess the precision necessary for making dependable sewing machines transferred over to guns. Singer was so good at it that the government had them switch over to manufacturing equipment for bomber airplanes. In all, Singer made only five hundred handguns."

"And Babe had one."

"It was from a *hakujin* officer who now lives in San Pedro." Key glanced at his notebook, some pages crumpled and looking like they were ready to get loose from the binding. "Name is Richard Klarman. He agreed to sell it to Babe after their victory in the Po Valley in Italy. There's an identifying serial number."

I didn't know how selling the Singer could be a true gift of gratitude, but I understood how a soldier could be attached to a gun. And Babe was always big on the latest gizmos—I remembered the attention he gave to his camera.

"So that's it." I had the evidence to present to Art but I felt deflated. "Babe did it. He killed his father."

Key raised his eyebrows as if to say that I shouldn't jump to conclusions yet. "There are some unusual circumstances."

"Like what?"

"Four set of fingerprints on the gun. One is Babe's and another Haruki's. The third belongs to his doctor, a Sidney Reed."

I pictured the psychiatrist in his majestic office overlooking the Colorado Street Bridge. "Dr. Reed? What does he have to do with the gun?"

Key pinched the end of the right side of his mustache. "Apparently Babe turned his gun in to Reed while he was getting treatment in the hospital in Pasadena. Reed returned it to him when he was released, thinking that Babe was of sound mind. The doctor contacted the police a few weeks ago when he found out that Babe had possibly harmed someone. He learned about Babe's father's shooting then."

Blood rushed to my head. I had probably been the source of Reed's initial concern. "The fourth print is still unidentified?"

Key nodded. "Strange that so many people handled the gun."

Who could that fourth person have been? Was there a possibility that person was the shooter?

Key consulted his ravaged notebook again. "Oh, and the police retrieved Haruki Watanabe's car."

"Where was it?"

"He was using a spot in the city hall parking lot. That goes for a premium. He brokered a deal with the DA's office. Free parking for free transportation. Someone from Arroyo Grande knew him from his racing days and vouched for him."

I was frankly shocked at Mr. Watanabe's level of connections. Who knew that stock car racing could garner him such influential perks? "The San Mark manager mentioned that some *hakujin* big shots would come around the apartments from time to time."

"The last client he drove before he got shot was a DA who's working on the Ku Klux Klan case."

I shuddered. Art would talk about the state revoking the KKK's charter from time to time at dinner.

"You know about that court case?" The private investigator asked me as if I were some sort of ding-a-ling.

"Of course! The state is trying to stamp out the KKK here." The incident of the burning cross on the lawn of that Jewish fraternity at USC surfaced in my mind.

Key squinted as if to measure my true comprehension. "More or less," he said.

"Do you think anyone would want to kill Mr. Watanabe? Just for driving this lawyer around?" The morning sunlight was starting to come through Mr. Wakida's broken venetian blinds.

"Well, it looks like those Jew haters are still around Los Angeles, but there hasn't been any related incident of violence, at least that we know of."

In some ways, I was relieved, but that observation didn't help us in identifying any suspects.

"Well, there's this doctor, too. Rented a space for his clinic at Nishi. Somewhat mysterious," Key said. "His name is Hodel."

I recalled that Charles had mentioned that a *hakujin* doctor had made some house calls to Mr. Watanabe's apartment.

"Treated clap. Rumored to have performed abortions."

"Really?" The illegality of abortions was an issue that I had become most familiar with in Chicago.

"But he's overseas in China. Left for his government assignment in the beginning of the year."

I adjusted the long strap of my purse. It didn't seem that Key had come up with any solid leads other than the evidence implicating Babe. "No other suspicious clients?"

"It could also have been a random act of violence involving a resident of the San Mark. But Mr. Watanabe wasn't close to anyone who lived there, correct? Was there anyone who could have known about the gun?"

I hated to think about it, but Charles sprung to mind. He was at the hotel at all times. He had a master key and it would be quite easy for him to go into Mr. Watanabe's room and snoop around. I had, however, developed a good rapport with Charles. I hated to think ill of him.

"You know who it could be." Key's eyes flashed. He looked more ridiculous than ever in that safari jacket. I wondered if he ever washed it.

I took out the ten-dollar bill from a zippered compartment in the purse and laid it atop some strewn papers on his desk. "Here," I told him. "As we agreed."

"I can do more research." Key's curiosity had been stirred.

"Sir, I'll be broke after you're finished with me. You've been most helpful. Really you have."

After I left his office, I noticed the beauty parlor's door was propped open. A couple of Nisei women were seated underneath hair dryers and glanced at me curiously, probably wondering what in the world I would be doing in an insurance man's office by myself so early on a weekend morning.

I considered whether I had wasted good money on the private investigator. Babe's pistol had been discovered in the same dingy room where Mr. Watanabe had been shot. This should be an open-and-shut case, yet Key also presented new suspects. A lawyer who was trying to kick the KKK out of California. A phantom doctor in China. And there was

Charles. Could Mr. Watanabe's killer have been under my nose this whole time?

Since I already was in Little Tokyo, I set out for the San Mark. I wanted to get up close to Charles and look straight into his eyes. I couldn't remember exactly what color they were—maybe a light brown—but I felt that I could trust them more than his words.

Willie Mae was back behind the chicken-wire window. She had obviously forgotten my name but not my face. "This will be the last month for me to be at the San Mark." Based on her huge smile, this was a cause for celebration. "My husband found a house. In a place called Compton."

"Oh, that's wonderful," I said. I mentioned nothing about the number of Issei farmers who had had to abandon their flower ranches and vegetable farms in Compton during the war.

"I suppose that you want to speak to Charles. He is having a meeting with some highfalutin men in city hall."

The mention of city hall flagged my attention. "Is that a regular occurrence?"

"Oh, he hobnobs with all sorts. Just not with many women. Not sure if he likes them."

Willie Mae was certainly a fount of information, solicited and not. I wished that we had a chance to get to know each other better before she left for Compton.

"What do you know about Charles's background?"

"From Frisco. Pretty resourceful. Can fix anything with the aid of a hairpin."

Charles had been in the army, so he knew how to use a gun. From Art's letters, I knew that part of military training was to climb up and down a rope ladder that extended a hundred feet off the ground. Traveling down a fire escape would be no problem for a former soldier.

"How did he come to the San Mark?" I asked.

"To tell you the truth, I'm not sure. He said that he came to work in the defense factories like my husband. But he ended up here instead. Why an able-bodied man would want to manage a dump like this is beyond me."

I had come to the same conclusion. And why had Mr. Watanabe been living here, of all places? The San Mark attracted people with secrets, that was for sure.

I went to the side of the San Mark and gazed at the fire escape. It wouldn't be hard for a man—or even a woman—to climb down those steps and ladders. Across the way was a windowless warehouse; no witnesses could readily see someone scale down the building. If someone wanted to shoot a man in cold blood in Bronzeville, I'd say the San Mark Hotel would be the place to do it.

CHAPTER 14

Before going to Chicago, I hadn't been the type to read news-papers on a regular basis. Working at Chicago's venerated Newberry Library and dating Art had changed me a bit. Instead of merely glancing at the headlines, I'd absorb the top couple of paragraphs and sometimes even read an article until the end.

Now in Boyle Heights and having access to all these news-papers from Mom's professor customer, we'd become our own kind of newsstand. I didn't care for the radio, as it reminded me of those constant daily briefings early in the war, especially after Pearl Harbor. My stomach had churned whenever I heard that Japan or Germany was extending their reach. When the government forced us to give up our radios, I'd found the respite from war news a bit of a relief. Instead of the doom-and-gloom announcements from excited *hakujin* men, we'd spent our last weeks in our wood-framed Tropico home listening to the voices of our family.

Since I had more time on my own now, I would spend some early evenings lounging in Pop's easy chair, my stockinged feet resting on an ottoman, a cup of hot tea on a side table. I'd start off with the *Rafu Shimpo* because its two pages of English were easy to scan. I wanted to make sure that I read any stories that were credited to Art, although he didn't get a byline on most of them. The columnists—like the two Marys, Henry, and Harry

Honda—were kings and queens; they gave life and personality to the pages. Some, like Mary No. 1, pushed readers to expand their thinking while others reflected more on who we really were—confused by our return to Los Angeles and scraping by the best we could. Next was the JACL's newspaper, the *Pacific Citizen*, which was one of the four non-camp newspapers that had continued publishing throughout the duration of the war. Everyone read the crime stories with Japanese American victims— and the most notorious incident involved a Nisei veteran who had been murdered in Stockton. His convicted killer, only a youth, faced the gas chamber. The police's administration of a truth serum, "a drug used during the war to quiet victims of hysteria," had resulted in his confession. No one that I knew challenged the ethics of using a tonic to extract the truth.

After catching up on the Japanese American news, I went straight to the *L.A. Times* and *Daily News* and the two Black newspapers, the *California Eagle* and the *Tribune*, the latter being the one Hisaye worked at. As I went through the papers, I looked for any mention of the hearings to ban the Klan from Los Angeles. Those stories were buried deep in the newspapers' pages. A hearing led by Attorney General Robert Kenny was taking place at the California State Building on First Street, just a few blocks west of Little Tokyo, across from the *Los Angeles Times* building and next to city hall.

Kenny, that name sounded familiar. Hadn't Charles mentioned that Mr. Watanabe had driven a government man named Kenny? I felt a push to attend the proceeding even though I had no business going. *Do I dare?* There was no danger that Art would show up; he had said that the linotype machine operator, Joe, was going on his honeymoon, so Art had to fill in for a couple of days. But I had already infiltrated places that no respectable young Nisei woman would enter. I was fully aware that I was pushing my luck.

After calling in sick the next morning, I drove over to the California State Building, hoping to secure some parking that wouldn't cost me an arm and a leg. I circled the block and pulled into a space on the street where a sedan was leaving. I walked into the State Building and was overwhelmed by its high ceilings and beautifully designed stone flooring. I wasn't quite sure how I would find the location of the hearing in this vast structure, but then I spied a young man carrying a white robe over his arm. *He must be connected*, I thought, and followed him to a set of elevators, decorative zigzags over each door. As I got in the elevator car after him, I found myself surrounded by *hakujin* men in suits. I moderated my breathing. *I have a right to be here. I have a right to be here.*

When I walked into the hallway toward the hearing room, I saw a huge cross standing larger than a *hakujin* man and lined with red light bulbs. A man—or at least I presumed it was a man—dressed in a Ku Klux Klan white hood and robe posed in front of it. I felt woozy and sick to my stomach. These symbols of hatred were living and breathing. Why was this spectacle allowed in a government building? I'd thought this was a legal proceeding. I wanted to run, but I forced myself to stay.

Once I entered the hearing room, I was surprised that it was so small. It looked like a law office, with rows of uniform books lining one wall. There were only a couple of dozen seats for the public and I felt completely out of place. As I scanned the seats, I spotted a familiar face: Henry, Art's editor, with another Japanese man seated beside him. Henry gestured for me to join him. Seeing no way to refuse, I made my way to him.

"Fancy seeing you here," Henry said. "This is Hashida-*san*, the Japanese editor."

Art hadn't mentioned Mr. Hashida much, probably because Art's Japanese was so poor. His mother was a Nisei, and she and Art's father spoke mostly English at home. In contrast,

Rose and I had attended Japanese school on Saturdays, an experience that we most detested, Rose, because she would rather have been socializing with friends, and me, because I hated to be stuck indoors on a weekend morning.

I bowed toward Mr. Hashida. Luckily, before Henry had a chance to identify me to the Japanese editor, the proceedings began. The judge had an Italian last name; his hair was jet-black like a Japanese and his nose a bit hooked like a pecking bird's. Much of the language in the courtroom was over my head, but I got the general gist—that the California state attorney was trying to revoke the KKK's charter because of its practice of bigotry and racial hatred. I stared at the attorney general's back as he spoke. Robert Kenny was a heavy man with an extremely short haircut, perhaps freshly groomed for today's public proceedings.

Kenny asked a number of KKK members to come forward to testify. Some were belligerent and others were reluctant to confirm that they still belonged to the organization. Some were definitely true believers who wanted all to know their devotion to keeping the US as white as possible. One of them was a *hakujin* man with hair styled in a mini-pompadour. I didn't catch his name but from time to time Kenny referred to him as a Kleagle, whatever that meant; I gathered it designated him as a top dog. He was defiant and proud, even shouting at one point, "The mission of the Klan is sacred." I practically shook in my shoes to hear that his belief took religious proportions.

The hearing was recessed with a decision to be rendered later that afternoon. Henry, after saying a word to his Japanese colleague, returned to me. "Time to grab a quick lunch?"

"Don't you need to file your story?" I noticed that Mr. Hashida had shuffled off with his notebook.

"This will be covered in the *Daily News* and *L.A. Times*. No need for the English section to go on and on about it. I was just here to help Mr. Hashida with translation. Unfortunately he can't wait until the judge's ruling to write the story."

I tugged at my sweater. I wasn't keen on spending one-on-one time with my husband's boss. "Well, honestly, I shouldn't be here at all. I called in sick to work."

"Just to come to the hearing?" Henry seemed impressed. "Well, you have to eat. Let me at least spring for a sandwich and some coffee."

Instead of walking to nearby Little Tokyo, we went to the café near the *L.A. Times* building. It was frequented by city office workers, harried lawyers, and poverty-stricken journalists, judging by their threadbare jackets and scuffed shoes. I appreciated the café's air of anonymity. No one I knew would spot me there.

"Well, Aki," Henry said, after taking the first bite of his bologna sandwich. "I was meaning to ask you, is Aki short for Akiko?"

"No, just Aki." My maternal grandmother had the same name. "Ko," which literally meant *child*, was a diminutive, like saying Jimmy for Jim or Dotty for Dot. A generation ago, it had not been fashionable to add "ko" to the end of women's names.

"And do you have an American name?"

I shook my head. I had heard from my parents that they were considering Annabelle but it just hadn't seemed quite right. My birth had been difficult, taking quite a toll on Mom, so filling out the proper paperwork for my birth certificate wasn't at the top of their minds. It had bothered me at first when my teachers and some of my classmates struggled with my name, but I later appreciated it, as I didn't have to choose to use an American name over a Japanese one.

"What do you think about the attorney general?" I brought the conversation back to the hearing.

"Kenny? Hard to figure. He's been going after us in the

escheat cases. There's one in Santa Ana right now as a matter of fact." He took a big gulp of his black coffee. "He's also trying to take a case against a Terminal Island fisherman to the Supreme Court. The fisherman got his license revoked just because he's Japanese."

How horrible. "So he hates both the Japanese and the KKK?" I said in a soft voice, not to alarm all the *hakujin* seated around us.

"I think he's a typical government lawyer in some ways. Has to defend the law as it stands. But last year he also spoke out to sheriffs in California to look after us Issei and Nisei as we returned. Said that we were Japanese Americans and not 'Japs.' That it was their duty to protect us from racist terrorists."

I was so confused. Was Kenny a good guy or bad guy? Or maybe he could not be easily classified. "Do you think that he has any skeletons in his closet?"

"Not that I know of. You've heard something?" A patron with a heavy white beard shuffled past us with a tray holding two corned beef sandwiches.

"No, no," I said, horrified that I may be spreading rumors. "By the way, what's a Kleagle?"

"It's a high-ranking officer within the Klan," Henry explained to me. "Heard from a source that the Kleagle who testified was passing out cards recruiting new KKK members. On the back of it was his Eagle Rock address."

"Eagle Rock? That's not far from here." It was, in fact, only a few miles away from my original home in Tropico. During the hearing, Kenny had mentioned a cross burning in Big Bear in the San Bernardino Mountains. That was out in the wilderness where mostly *hakujin* lived. I shuddered to think that such racial and religious hate could be right here in Southern California.

The Kleagle was the one who had been highly excitable,

declaring his devotion to the KKK with religious fervor. I couldn't help but notice that underneath his jacket, he was wearing an empty pistol holder. Was that a warning that he was preparing to use violence? Could this Kleagle's and Haruki Watanabe's paths have crossed? Was Mr. Watanabe, as Kenny's driver, privy to information that had led to his death?

Considering these questions, I silently munched on the last bit of my sandwich as Henry got up and paid the bill.

"By the way," he said as we made our way out. "Sorry to have kept your man out so late the other night."

I tried to maintain a blank look on my face as I felt anxiety rush into my head. Art's coming home drunk certainly triggered my fear that alcohol abuse would permeate my family life, just as my father's problem had.

"We all drank too much at that Mexican restaurant. Just hearing Kenji's story made us mad as hell."

"Yes, of course," I said, having no idea of what he was talking about.

"To lose the use of your arm on the front lines like that and be sent home to Hawaii in the hold of a naval ship, just like a miserable prisoner. I don't know what the navy was thinking."

I wasn't doing a good job in masking my confusion, and Henry stopped in his tracks before reaching Los Angeles Street. An office worker bumped my elbow as she rushed toward the green light. "Art didn't tell you the whole story, did he?"

I shook my head. Henry related the nuts and bolts: wounded Nisei soldiers recuperating in a San Francisco army hospital had finally been sent to their families, only instead of being treated like heroes in staterooms and cabins, they'd had to suffer the journey in cots below deck, with subpar foods. "Kenji said now that the war is over, no one cares about the Nisei soldier."

"That's really awful," I exclaimed.

"That figures that Art didn't disclose much to you. He likes to look on the bright side of things, doesn't he?"

I hadn't thought much about it until now, but in that way, Art was like my sister, Rose. No matter how bleak a situation was, they would try their hardest to will the circumstances into a more positive direction. Rose, unfortunately, had sacrificed her life. I was struck that the same could happen to Art as well.

As we walked on First Street, I could hear the faint pounding of percussion from a couple of blocks away. I stopped Henry before we got too close to Bronzeville. "Could you do me a favor?"

Henry looked at me curiously, a toothpick hanging from his mouth.

"Don't tell Art that you saw me here today."

Henry pulled out the toothpick. "You want our lunch to be off the record."

"Yes, could you?"

"I understand. We all get a bit paranoid at times. I stayed home last December seventh. Didn't want to give any yahoos a chance to take a crack at me."

Pearl Harbor Day didn't affect me like it had Henry. I had gone to Henrotin Hospital like I had every Friday. I did notice the headlines of the local Chicago newspapers, celebrating the hanging of a Japanese war criminal. But that didn't have anything to do with the Nisei or me.

No one seemed to look at me askew. Most of the hospital staff knew that my husband was overseas with the US Army. "Well, it wasn't that big of a deal for me in Chicago—" I started to respond truthfully when Henry waved me off.

"I've learned that it's not my place to tell another person how to deal with this problem of being Japanese in this country," Henry said.

I felt like interjecting that my presence in the hearing room had had little to do with my views on politics. I was, instead, trying to save my marriage. But as Henry was Art's editor, it would be highly inappropriate for me to confide in him.

"If the judge rules against the Ku Klux Klan, will that be the end of them?"

Henry stared at me dispassionately. "What do you think?"

"I hope so."

"The decision may keep them underground for a while. Unfortunately, I think that our children and even our grandchildren will be dealing with the likes of the KKK."

On Monday, May 27, Reverend Kowta made good on his offer for Evergreen Hostel to take in the Iida family. While Chole helped Mrs. Iida and Shiz pull together their meager belongings in the hospital, I drove over to Winona in the hospital sedan to collect the other Iida children. Since everyone was overtaxed and busy, I made the trip alone. I found myself relishing the drive along this strip of Highway 99, imagining myself trekking past Burbank to the mountains or maybe the beach. The rumble of airplane engines broke my reverie and I steadied the steering wheel. I would be entering the world of Winona soon.

I had read in the *Rafu Shimpo* that the Magnolia barracks, as well as other temporary housing units in places like Long Beach, had closed, sending more homeless sojourners to Winona. Housing administrators had pledged to improve the conditions of the trailer camp, but I didn't have high expectations.

I couldn't quite remember where the Iida's family's trailer was located and wandered around the camp a bit before finding it. The neighbor was handwashing laundry outside in a metal basin.

"Ah, *kangofu*-san!" The neighbor called out, brushing away stray hair from her face with the side of her arm.

I was honored to be called a nurse and I asked where the Iida children were. The neighbor gestured with her chin toward men squatting around the fighting ring for teenage boys. My anger returned. Did everyone think that this activity was fine and dandy?

I marched to the circle, eliciting responses from some of the spectators.

"Oh, it's lil Miss Goody Two-Shoes."

A soft chuckle rippled through the crowd in response. Obviously someone was enjoying himself. I narrowed my eyes and surveyed the gathering of men. In the circle of miscreants was Ken Kanehara, a cigarette behind each ear and another lit one in his mouth. With the closure of the Magnolia barracks, Ken had apparently landed in the hellhole of Winona.

"You're not following me, are you?" he said, as if we were old friends. He repulsed me more than any person I had recently come across.

I chose to ignore Ken and addressed the rest of the men. "You know that it's awful to use children for your amusement."

Ken made a face and fluttered his fingers, insinuating that I was as annoying as a squawking bird.

I felt like slapping him but I knew that wouldn't solve any problems and might, in fact, create more. My presence had dampened the enthusiasm for the gladiator game and most of the men dispersed.

Ken plucked the cigarette out of his mouth and blew smoke in my face. "You're here to speak to Babe, I guess."

My heart felt like it stopped. *Babe is here?!* I decided to play it cool as a cucumber. "Yeah, have you seen him?" I tried to say as casually as possible, but my voice instead sounded strangely high-pitched.

"He's with my old man in our trailer."

I whirled around to see which trailer he was speaking of. A

skinny boy wearing no shirt had apparently been eavesdropping and pointed at a trailer around a hundred yards away.

Before Ken could stop me, I trotted over to the trailer's open door and went inside.

"Ah, *konnichiwa*." The toothless Kanehara elder waved from his bed. I don't know if he was hoping for another rice cake, but I rudely ignored him to face the man who I had been searching for the past few weeks.

I was probably the last woman that Babe wanted to see. His mouth fell open, releasing a mash of chewed apple onto his dingy T-shirt.

"Hello, Babe," I said to him.

Babe brushed away a bit of apple from his chin. "Is Art here?"

"No, he's not. And I'm glad. Do you know how much trouble you've caused him? The police have been by the house a couple of times."

"What for?"

"To find you. Apparently you put our address as your permanent one. They think you are living with us."

Fear consumed his face. "He's okay, though, right?" He obviously didn't care two hoots about me.

"Yeah, why wouldn't he be? What's going on, Babe? And why were you in Skid Row in a peep show movie house with a reported gangster? If you care about Art, you have to tell me what's going on."

Babe gritted his teeth and squeezed the half-eaten apple in his right hand.

Seeing the fragile figure of Mr. Kanehara brought to mind the late Mr. Watanabe. "And I know about how you treated your father. Those weren't injuries from him falling down the stairs." I refrained from bringing up the Singer gun and straight-out accusing him of murder. Winona was his turf, not mine.

In a sudden burst of energy, Babe flung the apple out the open trailer door.

"Go back to your little house in Boyle Heights. Stay away from here."

My chest tightened. I couldn't let Babe shut me out. He might be the only person who could explain what was tormenting my husband night after night.

"What happened in the war, Babe?" I asked him. "What happened to you and Art?"

His beefy body shook like it was going to explode. "Go home. Make Art forget that he ever knew me."

I stumbled out of that miserable trailer, almost tripping on the last stair onto the packed dirt. Now that would have been something—falling on my face and maybe suffering a broken nose.

The two Iida children, whom the neighbor had informed of my arrival, ran to my side. Jerry, able to hear Babe's bellows, looked frightened. I tousled his hair to alleviate his worry, only to find my hand coated with oil. These children desperately needed a bath. "You'll be in a safe place soon," I whispered in his dirt-coated ear. "Just stay out of such *kitanai* places from now on, okay?"

Jerry nodded. He didn't seem to want to revisit the nastiness of the peep show theatre, either.

I followed them to their trailer and together we stuffed their meager belongings into soiled pillowcases, their makeshift suitcases.

It wasn't until the three of us were in the sedan that I realized I hadn't told Babe that I had received the *senninbari* from the laundry woman. "Serves you right," I murmured. Oblivious to my agitation, Jerry and Yoko were in the back seat, playing with the armrests and peering out the back window. I was Japanese enough to feel a responsibility to give the precious handmade item to Babe as soon as possible. *I'll do it next week,* I told myself. *It's not like he's at war right now.*

Before starting the car, I turned back to the children. "Settle down," I commanded them. "This is going to be a long drive."

It was a couple of hours before I was able to leave the Evergreen Hostel. It did warm my heart to see the Iida family reunited. Mrs. Iida especially had a beatific expression on her face as her children ran wild throughout the grounds of the hostel. After being confined so long in dirt, desert, and concrete spaces, they finally had some grass to play in. As I hiked home on Evergreen, I looked forward to tearing off my nurse's uniform and my sweaty bra, and to soaking in a Palmolive bubble bath. I would have to wait. As I turned on Malabar, I noticed a figure seated on our porch. I feared that it was another law enforcement officer but as I got closer, it became clear that it was a woman.

"Chiyo, what are you doing here?" I said, opening the low metal gate to our concrete walkway.

Chiyo wasn't dressed in one of her splendid outfits this evening. She wore a pair of loose high-waisted jeans, saddle shoes, and a short-sleeved shirt with a Peter Pan collar, an ensemble I had seen her wear in her Chicago apartment. "I didn't know where else to go," she said. She didn't have any makeup on her face, and her eyes were terribly swollen, creating lopsided double eyelids.

I was familiar with that look. Time after time in Chicago I had taken an ice pick to the block of ice in our refrigerator so I could collect some cool shards to help reduce the puffiness around my eyes after a good cry.

"We had an awful fight," she said, sitting down on one of our uncomfortable wooden patio chairs. She didn't have to say who "we" was.

"What about?" I lowered myself into the other one.

"Do you know Mildred Yamato?"

I knew who Mildred was but had never had an opportunity to say much to her except for "hello" and "see ya." She was tall and striking, with long legs atypical for a Nisei woman. She had been in Rose's circle back when we were attending John Marshall High School.

"They are old friends," I told Chiyo.

"What's wrong with her? She's almost twenty-five and not married. No boyfriend either."

I actually didn't know of Mildred's ever having a beau, but then I had never had one until Art. "I don't know, some girls aren't interested in marriage." I myself had fallen into it. Who knows what would have happened if we hadn't been sent off to Manzanar and Chicago?

"Well, at least she should have the good sense not to be calling a married man at all hours."

"Isn't she Roy's secretary?"

"I know." She pressed a handkerchief over her swollen eyelids. "But it gets people's tongues wagging. I even caught the Sandovals giving each other looks."

"Talk to him about it, Chiyo. You can talk to Roy."

Chiyo released a deep breath. "He's been under a lot of pressure. And I hate to say it, but your father isn't helping. All these former workers are depending on Roy to save the day. But to tell you the truth, I don't think that the produce market can be returned to us."

My heart sank. I suspected the same.

"Every time I try to talk to Roy about any kind of problem, he says that I'm going off the rails. And whenever we go out, he's always flirting with the young waitresses."

I didn't know what to say to Chiyo. She knew Roy was a bit of a playboy. That had been his reputation in camp and in Chicago.

"Roy was always social." Why was I excusing his behavior?

"Social, is that what you call it? I was tricked by his letters from Europe! Because he had no other women to distract him."

The French woman that Art had seen Roy with came to mind.

Chiyo squeezed her eyes shut but she was all cried out. She had escaped into her own world. "I'm thinking a baby will change his mind," she announced.

"Are you pregnant?" I inadvertently looked down at her stomach. It did pouf out slightly, but Chiyo had always been more on the chubby side.

"No, no." She waved her hands over her lap. "But I have a plan."

"What are you thinking of doing?"

"We are using rubbers." Chiyo was always straightforward with the most intimate of information. "I'm thinking of maybe poking holes in them."

I almost slipped off of my chair. I had never imagined that Chiyo was capable of something so underhanded. "You can't do that. You need to talk to him. Bringing a baby into this world is a big decision. Both of you have to be behind it." I was too familiar with the pressure that I felt from Art.

"He doesn't realize how good it will be for both of us," she said definitively. She had made up her mind.

I realized at this point nothing I could say would make her reconsider. I wasn't going to tattle to Roy, even though he was our oldest family friend and my father's former employer. Once he married Chiyo, they were committed to embark on their own journey. I was afraid for both of them, but then who was I to give out free advice?

"Are you locked out, Aki?" Art had come home on time for once, carrying his briefcase and wearing a felt hat. My heart leapt, and I was surprised that my body still tingled when I saw him after a long day.

"Oh, no. Chiyo came by. We were just enjoying the sunshine." My comment didn't make much sense as the bungalow porch was too shaded and dark. And based on the tuna fish sandwich mishap, we both knew firsthand that the porch wasn't built to make socializing comfortable.

"Hi, Art." Chiyo was able to manage a bright, wholesome smile.

"Where are you and Roy living again?"

"West Thirtieth."

"That's quite a trek."

"I drove over." Chiyo gestured toward a truck with TONAI PRODUCE painted on the doors. It must have been one of the few from the Tonai family fleet that had been salvaged. "I'm used to driving. I learned to drive on the farm when I was twelve."

"Is everything all right?" Art, perceptive as ever, noticed Chiyo's tear-stained face.

"Oh, yes. Allergies, you know." Chiyo abruptly rose. "Well, I better be going. See you two again. Soon, I hope."

As Chiyo easily swung herself into the flatbed truck, I could picture her driving around the perimeter of her family's vineyard. She was a long way from home and a part of me speculated whether she might be happier in a place like Fresno where she could be herself, an honest, straightforward, happy-go-lucky farm girl, rather than a business wife married to the playboy king of the produce market in Los Angeles.

Art cleared his throat as I remained seated on the ledge. "Listen, I had a talk with Henry."

I felt my chest tighten. Had Art's editor snitched on me? My mind whirled to come up with an adequate defense.

"I told him that I need to pull back from all these reporting assignments. I make more money selling ads, anyway."

"I don't understand," I said.

"I realize that I haven't been home much. We haven't been able to spend much time doing fun things. Heck, I haven't even seen Grauman's Chinese in Hollywood yet."

"But you love writing," I said.

"I love other things more."

I let Art's simple statement wash over me. I was such a fool. Why did I let petty jealousies take over my thinking?

I stood up and took his briefcase from him. "Let's go inside."

A rib roast was waiting for us on the dining room table. In addition, there were potatoes and fresh carrots from Pop's friend's garden, and a wedge salad with creamy dressing dribbled over the lettuce. My mother, perhaps sensing that we could all use a pick-me-up, had produced a small feast.

"Yuri, you've outdone yourself," Art said after we'd all practically inhaled her culinary masterpiece.

"*Gochisousamadeshita*," Pop agreed.

"I'll do the dishes," I volunteered, feeling a lightness in my step from my earlier conversation with Art. As I was collecting the dirty dishes from the table, the phone rang.

Mom went to answer. "Hallo." Our phone sat on a small table that was covered with a doily she had crocheted to protect its surface. "Yes," she said in English. "May I ask who is calling?" Based on my mother's formal tone, I knew that she was addressing a stranger. "Oh, *hai*, Koyano-*san*, *ne*. Wait a minute." Mom held out the receiver. "Art, Mary Koyano."

Why is Mary No. 2 calling the house for my husband?

Art also looked genuinely puzzled. He wiped his mouth with his napkin as if Mary could see him over the telephone line.

He turned his back to the table as he took the call. "Hello. Oh, hi, Mary. Yes, Henry is right. He was my best man." Pressing the receiver to his ear, he remained silent for a minute.

"Where did this happen?" he finally said, his voice sounding distant and professional, like he was interviewing a source for the *Rafu*. "Yes, yes, I understand. I appreciate you telling me, Mary."

He ended the call without even saying goodbye. All three of us knew that Art had been informed of something very serious. We waited silently.

Art turned toward us. All the color had drained from his face. "City News Service received a report about a shooting victim in Burbank. A police source leaked that it's Babe."

CHAPTER 15

Art was the one who was called to identify the body, as Babe didn't have any blood relatives in Los Angeles. I insisted on accompanying Art to the coroner's office.

"No, I don't want you to go," he said.

I knew what it was like to see a loved one drained of life. I had been in that position two years ago. I wasn't going to let my husband go through that alone.

"Let me at least drive you," I implored. Art's hands had been shaking ever since he received that initial phone call from Mary No. 2. He finally relented, realizing that he might not be able to navigate unfamiliar streets, especially at night.

My father had retreated to the bedroom almost immediately after Mary's call. My mother joined him shortly thereafter, leaving the cleanup entirely to me. The news of a young dead Nisei had certainly stirred a bad memory in all of us. In our dark living room, I was drawn to the gold urn on the mantel. *Don't forget about me*, my sister seemed to say to me.

The coroner's office was located in the Hall of Justice, an intimidating granite block that housed courtrooms and even a holding cell. Since it was evening, the downtown streets were clear and I was able to find an open parking space right in front. "You sure?" I asked him as he pushed the car door open.

"Yes. You stay here."

Alone in the Model A, I felt shaken to my core. I had just spoken to Babe several hours earlier. I opened the glove compartment to find anything to divert my attention. Instead, I discovered Mrs. Senzaki's *senninbari*, which I had stored in there to give to Babe the next time I saw him. I felt a pang of contrition. I should have given him the lucky belt today. If I had, would he be alive?

It seemed like Art had been gone for hours when I finally spied him stumbling toward the car, the silhouette of a zombie instead of the tall ex-soldier that I had been living with. When he collapsed in the passenger seat, I could see that his face was twisted in pain.

"Are you okay?"

Art buried his face in his hands. His sobs were intense and haunting; the noises didn't sound human. I had heard similar groans on the hospital ward in Chicago, but when such grief emerges from your spouse, it takes on another dimension altogether. I felt that a spear had been thrust into the side of my body, tearing into my organs and any other soft matter. I pressed my right arm around his curved shoulders, hoping to be that life preserver that he could hold on to. I regretted all the times when my petty jealousies had caused me to come to the wrong conclusions about his integrity and commitment. I needed to change, I realized at that moment.

I don't how long Art wailed in my father's old Model A in front of the coroner's office. It felt cathartic even to me, and I didn't share the same feelings for Babe. But Art grieved the loss of his friend and I connected to that loss. If only our family had cried like this for Rose, maybe our recovery wouldn't have been so prolonged and tortuous.

I didn't have a handkerchief in my large purse for Art to blow his nose. My *oshiri* was up in the air as I searched the back seat of the car for jackets with balled-up tissues in a pocket. I finally came up with an oily rag that Pop had probably used to wipe his hands after working on the car.

A loud tapping noise sounded on the driver's side window and I almost screamed in response. It was a security guard, dressed like a policeman.

"Everything okay in there?" he asked through my closed window.

Art was still crumpled against the passenger's window while I slid back in the driver's side.

"Yes, we're fine," I said. The guard nodded and sauntered off down the sidewalk around the granite fortress.

Art blew his nose into the rag. "Remember Thirty-First Street Beach?"

"Yes, of course. How can I forget?" That had been our favorite place in Chicago for romantic encounters. One night when we were canoodling in Art's family pickup truck, a police officer interrupted us before we got too far.

"Is there someplace we can go and park? Someplace safe?"

My mind whirled, considering the possibilities. I turned on the car and checked the fuel gauge. Fortunately for us, my father was the type to always fill up the gas tank. I knew of a place, but hadn't been there in at least five years.

As we drove down Figueroa Street, Art rolled down his window, allowing the cool air to whip through the car. The wind burst was a little too much for me but I wasn't going to make a fuss. The sound of the tires rotating against the freeway's asphalt provided a meditative rhythm. We were on our way to the ocean. To help mend our fragile relationship, we should have done this weeks ago.

When the air began to smell of salt and petroleum, I knew that we were getting close to our destination. The sun had gone down about an hour ago, and a faint image of a full moon hung behind a curtain of clouds. Even the celestials were hiding from us.

Once we reached Wilmington I drove west and then south. When we could hear the crash of the waves, I found an open spot and parked the car.

"Where are we?" Art, who had nodded off, straightened in his seat. He had oil smudges around his nose, but I didn't bother to tell him. It didn't matter.

"This is White Point. The Royal Sands Resort."

The site didn't look like much of a resort tonight. Where there had once stood a two-story hotel with a long saltwater swimming pool, only a concrete foundation remained. The large iconic fountain that had marked the front lay in ruins.

Art helped me through the rubble, large boulders extending into the water where a barge once stood. We finally found a flat and dry rock to sit on. With the hiding full moon above, the tide seemed to be coming in, higher and higher.

"I know how you're feeling," I told him. "I was the one who identified Rose at the Chicago coroner's office."

"I didn't know," he said.

How could he? I had never told him.

Art stared out into the black sea. "To see him like that on that gurney. His face disfigured from the gunshot wound. It reminded me of the war."

My heart ached but I kept silent. I knew that it wasn't time for me to speak.

A particularly large wave crested in the distance and a large bird, maybe a pelican, soared above us. "We were in Italy in a place called Po Valley," Art began. "We were attached to the 92nd division, a unit of all Black men."

"Negroes?" I was surprised. My co-worker at the Newberry, Phillis, had a brother who had fought in the Pacific, but my understanding was that not many Blacks were assigned to the front lines.

"Oh, yes, furious fighters. The 92nd was the only Negro

division that fought in Europe, I think. They've gotten a bad rap from their *hakujin* superiors who spread rumors that they lacked battlefield skills."

Like the Black soldiers, Japanese Americans also could not serve as officers in the US military—the only exception I knew was John Aiso, a Harvard Law School graduate who used his Japanese language to distinguish himself at the Military Intelligence Service Language School.

"In a way, they had it harder than us Japanese," I commented.

Art nodded. "The 92nd led a diversionary attack all the way to Massa, an oceanside town in Tuscany. It was dawn, even before the sun was up. We advanced, but then we were hit by a barrage of enemy fire. One of us was wounded and medics had just taken him away. It was just Babe and I who were left behind in this hidden woody area."

Art's hands were trembling and it took everything I had to not touch him. I had to allow him to travel back to the front lines without any present-day attachments thwarting his journey.

"And then this German stood up in this slop of mud, holding something in his hands. I could have sworn that it was a sharp end of a knife. I yelled and then Babe took out his knife from his belt. And like they taught us in basic training, Babe held this man's neck in the crook of his arm. He then sliced the soldier's neck as easily as carving open a summer watermelon. Blood shot out, and I was bathed in it. I couldn't get his blood off of me. Later the medics thought that it was my blood."

"Oh, Art." My throat was so dry that my voice lost almost all resonance. All we could hear was the crashing of the waves.

"When Babe checked if he was dead, I looked at the soldier's hands. He wasn't holding a knife. It was a picture. Of his sweetheart, most likely."

I covered my mouth. I pictured my bloodstained husband making this awful discovery. Art wasn't meant to be warring with guns, knives, and bombs. He was a gentle and kind wordsmith who spent his days in Chicago cleaning up the Japanese mausoleum at the Montrose Cemetery and attending journalism classes. "It wasn't your fault. Or Babe's either. It was war, Art. Of course you expected an enemy soldier to have a weapon in his hand."

Art's chest expanded and contracted as he took deep gulps of salt-tinged air. "I never wanted to see that photo again. But then when we had time for R and R in France I saw it. That damn Babe was carrying the woman's photo in his wallet."

"What in the world—"

"He was never quite himself after that. And now he's dead." Art covered his face with his fists.

"You can't blame yourself, Art," I said softly.

"I could have tried to help him more. In Bronzeville, at least." Art turned to me and the black smears by his nostrils made him look like a midnight prowler. His voice was tender as he confessed, "You were right. I lied to you. I told you that I hadn't seen Babe. He didn't want anyone to know where he was. But I did see him in Little Tokyo, the morning I arrived in Los Angeles. It was the only time. He had written to me that he was in a terrible situation. I think it was about money."

"Gambling?"

"I don't think so. Babe wasn't a gambler. But his father was. As soon as Babe was old enough, he made sure that their farm was in his name. Babe was worried that his father would sell off the land to pay his debts. But as it turned out, the government took it away, anyway."

It was strange to hear Babe's side of the story from Art. Before, I had felt such sympathy for Mr. Watanabe because I had seen him in a most desperate situation. But I was learning that he wasn't completely innocent, either.

"Babe didn't have a good relationship with his father. His mother had died young." Art gripped the sandy surface of the rock we were sitting on. "When I met with him that day I arrived in Los Angeles, he was acting erratic. He told me that he had a plan that would solve all his problems. That I shouldn't worry, but that he needed his privacy for a while. That I shouldn't try to contact him anymore, but he would reach out to me in due time."

Art's eyes were dark pools.

"And I kept something else from you."

I tried to swallow but the dryness in my throat prompted me to almost gag instead.

"A white man came by the newspaper a few weeks ago. He was asking me questions about Babe. Like what places he frequents. I told him that I didn't know."

"What did he look like?"

"Light skin. Freckles."

"That sounds like one of the men that came by the house."

"The coroner told me to call the police tomorrow. They apparently want to talk to me."

The flat rock underneath us felt uncomfortably cold. "Maybe they should speak to me instead."

Art fully turned to me, his voice now more urgent. "What do you mean?"

"I saw Babe earlier today," I confessed. "At Winona. He was staying at a friend's trailer. I happened to be picking up the Iida children to bring them to Evergreen Hostel."

"How did Babe seem?"

"He was in a bad spot, Art. He didn't want you to be involved."

"Well, I don't want you to be involved," Art said. "I'll deal with the police. You don't have to be a part of it."

I should have protested, but I was relieved. I didn't think I could share anything worthwhile to find Babe's killer, anyway. If those men who came looking for Babe weren't policemen, I didn't know who they were.

The tide was almost lapping at our shoes. "We better go back," I told him. I rose and took his hand. Art kept his hand on my shoulder the whole ride home.

CHAPTER 16

The next morning Art called the original LAPD detective, Carl Miller, after we both contacted our respective employers to take the day off. Within an hour, Miller arrived at the house with his partner, Ben Pease. Art had me and my parents retreat to our respective bedrooms while he dealt with them in the living room. Of course I pressed my ear against the door to hear what I could of their conversation.

I recognized Detective Miller's voice. "It was a mob hit, no question about it."

I felt as though my heart had stopped beating.

"Why would gangsters want to kill Babe?" Art asked.

The other detective answered in a low, more monotone voice, and I couldn't catch every word he said. Basically they had an informant in the Burbank operation. Babe had stolen money from the gangsters.

"I'd be careful, Mr. Nakasone." Detective Miller pronounced our last name like it rhymed with "macaroni." "These men will want their money back. Since they couldn't get it from the deceased, they will try to involve anyone else in his circle."

"But I had nothing to do with any of it."

"They know that you are friends," the lead detective added. "You are settled and have a family. You have a lot to lose and they know that."

Pease then said something, nothing that I could comprehend through the door.

Miller spoke up again: "We can assign a man to park outside your home, but the department is a bit shorthanded right now. I'd advise that you move out until this all blows over."

A shuffling of bodies, footsteps, and the front door opening and closing. Sensing that the policemen had left, I came out. Art was standing in the middle of the room, a slight swelling around his eyes from the upset last night. In that moment, he looked like a college student confused about the course of his life.

"Don't worry, Art. I'm not frightened." The moment I said it, I realized that I was speaking the truth. The government had taken our past away. Rose was dead. Yet I had survived. Art had experienced hell on the bloody battlefields of Europe. Anyone seeking to harm our family would have the both of us to contend with.

We still needed to take the detectives' warning seriously and decided to move my parents to Chiyo and Roy's house in South Los Angeles. I expected protests, but my parents were relatively compliant. We didn't share the specifics with them, but they did understand that we were under some kind of threat because of Art's association with Babe.

Thirtieth Avenue was the home for a number of former Issei and Nisei produce workers and in that sense, Pop would be among his people. Mom didn't *monku* much because she was going to be closer to her customers. As her hip was giving her problems, the shorter commute was definitely a bonus.

"You come, too," Mom insisted as I helped her pack. Art, meanwhile, was calling Mary No. 2 at City News Service to get any updates on Babe's murder.

"No, we have *sekinin*," I told her. Responsibility to what? To our jobs? To find out what happened to Babe? I was ambiguous, but the Japanese language is useful in that it sometimes requires the listener to fill in the blanks.

"Be careful," she said in Japanese. She said it so quietly that I couldn't help but take heed.

Leaving my mother to gather her toiletries, I went to my secret compartment in the floor of our bedroom closet, removed the loose floorboards, and carefully took hold of Rose's gun. I checked the chamber—there was one bullet still in there. I placed the gun in the safety of my pocketbook.

I sat behind the steering wheel of the Model A again, because I was more familiar with the streets of South Central than Art and didn't have the energy to give him navigation instructions.

"Tonai-*san, kinodoku desu ne,*" my mother commented from the back seat. *Kinodoku, kinodoku,* a word I had often heard during my childhood. I'd heard it said when someone lost their child in an accident, or when a friend did a favor at a great expense to themselves. *Kinodoku* literally means "spirit's poison," and its use indicated how much we didn't want to burden someone even more. We were indeed imposing ourselves on Roy, and especially on Chiyo and Roy's mother. The Sandovals had just left to move in with relatives in Pico Rivera, but the new Mrs. Chiyo Tonai had only been young mistress of her first marital house for a few days. Now the newlyweds would have to share the abode with my parents. I wondered if they would sense that Roy and Chiyo's marriage was not on the strongest footing.

When we arrived, Roy asked for Art's help in turning over the mattress in the Tonai guest room. "Pablo and Hortencia mentioned that the middle is starting to sag," Roy said. "Don't want the bed to be too uncomfortable for your parents." While we moved my parents in, Mrs. Tonai stayed in her bedroom, not bothering to even say hello to us. I was worried my mother's presence would be stressful for Roy's mother. They never had been very close; Mom was the type to get more active during times of trouble, while Mrs. Tonai had opted to retreat.

"Sorry, Chiyo," I told her as I moved in the second of my parents' suitcases. "I imagine that this will be just for a few days. Until this Babe Watanabe situation calms down."

As soon as I spoke I wanted to clamp my hand over my mouth. I had never intended to mention anything about Babe. Art and I had decided to tell Chiyo and Roy that we were doing repairs and needed my parents to vacate the Malabar house for a short time.

"What about Babe Watanabe?" Chiyo asked. She had been at my wedding in Chicago. Of course she would know Babe.

"Ah—" I was tongue-tied. I didn't know whether I should resort to the manufactured story that Art and I had concocted earlier. Even though I had been getting a lot of practice in telling lies, I knew that my skills had not markedly improved. "Well, you probably will hear about this soon enough, but Babe was killed yesterday."

Chiyo's mouth fell open. I knew that she was ready to receive any lurid gossip that I would be sweeping her way.

I didn't go as far as to mention the police's early-morning visit or Babe's involvement with the underworld. "It's been such a shock for Art," I said. This I could say truthfully. "Art being Babe's closest friend, there's a lot we need to take care of. Art hasn't been the same since experiencing combat. We thought that it would be best if my parents were away for a little while."

Chiyo pulled out a tissue and dabbed the edges of her eyes. "Unbelievable. First his father and then him. What is going on in this world?"

Babe's demise had hit Chiyo harder than I expected. "I didn't know that you knew him that well."

"Everyone in Gila River knew him, Aki. He was quite the star."

Oh, the Gila River connection. I had completely forgotten. "Really?"

"That's why I was so surprised to see him at your wedding ceremony. And him dropping his camera and ruining your wedding photos. That was so awful." Leave it to Chiyo to remember a distressing incident. "Esther was so wild about him."

Aki wondered who Esther was, but before Chiyo could prattle on about camp gossip, Art signaled that it was time for us to leave.

"Again, thank you," I said to Chiyo. "And we don't want the news to get out too fast about Babe."

Chiyo nodded, and she placed her index finger over her mouth. "My lips are sealed."

On our way back to Boyle Heights, Art and I discussed why Babe would involve himself with gangsters. "He must have completely lost his mind," Art said while I navigated Figueroa toward downtown. "If only we could find someone who knew what he was up to after being released from the hospital."

I pursed my lips before speaking. It was time for me to come clean about Key Wakida. "I hired a man to dig up information on Babe. A private investigator."

"Aki!" Art, who was not money-obsessed, didn't bother to ask how I had come up with the money to pay the PI. "Why would you do such a thing? You know that Babe was like a brother to me."

"I did it because I needed to know if Babe killed his father. I didn't want you to get hurt. And you weren't completely honest with me, either. I was beside myself."

We traveled in silence for a while.

Once we stopped at a stoplight, Art unclenched his teeth and let out a deep breath. "So what did this private investigator find?"

"Hiring him was actually a waste of money. He found out what the police had discovered. The gun that was used in Mr. Watanabe's murder was found in his apartment. It was a gun made by the Singer sewing machine company."

"I remember that gun," Art said. "An officer sold it to Babe."

"There were four sets of fingerprints on that gun. Mr. Watanabe's, Babe's. Also the prints of Babe's doctor in Pasadena who had been hanging on to the gun while Babe was hospitalized. And a set of prints from another person. Unidentified."

"Could it have been a gangster's?"

I shrugged. "I don't know."

The light turned green and I drove forward. City hall loomed in the distance. "Do you know a man named Ken Kanehara?" I asked.

"The name doesn't ring a bell."

"That's whose trailer Babe was staying in when I saw him yesterday. I think they met on Skid Row. A gangster's hangout. The young Iida boy from the Winona trailer park had even seen him there. They were running numbers."

Deep in thought, Art rubbed his chin stubble. "When Babe was writing me letters from the hospital, he mentioned that there was something important that he wanted to tell me. But he had to do it in person. When I finally saw him in Little Tokyo, he said that he couldn't speak freely. He was jittery, not quite himself."

I refrained from making a face. From my brief interactions with him, he had seemed all jitters. "Did he give you a hint about what it was all about?"

Art shook his head. "He must have concocted the plan to rob the gangsters by then."

The Model A shook as we hit a pothole.

"I don't know what he was planning to do with the money

that the police had said he had stolen," Art continued. "What had happened to him while he was in Los Angeles?"

"Maybe Ken will tell you," I told Art. I hadn't had much luck with him, but maybe he would be more forthcoming to Art, a man, than me.

"Then let's go to Winona."

From Mary at City News Service, Art knew the address where Babe's body had been found. As Art had seen at the coroner's office, Babe had been executed with one gunshot to the face. Based on physical evidence, the police had concluded that his body had been moved after death to this location on South Mariposa Street near Riverside Drive. Since the address was on our way to the Winona trailer park, we made a quick stop. Not far from the Magnolia barracks, the site looked like a dirt farm with a horse stable in the distance. Small birds twittered in nearby trees. What an odd place to dump a dead body. This neighborhood resembled a scene in a movie set in the Midwestern countryside.

While we were parked, a shiny sedan turned into a dirt driveway toward the horse stable. The face of the *hakujin* driver was familiar. "I've seen that man before," I said to Art. "He came to the house with the other two men. He was wearing the Burbank police uniform."

Art and I exchanged looks. Was this officer in cahoots with the mob? We knew of plenty of cases of police corruption in Chicago. Could it happen here?

"Let's get out of here." Art's voice was insistent.

When we arrived at Winona, there was no sign of the boxing matches involving children. No outdoor soup kitchens, either. In fact the trailer park seemed quite deserted. Far from evoking a sense of calm, the absence of a living soul gave the trailer camp an eerie feeling, as if a Western gun battle might be unleashed at any time.

As all the trailers looked quite similar, it took me a few tries before I found the one where the Kaneharas lived.

Art trailed behind me a few feet. He seemed transfixed by the trailer park, as if he could not believe what he was seeing.

I didn't have to rattle the door of the Kaneharas' trailer, because it was already open. Mr. Kanehara was lying on his bare mattress with his eyes open. He was so still that I feared that he had expired in the heat. But he blinked and held up his skeletal arm as a greeting.

"*Konnichiwa*," I said, trying to keep my voice bright and cheery. "Is Ken home?"

He jerked his head toward the back of the trailer.

I marched up the metal steps with Art at my heels. He had to duck and crouch down; the trailer couldn't accommodate his full height.

I smelled blood in the dark corner of the trailer. Art was familiar with the smell, too. I wanted to run away but that wasn't an option.

As my eyes adjusted to the darkness, I could see Ken seated on another mattress. He, too, was so motionless that I was frightened. I preferred the jaunty, rude Nisei man who had spoken so irreverently to me.

He hadn't heard us enter but now registered our presence. "Don't take one more step," he said and held out a BB gun, hardly more than the toy I had seen the Fujita boys use to terrorize neighborhood pigeons. He had no idea of the real gun that was in my purse.

I put up my hands. "Ken, it's me. Aki Nakasone," I said. "This is my husband, Art."

Ken lowered the BB gun. I took a few steps forward only to stifle a gasp. His face was completely ravaged. His nose was broken and there was a gash below his left eye, which was swollen shut. Based on the consistency of the blood on his face, this beating must have happened as recently as yesterday.

"Do you have anything clean in here? Maybe a sock or T-shirt?" Piles of soiled clothes lay all over the floor. I couldn't fault the Kanehara men for that, at least. It wasn't like laundry facilities were nearby.

The father moved from his mattress and slid a worn suitcase out from underneath his bed frame. Flipping open the lock, he pulled out a folded handkerchief from an inside compartment. It looked like a woman's handkerchief, embroidered with a pink tulip.

"*Daijoubu?* Okay? It's going to get bloodied," I told him.

Mr. Kanehara sucked in his lips. "Go ahead," he said in English.

I went into the restroom, avoiding the big hole in the floor. I found a thin sliver of soap on the side of the sink by the wall and did my best to rub it into a lather with the moistened handkerchief.

By the time I returned to the trailer, Art had established some kind of rapport with Ken. Art was seated on an orange crate, which apparently was the Kanehara's stand-in for a chair. Of all the things they could talk about, they were discussing baseball. Men and their sports, the ultimate topic of comfort.

I dabbed the end of the wet soapy handkerchief on the open wound and Ken winced. "You have to go to the hospital, you know," I said. "You probably will have to have your nose reset. And maybe get some stitches."

"You can't do it?"

"I don't have my first aid kit. And if you don't tend to your nose properly, it may be crooked for the rest of your life."

"Well, I was never going to be a beauty queen," Ken commented drily. He tried to release a few chuckles but then grimaced in pain that seemed to be coming from the lower part of his body. The way he was seated seemed abnormal, with a blanket only covering his left side.

"Is something wrong with your leg?" I asked.

"Broke-*shita*," the father called out from his mattress in a mishmash of English and Japanese.

Ken was obviously trying to hide the full extent of his injuries. I pulled the blanket from his leg and almost lost my breath. His leg had been beaten to a pulp. His pant leg had been torn off, either by his attackers or himself. This flesh looked like ground raw meat; a piece of bone was even visible.

"Who did this to you?" I asked.

"Who do you think?"

I was too afraid to even hazard a guess.

"They found out Babe was living with me. These two men arrived when Babe happened to be out. They brought hand tools, a hammer and a handsaw. Only they weren't here to do home repairs."

Art asked for a description of the men. One was the size of a gorilla, Ken said, with part of his ear gnawed off. The other wore a Burbank police uniform, only it seemed faded, an older version of what the local police wore today. Art and I exchanged glances. That fit the description of two of the men who had come by the Malabar house when I was alone.

"We'll have to take him to the hospital," I told Art.

I expected Ken to put up a fight, but he must have been feeling quite terrible because he acquiesced almost immediately. Art pulled Ken from his corner perch—not a simple matter as Ken only had limited strength to assist. Mr. Kanehara sat up and watched as his son was moved. When they reached the door, Ken handed him the BB gun.

"After *byouin*, he'll come back," I told the father. Mr.

Kanehara bent down so low that his face was almost touching the tops of his knees.

"*Osewa ni narimasu. Osewa ni narimasu,*" he kept repeating as if it were a chant. *We are in your debt. We are in your debt.*

Art had Ken wrap his arm around his shoulder as he practically carried Ken to the car. I felt as if I was running an ambulance service back and forth from the trailer park to the Japanese Hospital. It didn't bother me because I was at least being helpful to the residents. Winona was definitely not an ideal place for healing.

Just as Shiz Iida and her mother had ridden in the back seat, Ken lay down with his wounded leg extended. I told Ken not to cover it as exposure to fresh air would be better than any makeshift bandage we could manage to come up with in the filthy trailer.

Ken's pain tolerance was high; he did not *monku* one bit when the car bounced on occasional potholes on the highway.

I gazed at him from time to time in the rearview mirror. I couldn't help but think of an alley cat who had lived in our neighborhood back in Tropico. She had disappeared during her last days on this earth. My father had discovered her dead carcass in a shaded corner of our rental property, at the base of a wilting fig tree.

"You were prepared to die in that trailer." I said out loud what I was thinking.

Ken's eyes pooled with tears. He attempted to brush them away with his forearm. "I didn't want to die in front of my father."

I couldn't say anything in response. I kept my eye on the highway as we drove past lines of telephone poles. Art was so quiet that I first thought that he had fallen asleep. Taking a quick look, I saw that he was fully alert. His eyes were focused on the road but his mind was probably on Babe, or who knows what else—maybe the war wounds he had seen in the woody hills of Italy.

"Hey, you have a cigarette?" Ken asked from the back seat when we were on the border of Glendale.

Art pulled out a pack from his shirt pocket. He tapped out a cigarette, put it in his mouth and with his metal lighter, lit the end, and then transferred it to Ken's trembling hands. Usually I would have told smoking passengers to open their windows. This was not the time for all that.

Ken took a long drag. "So you were in the trenches with Babe, huh?"

Art, who had lit himself a cigarette, blew out a stream of smoke. "He saved my life at least a couple of times. He had that golden arm, you know. He was the best at throwing grenades into machine gun nests."

"He talked about you, you know. He called you South Side."

I'd never heard Babe's nickname for Art. It was appropriate, referencing his birthplace, as much as Tropico was Hammer's nickname for me.

"His father was a mean son of a bitch, did Babe tell you that?" Ken leaned forward and spat out the words. I felt some saliva hit the back of my ear.

I could tell from Art's lack of response that the answer was yes.

"Whatever Babe did, it wasn't good enough. But he still loved his pops. Wanted to make him proud."

The road was rough in Glendale and our old Model A lurched forward a couple of times. "Sorry," I said to my two male passengers. They didn't seem to care.

In his weakened state, Ken gave up all the information he knew, as if the Model A were a moving confessional. "Babe stole from the mob. They're running a gambling joint at this horse stable in Burbank." Art and I exchanged glances. We had inadvertently trespassed on gang territory this morning. "He went in there with his army gun and a pillowcase over his face. Stole a thousand dollars of casino money. How did he think that he was going to get away with it?"

I was dumbfounded. Why had he taken such extreme measures? A thousand dollars would have covered the cost of a car or a down payment on a house.

"A *bakatare*. And he was working with one of the gangsters, an *inu*."

"You mean the robbery was an inside job?"

Ken nodded. "The wiseguys who got me were out for blood. Not only Babe but one of their own, too."

"Did Babe steal the money before his father was killed?" I asked.

Ken nodded. "A few nights before."

For a moment, the only sound was the squeaking of Pop's jalopy. I imagined that we were thinking the same thing: Mr. Watanabe must have also been killed by a Chicago gang. But, I thought, why with Babe's gun? Why use the Singer .45 when they had their own tools of their dark trade? "The money is still missing?"

"Babe said that he hid it in his father's room at the San Mark. The money was in a rice bag in a vent next to the bed. He sent me over there to pick up his camera and told me to check the vent. But the Negro man was a stickler and I couldn't get in."

"Maybe the LAPD found it?"

"Could be. Or anybody who lived in the San Mark. A lot of desperate, hard-luck people over there."

I didn't want to believe that Charles had been involved in stealing the money. I didn't mention his name.

"It's my fault that Babe's dead." Ken rested his head against the car door. "I gave him up. I told the wiseguys that he was across the street buying cigarettes and the next thing I hear from Skid Row friends is that he's dead."

After a few minutes, Ken's snores reverberated from the back seat. He had fallen into a deep sleep.

As I continued to drive, Art and I tried not to talk about anything related to Babe or his father, but my mind was swimming with thoughts and worries. Art's was, too, because midway through our conversation, he seemed lost, completely disconnected.

"Art, Art, are you listening to me?"

"Oh, yes, darling, I'm sorry. What were you saying?"

"Oh, nothing." I couldn't remember myself.

As we reached Boyle Heights, I looked out the windshield at the line of brick storefronts on First Street. The streetlights were dim and I imagined sedans filled with gangsters parked in alleys. Would the violence that visited Ken befall us?

CHAPTER 17

Nurse Honma was at the hospital when we arrived with Ken. "Bringing more patients to the hospital in your car. What a nice side business," she said to me in Japanese, her voice laced with sarcasm. To Art, who obviously couldn't understand a word, she smiled, revealing a line of perfectly shaped teeth, which I was convinced were false.

Once she got a good look at Ken, she said to me, "He should contact the police."

"*Hai, hai*," I answered, but we both knew that my "yes, yes" was merely an acknowledgement that I had heard her, not any kind of agreement.

"You're in good hands," I told Ken, who had been placed in a wheelchair.

"What about my old man? What's he gonna do without me?" Since the war had started, it seemed like we Nisei were always leaving our family members.

"I'm sure you'll be back in no time," I assured him.

I didn't expect a thank-you from Ken and didn't receive one. I'm sure that he viewed an expression of appreciation as a sign of weakness.

In the car, however, I complained to Art about his lack of gratitude.

"Give him a break, Aki. Life has dealt him a bad hand. He

probably feels that there's not enough in him to give another person a pat on the back."

I was surprised by Art's defense of Ken, but that's how my husband was. He was a superior human, especially in the area of humility versus pride. He was always willing to give a person the benefit of the doubt, whereas I liked to go straight to doubt. And right now, I was doubting the one person I knew the best at the San Mark. Could Charles, a fellow chop suey lover, have set up Mr. Watanabe and taken the stolen money?

As I turned on Malabar, the Model A backfired, which it was in the habit of doing after being driven for long spells. I jumped. I was on edge, for sure. My heart sank further as we neared our house. Instead of chasing each other or playing stickball, four of the Fujita children were standing frozen in our driveway. The youngest one, still in diapers, was barefoot. I knew that something was wrong.

I parked the car across the street. The exterior of the Fujita house appeared intact, as did ours. I approached the oldest Fujita child. "What happened?"

"A *hakujin* man was in your house."

"Kilroy was making a racket," another Fujita boy commented.

"Did you call the police?" Art asked.

"We were waiting for our parents to come home."

Art and I hurried inside. The house had been turned upside down. Much of our precious china, saved by the San Fernando farmer, now lay in ruins on our hardwood floor. I was thankful that my mother wasn't there to discover the damage. While it seemed that she weathered the storms of our lives with her characteristic stoicism, I thought this last straw would do her in.

Out of habit, my eyes went to the mantel, the resting place of Rose's ashes. The mantel was empty. "No, no," I cried out.

Panicked, I kicked away glass shards on the floor, desperate to locate the urn without slicing my fingers. I scanned the breadth of the living room. And there, lying on its side by the kitchen door, was the gold container. It was unbroken, and beside it was the canvas bag holding Rose's ashes. I plucked both from the wreckage and, stuffing the ashes back in the urn, returned them to the mantel. I wasn't going to leave my sister's remains on the floor.

Art, meanwhile, was on the phone with police. Detective Miller wasn't available, so he spoke to Ben Pease. "Yes, yes. The place is a mess. The neighbor children say they saw a thin white man walking from the house. Uh-huh. Uh-huh. That's fine."

While Art continued his conversation, I went into the kitchen. The freezer door was ajar, liquid dripping onto our floor. The once-frozen bluefin tuna from my Terminal Island friend sat in a pool of water with other melting foodstuffs. Both the flour and sugar cannisters were overturned on the counter.

From the kitchen, I went into the hallway, noticing that the back door's window was broken. That was apparently how the intruder had entered our house.

In both bedrooms, the vandal had ripped the sheets from the bed and shoved the mattress from its box spring. My blood boiled when I saw our freshly laundered and folded clothing piled on the floor.

Then I remembered my Maytag money, which I had stuffed in the leg of a wool undergarment Mom had knitted for me in Chicago. I tore through my cotton panties and bras—there, I found the long underwear and the money. The unassuming homemade item had secured my savings.

I then checked our closet. The culprit had torn away the floorboards and discovered my hiding place. Thank goodness I'd had the gun in my purse. I almost swore when I spotted

Rose's photo facedown on the floor. I picked it up, brushing away the dirt that had muddied its glossy surface.

Art appeared in the bedroom door, our ceiling light creating shadows on his smooth face.

"A patrolman will be here in an hour. Leave everything where it is. He says most of the detectives have gone home." He was quick to spot the torn floorboards in the closet. "What's this?"

"Um—" There was no sense in being coy after all that had happened. "My secret hiding place."

"What did he take?" Art peered into the empty metal bento box, its lid open, only crumpled issues of the *Chicago Tribune* inside.

"Nothing."

"It looks like something was in there."

I pulled off my purse and slid the gun onto the bare mattress.

"What the hell, Aki."

"I brought it from Chicago. My sister got it for an ex-roommate."

"Why would your sister go to such lengths—"

"It was for protection." I took a deep breath. "You see, my sister was attacked. Sexually."

"The rapist." Art's voice was rough and barely audible. He knew at least one of the culprit's victims. I told him the whole story. I had felt shame before but as I disclosed everything that happened, I sensed Rose was right beside me, coaxing me on. *Don't be afraid to tell the truth. That's how you will keep me alive.*

"I'm so sorry that happened to your sister. And to you."

There was a pounding at the door. The police had arrived.

Art quickly took the gun and returned it to my purse.

After the patrolman came and went, we hardly slept. I changed into my nightgown but Art stayed in his street clothes. We hadn't eaten much of anything that day but it didn't matter because our stomachs were wrecked from the stress of the break-in. That night Art slept with Rose's gun under his pillow.

CHAPTER 18

The next morning I climbed out of bed first and began to clean the kitchen. The night before I had thrown what I could back in the freezer, but what I couldn't salvage went into the rubbish bin. I even tried to save some of the spilled sugar and flour. It's not like we were flush with money, especially for a four-person household.

I was mopping the sticky and grainy floor when from the kitchen window I saw Art head to the garage. Several minutes later, the sound of hammering proceeded from the north side of our house.

I went down the hallway and saw that he was covering the broken door with leftover wood that the previous owner, Abe Zidle, had left.

"This is just awful," I said to him after he was done hammering. I handed him a cup of coffee.

Art's eyes were bloodshot. At least he had changed into some fresh clothes. Seeking comfort, I had put on a pair of dungarees and a T-shirt.

We sat on the porch for some respite from the chaos of our house. Art went to the Model A to retrieve a pack of Lucky Strikes from the glove compartment. "What's this?" The cigarettes now in his shirt pocket, he returned with another item, the *senninbari*. "It looks like a Japanese belt one of the boys in my company wore. It was from his mother. She stitched a message, *God bless*. He claims that protected him on the battlefield."

I felt a now-familiar pang of guilt and clutched my cup. The half-drunk coffee was lukewarm. "Oh, a Gila River lady gave me that to give to Babe. She and some other ladies in Gila River made it for him. It was supposed to protect him, too."

A sparrow landed on a thin branch of a Japanese maple tree that my father, in a moment of deluded optimism, had planted in the front yard. The sparrow hopped from one bare branch to another. Only a few yellow leaves sprouted from the lowest branch, which was shaded by the Fujitas' overgrown ficus. Japanese maples didn't do well in the heat of Southern California.

"Remember I told you about the freckle-faced man who came to *Rafu* to ask me about Babe?" Art said. "Who knows that Babe and I were friends?"

"People who went to our wedding, I guess. And that doctor in Pasadena."

"What doctor?"

"You know, Babe's doctor. He's the one who had taken away his gun while he was hospitalized." I drained the last bit of cold coffee. "And there's also Charles."

"Who's Charles?'

"That Negro man at the San Mark. I think that he may know something."

"Then I think we need to pay him a visit."

"Now?"

"Now."

"Are we taking the car?"

Art was already out the door and heading for the passenger's side. I wasn't sure how it had happened, but it was now established that I was the main driver for the household. I ran into the bedroom for my purse. That's when I spied the gun peeking out from underneath Art's pillow.

I stuffed the gun back in my purse. I understood now how a weapon could transform a feeble person into a bully. I was tired of being pushed and manipulated. It was time for me to push back.

I couldn't find an open spot on First Street, so I parked north of the San Mark in an empty lot. This area was dangerous, but I figured that no one would want to steal the Model A, even for spare parts.

In the receptionist booth was a young Black man with fuzz over his lip, a weak attempt at a mustache.

"Is Charles here?" I asked.

"Elevator stopped at the second floor. He's gone to fix it."

As soon as he spoke, I realized that Willie Mae's replacement was probably only a teenager. He was slim and short, only a few inches taller than me.

I cleared my throat, trying to sound as authoritative as possible. "What's your name?"

"Why do you need to know my name?"

"We're family of the Japanese man who was shot in room 302. I think everyone here knew him as Mr. Wat."

"Yes, ma'am."

"Your name?"

"Freeman Clark."

"Freeman Clark, we're here to pick up Mr. Watanabe's things." Art, catching on to my charade, jumped in.

"We threw everything out," Freeman Clark told us. "We had to. Nobody claimed his things and people wanted to move in."

"Oh," I said, "what a shame." I kept my voice as steady and soft as possible. If anything, I had the power to disarm with my seemingly harmless appearance.

Freeman Clark seemed a bit agitated as he crossed and then uncrossed his arms over his white shirt. I took a closer look. It rested a little stiffly on his slender frame. *Wait a minute.*

I went over to the open door of the receptionist booth and pulled at the side of his shirt.

"Hey—" The teenager lurched back but I held on tight. I took a big whiff of the fabric. I smelled sweat and oil, but more than that I could identify the fragrance of cooked rice. "This is Mr. Watanabe's shirt!" I declared.

"No, ma'am, you are mistaken." The teenager tugged his shirt back, his voice cracking under the pressure of the situation.

"I know that smell. You took Mr. Watanabe's clothes."

"I didn't s-s-s-s-s-steal his shirts," Freeman Clark stuttered. "Mr. Charles said I could have it. That everything was free for the taking."

"What did Charles take?"

"He didn't take anything."

I narrowed my eyes. "He's lying, Art."

"Yes, he's lying." Art seemed to enjoy putting the screws on this teenager.

"Waitaminute. Sh." I put my index finger to my mouth. Even Freeman Clark stayed quiet, probably fearing the repercussions of wearing a dead man's dress shirt. *Tick-tick-tick.* "What do you hear?"

Art frowned. "A clock of some kind?"

I pushed my way into the tiny space, forcing Freeman Clark out of his booth. It was more like a cage, really, with wire mesh over the window. There was barely room for a tall stool in front of the counter. On the back wall was a painted grid with numbers and corresponding keys on plastic key chains hanging from nails. A couple of shelves held registration cards, hand tools, and a telephone. I heard the ticking emanating from a cubbyhole underneath.

As I tugged at the box, I heard protests from Freeman Clark. He was practically squeaking. "I wouldn't touch that. That belongs to Mr. Charles. He will be out for blood if you mess with his property."

The box turned out to be a soldier's wooden footlocker. Stenciled on the lid was the name CHARLES M. JONES, US ARMY. I grabbed a screwdriver on the shelf and jammed it behind the hinge barely holding the latch. The wood was damaged, probably from water exposure.

"You can't be doing that!" Freeman Clark was apoplectic but he knew better than to touch a married Asian woman. Art got in front of him, preventing him from gaining further access to me.

Crack! It didn't take much to break it open.

On top was a photo of a group of Black men in US Army uniforms posing in front of the Eiffel Tower. Below that was a glamour portrait of a beautiful light-skinned Black woman wearing pearls. Based on the gray hair around her temples, I assumed she was Charles's mother. What was I doing— invading this man's privacy? But then I spotted a glint of something golden below the photos. I pulled out a pocket watch, the same one I had seen Mr. Watanabe clutching back at the hospital the first time I had met him. It was still ticking, but the time was completely off. I turned the watch over. *Haruki Watanabe. Third Place 1934 Gilmore Gold Cup.* Irrefutable proof that Charles had pilfered a dead man's property.

Also in the locker was the small photograph of the *hakujin* woman that had been pinned to the door of Mr. Watanabe's room. That face seemed so familiar to me. I dug deeper in the locker and came across a suit and a few medals stuffed in white socks. No bundles of cash. I turned back to Art, who was standing outside the booth entryway. "No money," I said. "I don't think he took it, because why would he still be at the San Mark?"

"Let me check the room again. What was it?" Art asked.

"It's 302. You're not going up there, are you?"

"I want to give it a look-see."

"I'll go with you."

"No, you stay here, Aki."

"But I've been here before."

"Stay here," he directed me, and with his long legs went up two stairs at a time.

Freeman Clark was trembling at the foot of the stairs. It was as if he was conflicted about whether to leave his post or find help to deal with us unruly Nisei.

I knelt by the open footlocker and picked up the photo of the *hakujin* woman. She had thick, lustrous hair that fell over her shoulders. I had seen that sharp chin before. Was she in the movies? Thinking that it might help me to unravel Mr. Watanabe's secrets, I slipped the photo into the side pocket of my dungarees.

The elevator door made its terrible screeching noise. I was still in the receptionist's booth when I heard a familiar voice: "What's going on? Why did you let her in there?"

"She forced her way in, sir." Freeman Clark sounded like he was ready to cry. "I couldn't stop her."

Charles, his cap askew, saw the splintered wood and the metal latch with the lock on the floor of the booth. "You've broken into my things! You've committed a crime," he exclaimed.

I snatched Mr. Watanabe's pocket watch from the open footlocker. "Speaking of crimes, when did you take this?"

Charles's face fell. "I was holding on to that. If someone in the family showed up."

"Then why didn't you give it to Babe's friend when he picked up Babe's camera?"

Charles didn't have a good reply. "Wasn't sure if I could trust that fella."

"Did you happen to take the watch after you shot Mr. Watanabe in cold blood?"

"You can't think that I would do such a thing." His eyes narrowed in the darkness of the San Mark lobby. His voice sounded threatening and I wished that Art had stayed behind with me. I dropped the watch in my purse, hearing it ding against the gun.

"That's not yours to take." Charles blocked my exit from the reception booth.

"She said that she was a blood relative," Freeman Clark said.

"She's not a blood anything."

Charles yanked my purse from my shoulder. I tried to stop him, but the hotel manager was strong and wiry. He was easily able to wrestle the bag from me.

The gun clattered to the floor.

"What the hell—"

Freeman Clark's mouth fell open.

Charles scooped up the gun before I could react. He aimed it at me. "You get out of here."

Art, perhaps sensing trouble, came bounding down the stairs.

Charles gestured with the barrel of the gun. "You, too," he said to Art.

We both held up our arms and backed out to the door. I thought that I might collapse in fear. Were our lives going to be cut short before we reached even our first year of marriage? I prayed that at least Art's life would be spared. Once we were in the sunlight, we ran to the Model A, leaving my sister's gun in a stranger's possession. I had thought that Charles could be a friend, but it turned out that he was a run-of-the-mill thief.

Kilroy loudly announced our arrival as we got out of the Model A. Inside the house, however, the piles of our damaged belongings haunted us like silent spirits. We retreated to the bedroom. I shed my dungarees onto the floor and climbed into the bed with Art, who lay perfectly still.

I stroked his arm gently. "Are you okay? You hardly said anything to me on the drive home."

"You didn't either." Art's gaze was intent on a crack on our bedroom ceiling.

"I guess we are both in shock."

Art finally turned to me. "Why did you bring the gun to the hotel?"

"I didn't want anything to happen to you. I wasn't thinking. What should we do?" I was at a loss.

"We can't tell the police," Art said.

"But what if Charles did kill Mr. Watanabe? I mean, he stole his watch."

"I don't think he did it. It's just a hunch. Maybe soldier to soldier." Art sounded so definitive.

"I hope so," I said, not sure at all.

My whole body was still pulsating from the trauma of having a gun aimed at me. "How could you survive that day after day on the front lines? Your life being constantly threatened." I clasped my fingers together in an attempt to slow down my heart rate. "I can't even imagine."

Art reached for my hand and squeezed. "You try to think about the good things in your life. Simple things. Sometimes even the breeze cooling you down. Or a bird singing a bright song. I thought of you a lot."

We lay in the bed in silence for a while. At least we had covered the bare mattress with fresh, clean sheets after the police officer had left last night. The scent of air-dried linen was the simple luxury I could enjoy.

"Oh, I do have something else to show you." I crawled out of bed to retrieve my dungarees from the floor. I showed Art the photo of the woman that had been tacked onto the back of Mr. Watanabe's door. "This was in Babe's father's room. Does she look familiar to you? Maybe from Europe?"

"What? Who is she? I've never seen that woman before." He flipped to the back of the photo. "But that's Babe's hand-writing," he said.

There, in faint pencil that I had earlier thought was a smudge of dirt, Babe had scrawled, *My future wife.*

CHAPTER 19

With Chole's help, I was able to find another nurse's aide to cover my shift. I wasn't quite ready to return to work. Art, on the other hand, felt obligated to resume duties the next day as the newspaper was currently shorthanded. Since he was running late, I offered to drop him off at the *Rafu* office on Los Angeles Street, next to the liquor store that had displaced Iwaki pharmacy. Going home on First Street, I passed Asahi Shoe Store, San Kwo Low, and Mikawaya. As I waited at the light at the intersection of San Pedro, I drummed my fingers on the steering wheel. The photo of that woman, identified as Babe's future wife, burned in my mind. When the light turned green, instead of proceeding straight, I made a left turn on San Pedro.

This time I went to the intercom panel outside of the San Pedro Firm Building's door and found the button labeled E. YAMAMOTO. I pressed firmly and then heard a window open above. "Mrs. Nakasone." Elmer didn't seem surprised to see me. He threw down a key attached to a red string. I was able to catch the key before it fell on the sidewalk.

After opening the front door, I made my way up the stairs to Elmer Yamamoto's corner office.

"If your client is dead, is what he told you still confidential?" I said as soon as I stepped into his office.

"Of course." Elmer rose from his chair and leaned on his

cane to hobble closer to me. He accepted the key from me and I waited for him to return it to a nail on his wall.

"What if I know why he came to you?"

The lawyer gripped the handle of his cane. The skin on his hand was almost translucent, with visible blue veins extending to his fingers. "I'm listening."

From the open door, I heard someone walk down the stairs. "He wanted to get married to a *hakujin* woman. He needed some legal help as it's against California law."

"He disclosed that to you?" Elmer narrowed his eyes. I wondered if he adopted such expressions in the courtroom.

"In a way." Maybe not verbally. But he had left enough clues in the wake of his short stay in Los Angeles.

"You are very clever," Elmer declared for the second time. I was enjoying being in the lawyer's presence. Perhaps he was tired of standing, because he made his way back into the chair behind his desk. Through the window I could see children playing in the courtyard of Union Church. "Her parents weren't happy. Especially the mother. To be expected in this climate. I believe Babe's fiancée lives nearby in Glendale."

The Sunday school Rose and I had attended as children was located in Glendale, west of Pasadena. Both cities had plenty of wealthy old families who didn't mix with Japanese unless they were gardeners, maids, or laundry workers.

"For Babe to get married to a *hakujin*, he'd have to travel to another state, wouldn't he?"

"In a hypothetical situation, yes, a man of Japanese descent cannot legally marry a white woman in California. Plenty go up to the state of Washington to tie the knot."

"So that's where Babe was heading?"

"I know that Babe wanted a new life."

"A new life costs money."

"Yes, indeed."

Elmer and I had a stare-down. I took the woman's photo out of my bag and showed it to Elmer. "Do you know this woman?"

Elmer shook his head. "Is it her?"

"I believe so."

"If you encounter her, please tell her that Babe was prepared to risk everything for her."

After saying my goodbyes to Elmer, I strode out of the San Pedro Firm Building. In the sunlight I took another look at the photo of the woman. I'd had a nagging feeling for a while that I had seen that face, and now I remembered where.

I took the Model A to Pasadena instead of hopping on the bus. Most drivers were loath to travel on the Pasadena Freeway, with turns so sharp that sensitive passengers feared getting whiplash. I, however, enjoyed it. When Pop drove the family on it, I felt like I was on the Cyclone Racer roller coaster on the Pike in Long Beach. Now, driving solo, I thought about Mr. Watanabe navigating his stock car along his farmland in Arroyo Grande.

I parked in a lot across from the facility, which had recently been renamed McCornack General Hospital, according to a new sign. As far as I could tell, it seemed the same inside. Dr. Sidney Reed's name was in the same spot on the directory. Instead of taking the elevator, I chose to take the stairs.

The door of his office was open and I held my breath in anticipation of who I would see inside.

The psychiatrist, reading glasses perched on his nose, was standing in front of an open filing cabinet.

"Hello, Dr. Reed."

He seemed a bit stunned to see me. "You're Babe Watanabe's friend, aren't you?"

"Yes. He was my husband's best man in our wedding." I

couldn't remember exactly what I had told him when I had first met him.

"His demise was unfortunate." He could barely manage the words. His distress didn't seem to reflect a normal patient-doctor relationship.

Displayed on the filing cabinet were a couple of personal photos in stand-up frames. Both were in color, unusual for the time. One was a soldier in a naval uniform. The other one was of the doctor; a middle-aged woman with wavy salt-and-pepper hair; the soldier, only younger; and a girl with dazzling red hair. That was the same woman in Babe's photo.

"Is that your nurse?" I gestured to the family portrait.

"Yes, that's my daughter, Gloria." The doctor gazed at me over his glasses. His eyes were a brilliant blue and I saw sadness in his face.

"Where is she?" I asked.

"She's on her break. She's taking a walk on the Colorado Street Bridge." He pointed at a miniature figure in the distance through the window. "See, there she is. Why—"

"Thank you, Doctor," I said before he could ask any more questions. I ran down the stairs and across the tiled floor of the hospital. There was no need to hurry, but for some reason I felt desperate, as if I had been called to extend a hand of help in a storm of grief.

Gloria was resting her elbows on the concrete railing as she looked down at the dry chaparral below. Sedans sped back and forth behind her.

"Hello," I said to her, a little out of breath.

"Hello," Gloria responded. She didn't seem surprised to see me. Her face was drawn and pale, accentuating the red hair that was visible below her nurse's cap.

"I've never been on this bridge before." From the structure

I could clearly see the lavender-colored San Gabriel Mountains to the north and in the south, the canyon of the Arroyo Seco. I felt as though I was suspended over the earth and seeing my surroundings in a new way.

"They call this Suicide Bridge." Gloria's voice was monotone, no inflection indicating exactly how she was feeling.

"What an awful name for a beautiful bridge." My heartbeat quickened. Surely, the doctor's daughter was not considering doing anything dangerous. I sought to get her mind off the bridge. "You have such lovely hair," I said. I took out her photo from the inside compartment in my bag. "This photograph doesn't do it justice."

"Where did you get that?" she asked.

I handed it to her. "It was in the Watanabe apartment in Japantown. Look on the back."

Upon reading Babe's message, Gloria gripped the photo with her left hand, covering her mouth with her right. Her words were muffled, but I could still understand what she was saying. "I thought that he had gotten cold feet. We were going to elope."

"Here, let's sit down." I led her away from the railing to the east side, where a bench was positioned on some grass underneath the shade of an olive tree.

Sitting next to her, I could see the faint spray of freckles along the ridge of her nose and her cheeks. She looked much younger than she had in the grand setting of the hospital. "I really thought that he had run off without me. I should have never doubted him," she said. She didn't look at me. Instead she faced the length of the bridge, with its distinctive lamps holding three globes of lights.

I had doubted Babe, too, but I didn't share that thought. "My husband was very close to Babe," I said instead.

"I know who you are," she said. "Aki, right? Babe was the best man in your wedding in Chicago."

I was truly surprised. "You know about that?"

"Babe told me all about it." She sounded brighter, more reflective of her young age. "The delicious food. And how pretty you looked. He felt so bad that he dropped his camera and ruined your wedding photos."

A few sedans drove toward us. One was a convertible with a young couple enjoying the sun of Southern California. Here I thought that Babe hadn't given the incident a second thought, but he was actually pained that he couldn't deliver what he had promised. I felt embarrassed about the unyielding resentment I had carried over many months.

Gloria gripped the edge of the bench. "There were a lot of factors against us, but we were excited about getting married. He proposed to me right on this bridge. He didn't know that the locals called it Suicide Bridge and I didn't have the heart to tell him."

Why was it not a surprise that Babe would inadvertently ask a woman for marriage in a location notorious for death?

"When I didn't hear from him for days, I figured that he had abandoned me before we reached the altar. And then in the pages of the newspaper, there it was. S. Watanabe shot to death in Burbank. The story was barely one inch. But I knew that it was him." Gloria's voice had reverted to its monotone cadence. She was tying up her grief and putting it into a box, like my mother often did. I could picture Gloria wrapping her feelings in brown paper and firmly tying twine around the package.

She finally looked at me. "When was the last time you spoke to him?"

My arms grew limp. It had been the day he died. Babe standing in that wretched trailer, feeling so hopeless and angry. He probably realized then that there would be no happy ending for him and Gloria. He warned me that Art needed to stay away from him. In the same way, he knew that being close to Gloria would have put her in danger.

"I'm not sure," I lied to her. "But I'm positive that you were top of mind until the very end."

I felt the presence of someone beside me. It was Dr. Reed, his back bent so that his graying hair would not brush up against the olive tree. I rose from the bench. "Please," I said. "Sit down by your daughter."

That night, I told Art the whole story over some peanut-miso soup and rice. "Why didn't he tell me that he had a girl?" Art kept saying over and over again.

"Maybe by the time you got back to LA he had decided to solve the problem his own way and didn't want to involve you."

"Damn Babe," Art murmured. "This could have ended so differently."

CHAPTER 20

I returned to work the next day. The daily routine of fastening my cap onto my hair with bobby pins in the morning and washing my uniform at night was restorative. So was walking the hallways in my white loafers and checking on patients. I didn't even mind carrying bedpans full of *shishi* out to the toilet. It was mundane and straightforward. Even though there were life-and-death scenarios all around me, at least we were healers. We attempted to make conditions better, while outside the doors of our humble hospital, all bets were off.

I stayed late after some shifts, but today I wanted to get home to Art as soon as possible. I had finally begun to understand the close relationship between him and Babe as well as the darkness that followed him into his sleep. Right at five, I walked down the steps toward Fickett Street. Before I reached the sidewalk, I felt a pebble hit the back of my cap, which was already almost falling off.

I turned suspiciously. Boyle Heights, with its plentiful fig trees, was full of mischievous squirrels. Another pebble rolled my way at an angle from the side of the building. I trod slowly, ready to scream if need be.

I scrunched down, peering through an overgrown hedge in front of the hospital. I spied a Black man hiding in the back. It was Charles.

"What in the world—" I started to back away, ready to call the orderly on duty for assistance.

"Sh, sh." Charles's voice was raw and hoarse. "I'm in trouble. Only you can help me."

I stood by the hedge. I was exhausted from all the recent upheaval in my life and felt that I could not take any more.

"I killed the gangster who killed Babe. I used your gun."

I could barely process what Charles was telling me. Hearing "your gun," I felt my body grow cold. I was inextricably linked to this shooting.

I crawled through the hedge, feeling its brambles scratch the sides of my face and arms. Charles was leaning against the hospital wall. His clothing was singed and stunk of smoke. A tear in his plaid shirt revealed an open wound, swollen and pink against his skin, but no sign of blood.

"He shot me before he went down. I can't go into the hospital. But I need some medical attention."

With his sweat-soaked forehead and trembling fingers, Charles showed signs of being in intense pain.

"The doctor here can help you," I told him.

"No, no, he will call the police, won't he?"

If Dr. Isokane didn't, someone else probably would. Especially regarding a Black man who was wounded by a firearm.

"Where's the gun?" I asked.

Charles struggled to pull the gun out from the back of his waistband, and tossed it in front of him. "It's all out of bullets."

I reached out and gingerly fingered the handle toward me. It was coated in blood. I plucked loose pages of a soiled newspaper stuck in the brambles and wrapped the gun in them.

"You know it's only a matter of time before they will come after me. And one of them, I think, worked for the Burbank police department."

I understood who "they" were. The ones who had established

an illegal gambling operation in Burbank. The ones who had ordered Babe to be killed. How they could still be in business was beyond me. It certainly seemed that the police were looking the other way.

I released a stream of air through pursed lips and stuck the wrapped gun in my uniform apron. I wasn't sure if aiding a man who had gunned down another was the right thing to do. "I'm going to have to get our car. How did you even get here?"

"The streetcar," Charles rasped. His voice was becoming progressively weaker. "I covered the wound with a newspaper."

I was incredulous that he had been able to make it over here. "I'm going to have to tell my husband."

Charles swallowed and nodded. "I don't have any other place to go."

Before going back to the house to retrieve the Model A, I snuck into the hospital's medical supply room. My hands shook as I slipped a package of sulfa powder, a bottle, and a syringe into my paper lunch bag. As Nurse Honma kept a meticulous inventory of medicine and even bandages, my theft could easily be exposed. I was at risk of losing my job or even going to jail myself, but I didn't have time to worry about that now.

Clutching the bag of contraband, I ran all the way home. The neighbor across the street stared at me curiously and I knew that I would probably have to take Charles through the back door. Once safely home, I was able to catch Art at the *Rafu* over the phone. "Charles Jones was hiding outside of the Japanese Hospital," I whispered, even though there was no one in the house to hear me. "He shot the gangster that killed Babe with Rose's gun. He got injured himself but doesn't want to be admitted to get treatment. He wants me to help him."

Art was so silent on the other end of the line that I thought that our call had lost connection. "Art, are you there?"

"Yes." Art was now speaking in a hushed tone. "The police are all over Little Tokyo right now about the shooting. Wait for me before you do anything."

"I can't leave him out there. Someone is going to spot him."

"Aki—"

I hung up the phone before Art could try to change my mind. I stopped the car right in front of the hospital with the engine still running. It was the in-between time when people were being released from work. Risky, but I had no choice. I coaxed Charles from his hiding place, covering him in the blanket I'd brought as we quickly went to the Model A. I guided him to the back seat, where Ken had been a few days before.

Charles was quiet during the brief ride, while my mind whirled. *This is the end of everything. This is the end of everything.* I didn't see how any of us could get out of this predicament unscathed. This wasn't the time for reflection, I realized, but action.

About half an hour later, Art came barreling into the house. "Where are you?" he yelled.

"We're here," I called from my parents' bedroom.

I had removed Charles's torn shirt and cut off the remnants of his undershirt. The top layer of his burnt skin had stuck to his clothing. The wound itself was superficial but would have to be cleaned.

From the open doorway, Art could see that Charles was in no position to be a threat to either one of us. "How can I help?" he said.

I had retrieved some sulfa powder from my lunch bag and applied it in the area where the bullet had grazed his skin. Charles gritted his teeth but made no sound. With his chest exposed, we could see keloid scars crisscrossing his light-brown skin. I had seen keloids like these with my postsurgery Japanese patients—raised lesions that never flattened. This was not the first time that Charles had suffered from a bullet entering his body.

I filled up a glass syringe with a vial of precious penicillin that I had stolen from the hospital's supply chest. Our surgeon had connections in high places and we were occasionally stocked with the latest drugs. This would reduce the chances of infection.

After I completed the injection, Art got a glass of water for Charles and handed it to him. He waited until Charles took a few sips, the excess water dribbling down his chin. "Tell us what happened," Art said.

Charles took a few deep breaths. He told us that he had been working again on that broken-down elevator. He was walking down the stairs when he witnessed a heavy man with a disfigured ear pistol-whipping poor Freeman Clark. "He was going on and on about the money that Babe stole. That it had been hidden in his room and we must have taken it." Ever since he had taken Rose's gun from us, Charles had been carrying it with him everywhere he went. "I told him to stop and pulled the gun on him. He nicked me but I got him right in the heart."

The surface of Charles's eyes looked shiny as he gazed out one of our windows. Taking a life seemed to weigh heavily on Charles. Even though the gangster had been filled with malice and violence, he was still a human being. "We ran out of there. We knew his people would be on their way. The boy helped me onto the streetcar and I told him to get out of Bronzeville. In fact, get out of Los Angeles."

I felt for Freeman Clark. Based on the way he spoke, I guessed the teenager was a transplant from the Deep South like others in Bronzeville. Where would a young man like him end up?

I turned my attention to Charles. "Your footlocker at the

San Mark. I'm sorry that I broke into that. You were in the service?"

Charles nodded. "That's how I met Babe in the first place."

This revelation was a surprise to both Art and me. "But that's impossible," Art said. "I was by Babe's side the whole time in Europe."

"Babe and I were in the same army hospital in San Francisco," Charles explained. "We never ran into each other on the front lines. But we were all fighting in the Po Valley at the same time."

"You were with the 92nd," Art murmured.

Charles took another sip of the water. "Babe and I had the same ailments. Shell shock, combat fatigue, whatever you want to call it. I couldn't get words out of my mouth, can you believe it? Babe was in a bed right next to me. I knew the demons that he was fighting." Charles's voice was hypnotic as he pulled out his memories. "He told me that his land was being taken away and there wasn't much he could do about it. I was discharged weeks before Babe was and on my way to Los Angeles. I was told by other men of the 92nd who were from Los Angeles to stop by Little Tokyo. That Negroes were living there and I may find a place to live." Charles was losing his grip of the water glass and I took it from him. "I went to work in a defense factory in Long Beach but only lasted one day. To be around the military, I was through with all that. A job opened up at the San Mark and I took it."

I placed a cool compress on Charles's forehead and he nodded his thanks. "When a room opened up, I helped his father make the move from Arroyo Grande. I had connections with an officer who was working at city hall."

I was finally able to get a larger picture of who Charles was. First he had been a stranger to me, a worker in a low-income hotel. Then he became suspect, a dangerous figure who had pulled a gun on us. (Granted, it was our gun and I had broken into his property.) And now it turned out that he had cared about Babe as much as my husband had.

"Why didn't you tell me your connection with the Watanabes in the first place?" I asked, a little exasperated. We could have joined forces and maybe even prevented some of the tragedy that had befallen father and son.

"I don't find it easy to trust people. I actually opened up to you more than usual." Charles was definitely feeling better after my treatment. I figured that with him, actions spoke louder than words. "Babe, too. He was a different kind of person. No affectation. No false front. He didn't bullshit." Charles rubbed the back of his head. In all the chaos, his hair, which usually was styled impeccably, had lost its even shape. "We kept in touch when he was transferred to the hospital in Pasadena to be closer to his father. I went and visited him when I could."

"Did you meet his girl?" Art interjected.

Charles's large eyes widened further. "You mean that nurse." He made a faint snapping sound with his fingers. "I thought there was something going on between them."

"You didn't know that they were planning to run off and get married?" I asked.

"No, nothing like that. But then we didn't talk much about matters of the heart."

That didn't surprise me. I didn't like to spill much about my own romantic life, either. "What are you going to do now?"

"Well, I can't go back to the San Mark. Both the police and the gangsters will be looking for me. Also, who knows who is in cahoots with who?"

"You did say that someone wearing a Burbank police uniform came to our house with those gangsters," Art reminded me.

I remained quiet as I thought hard. Detectives Miller and Pease seemed like straight shooters. But in Chicago I had experienced firsthand the corruption of certain police officers. And who would give us—two Nisei, including a former Manzanar camp inmate, and a Black man—a fair shake?

"I need to get out of California now. Go east. I'll get to a train station and hop on a railcar," Charles said.

"You can't go anywhere right now," I said.

"No, I can't wait. It will be dangerous for me and it will be dangerous for you two."

There was a station in East Los Angeles not far from Whittier Boulevard. Trains traveled to Salt Lake City and who knows where else. Maybe Charles was right. It might be only a matter of time before either the police or the gangsters descended on the Malabar house.

I left Charles in Art's care and retrieved the rest of my Maytag washer money from my underwear drawer. I wasn't sure how far that money would take him. I stuffed the cash into a pillowcase. From the kitchen I threw in a loaf of bread and some cans of liverwurst. Finally, I added fresh bandages, tape, aspirin, and a package of yellow sulfa.

"Where's the gun?" I heard Art ask Charles in my parents' bedroom.

"I gave it to your wife. It's all out of ammo. Sorry about all that back in the hotel."

"We shouldn't have brought the gun," Art said, apologizing for my stupidity.

"You can have it, Charles," I said from the bedroom door. Retrieving my purse, I unwrapped the gun from the pages of newspaper and washed the blood off its handle. Patting it dry, I hid it underneath the other provisions in the pillowcase. If this weapon acquired for Tomi's protection would serve this man's needs, so be it.

I drove us down to Whittier Boulevard and headed east to the Union Pacific train station.

The lanes of the boulevard were wide and smooth without the presence of many pedestrians. As we passed billboards and vacant lots, I started to feel the familiar pang of dislocation that had visited me in both Manzanar and Chicago.

I parked the car across from the train station in East Los Angeles. For a moment we sat still as if we didn't want to leave one another's presence.

A train car rumbled through the station.

"I better get going." Charles opened the back door.

Art and I got out of the car to say goodbye. I handed Charles the pillowcase.

"What's this?" he asked, peering into the pillowcase.

"You'll find some money I was saving for a washer." I hadn't consulted Art about my gift and hoped he would understand. "And some fresh bandages, medicine, and tape. Make sure the wound is clean as it heals."

"You don't need to do this," Charles said.

"No, I do. I really do. And there's no way you can make it as a stowaway. Buy a proper train ticket."

Charles let out a deep breath. He knew I was right.

"I'm so sorry about how everything turned out," I said.

"Well, I'm better off than most. I have my two working legs and arms, and my head is finally on straight, at least most of the time."

Art took hold of Charles's hand and shook it hard.

"Be careful," I told him. "Please. I'll never forget you."

"I know." Charles smiled his crooked grin and limped over to the train station.

The murder of a gangster in the San Mark didn't end up in the *Rafu Shimpo*, but it was in the *Los Angeles Times* and *Daily News*. The *Times* mentioned his name, Fred "Ox" Shannon. According to reports, he had been involved in a bookmaking operation in Skid Row. He had apparently arrived recently from Chicago and was connected to a South Side syndicate called the Outfit. An LAPD spokesman was quoted saying that Ox might have been killed by another gang member. An investigation was ongoing. I just hoped that I would never see Charles Jones's name attached to the case.

Late that night while Art was taking a bath, the phone rang. I was almost afraid to answer it.

"Hello," I said tentatively.

"Mrs. Nakasone."

"Who is this?"

"It's Key Wakida."

"I never gave you my home phone number."

Key laughed. He was a private investigator, after all, and finding my number was probably easy as pie for him. "You and your husband have been in the middle of things, it looks like."

My heart began to pound. What did he know?

"Had a talk with my LAPD contacts yesterday. Your house was ransacked earlier this week."

"Nothing was taken. The police haven't told us anything."

"You don't have anything to worry about. It was a low-level gangster named Billy Utley. He was in cahoots with Babe."

"Really?"

"Billy and Babe cooked up a scheme to steal money from a gambling operation in Burbank. Billy told him the location and what time to hit it. But Babe pulled a fast one on him. He ran off with all the money without giving Billy his cut."

Why did Babe think he could outsmart a gangster?

"Police say Billy is the one who snitched to the Outfit about Babe. Detectives aren't quite sure who killed Ox, though. Nobody at the San Mark is talking."

I tried to calm my voice to mask my worries concerning

Charles eventually being identified as the killer. "How much do I owe you for this?"

"This one is on the house," Key replied.

"Well, thanks for calling," I said.

"Goodbye, Mrs. Nakasone. Hope to see you again in Little Tokyo."

Not if I can help it, I thought, hanging up the phone.

The next day I went to pick up my parents at Roy and Chiyo's place. We had stayed up all night to get the house cleaned up. Our china cabinet was half-empty. Without a doubt, my mother would notice. However, dishes could eventually be replaced—unlike lives.

I was so weary that I couldn't navigate the twists and turns of the Pasadena Freeway as I usually did. A few cars behind me honked their horns as the Model A crossed over the dividing line.

I had been so wrong about Babe. Here I had thought of him as a bumbling idiot because he had ruined my wedding pictures. But like Art said, those photos of our nuptials are filed away in my brain—I still carry them with me today. I don't have to have the physical ones to remember every detail—the sweet smell of the stephanotis corsage on Art's uniform or the smiles on the faces of our friends.

When I arrived at the Tonais', my father seemed ten years younger. He was clean-shaven and his eyes sparkled behind his spectacles. Roy, meanwhile, looked a bit peaked. "I hope my parents' stay wasn't too much for you all," I said to Chiyo as she helped me carry the suitcases to the car.

"He kept Roy up late every night," Chiyo whispered in my ear, "talking about how wrong the new owners are and how he was going to enjoy watching them lose the market."

I hoped that my father had not succumbed to drinking

during these late-night conversations. I couldn't ask, because I couldn't let on that he had problem, although I suspected the Tonais were well acquainted with his weakness for liquor from his conduct at parties before the war.

"How's Art doing?" Chiyo asked as we walked up the steps to the porch.

"Huh?"

"You know. I didn't tell a soul—even Roy. About Art having mental problems. I've heard of other boys dealing with shell shock, but Roy's okay."

Why did Chiyo sound like she was bragging about such a devastating subject?

I didn't doubt that Roy had emerged from the war relatively unscathed. He hadn't been on the front lines of the battlefield like Art and Babe. "Art's fine. Better than fine. He even got a promotion at work." Chiyo was apparently unaware of the poor salary of journalists at ethnic newspapers because she seemed impressed.

We lingered on the porch for a few moments. Chiyo obviously wanted to unload her intimate thoughts. "We'll need to turn the guest room into a nursery."

"You mean—"

"No, not yet. But soon."

I crossed my arms, holding in opinions that were threatening to burst out.

Chiyo abruptly changed the subject. "Esther must be heartbroken about Babe."

I couldn't help but sigh. Between her trying to trick Roy into fatherhood and gossiping about people I had never met, my patience was wearing thin. "You keep talking about this Esther. I don't know who that is," I said.

Chiyo's round face glowed with anticipation of sharing some juicy scuttlebutt. "Oh, Esther Senzaki. The laundry woman's daughter. You asked for her mother's information the other day. She was always a little high-strung."

"You mean Etsuko?" My attention was piqued.

"Oh, I keep forgetting about her Japanese name. Yes, Etsuko. She was a star softball player herself. Obsessed with Babe. Never missed a game of the Gila River Eagles. She was beside herself when he got drafted. I'm sure that she had planned to become Mrs. Watanabe someday."

I hadn't figured the surly young woman I'd met briefly in the laundry woman's apartment could be so passionate. I was gradually learning that I couldn't judge a person based on one encounter, mistake, or accident. I would continue to jump to conclusions throughout my life but I like to think those occurrences are now few and far between.

As I drove my parents home, my head pounded. My mother, who sat beside me in the front, kept talking about how Mrs. Tonai refused to leave her room so Chiyo was forced to leave meals on a tray outside of her door. And how Chiyo was a much better cook than I was, and that I should see if she could give me some lessons.

Again, "*Hai, hai, hai.*" I acknowledged that I had heard her observations. I was completely depleted from treating Charles.

Later when Art and I were in bed, I told him that I had been wrong about Babe. "Talking with Gloria completely changed the way that I see him," I said to Art.

"What, that a white woman could give him the time of day?"

"No, that she really loved him. That Babe was worthy of that much love and adoration."

"You really didn't think much of him, did you?"

"I don't know. I guess I never really knew Babe. Even though you had spoken so highly of him—"

"You didn't believe me."

"No, it's not that. He just didn't make a good first impression."

"You really resented him for not being able to deliver on the wedding photos."

I blushed. It was embarrassing now, after all that had transpired, that I could be so petty and self-centered. "Yes, and when I first saw him at the hospital, I feared the worst. I didn't want to even consider that he had abused his father, but who else could have done such a thing?"

"I'm starting to hear more stories from Hawaii about that. Some of our boys are having a rough time of it."

We both lapsed into silence.

"Well, it's over now. Mary had told me that the newspapers and police see it as gang warfare. Nothing about a Black vet from the 92nd." Art must really have believed what he had said because he promptly fell asleep, snoring after a few minutes, with no sign of nightmares plaguing him.

I, on the other hand, couldn't get to sleep. Whenever I had problems with insomnia in Tropico, Rose was the only one who could settle me down. I dozed a few minutes only to start awake. Finally, around five o'clock, when the rooster from a block away was crowing, I dragged myself out of bed and made myself a strong cup of green tea. From the living room table, I watched the sunlight wash over our porch. Something was stuck in my craw, a detail that I had seen but couldn't properly connect. I went to collect my hand-washed uniform, which I had tossed in a laundry basket a few days ago. I had failed to hang it up as I took it down from the line in the backyard and there were deep creases down the middle.

Setting up the ironing board in the living room, I smoothed out the wrinkles with a new iron with an aluminum plate that I had purchased on Brooklyn Avenue. I had brought one from Chicago, but the plate had rusted quickly. I preferred washing to ironing. Ironing required a certain precision that I didn't have—at least, not for purposes of personal appearance. I thought about Mr. Watanabe, how meticulous he was about his clothes. He had been a humble driver, but also a bit of a dandy. The bamboo basket left on the floor of his room had been bothering me this whole time. It seemed so out of place in a tiny bachelor apartment.

My goodness! The fourth set of fingerprints. I had assumed that a Burbank gangster had handled the gun, but now it was becoming clear that someone else had shot Mr. Watanabe dead.

Judging from the sounds from my parents' bedroom, they were starting to rise. I quickly put on my uniform and left before anyone could ask me any questions.

Mrs. Senzaki's door was open, like the last time I had visited. An Issei man emerged with a folded stack of white shirts. He bowed slightly to me and I returned the greeting. This morning the familiar smell of rice starch made me feel nauseated instead of nostalgically transporting me to my Tropico days.

"Senzaki-*san*." I stood in the doorway as she angled her hot iron around the collar of a shirt. I never was very good about collars.

"Oh," she said. Her body, which had been so involved in her physical task, now seemed deflated. She obviously suspected that I was here for nothing related to her small business.

I didn't bother to say a proper hello, a sign that I wasn't there under friendly circumstances. I crossed my arms. "You weren't telling me the whole truth, were you?"

Mrs. Senzaki gave me a blank look.

I dove in. "Laundry was delivered to Watanabe-*san*'s apartment the day he was killed."

"I was here, washing clothes."

What had Willie Mae said? She had first described the

laundry woman as a girl. Maybe she hadn't been wrong. "But Etsuko wasn't."

Steam seeped from the iron as it rested on the ironing board.

Mrs. Senzaki, whose cheeks were already pink, flushed bright red. "No, no deliveries to Watanabe-*san* that day."

A bamboo basket—a little larger than the one at Mr. Watanabe's—sat in the corner. It was the same tightly woven pattern. Could they be mates? Mom used to have a similar woven basket set that held her belongings when she came to America. "Then why was a basket like this one full of ironed shirts on the floor of Mr. Watanabe's room?"

"Anyone can have a basket. And why should I be responsible for how a bachelor tends to his living situation?" Mrs. Senzaki's speech sped up, the Japanese words slurring into each other. She was clearly agitated, quite a different woman from the one I had first visited. "You need to go, Nakasone-*san*. I'm quite busy."

"Did she see who shot him? Why hasn't she come forward?"

"Get out!" This woman who seemed so kind and congenial during our first meeting had transformed into a demon. Her shriek must have cut through the thin walls of the low-income hotel. I heard stirring in the adjacent rooms.

I didn't move. I tried to remember our first conversation. Mrs. Senzaki hadn't said outright that Babe had abused his father. But saying that he seemed demon possessed—she didn't have to share that with me, a perfect stranger. Was she that crafty, carefully planting seeds of suspicions regarding Babe's mental health? And why had she foisted that *senninbari* on me? To portray herself as a woman who only had the best interest of the Watanabes in mind?

"Get out!" she repeated, again and again. She grabbed hold of her steaming iron, yanked its cord from the outlet, and advanced toward me. I snatched the closest possible weapon, a broom, and was getting ready to defend myself when Esther emerged into the main room. "Stop it! Stop it, both of you!" She went to the front door and slammed it closed to any lookie-loos.

"I won't leave until I hear the truth," I said, my hands still clutching the broom handle.

"Her husband works for the *Rafu Shimpo*," Mrs. Senzaki warned her daughter. "Et-*chan*, go back into your room."

"No, Mama, I want to tell her. I wanted to tell the police, anyway."

"Et-*chan*!" Mrs. Senzaki was livid, a vein bulging on her smooth forehead.

Esther plopped down in a faded fabric love seat. She wore a loose knit skirt and plain white T-shirt. "It will be a relief. I haven't been able to sleep for weeks." Her smooth face revealed nothing of her insomnia. "I loved him. He was such a pure person. No one is as pure as he was."

Her plainspoken declaration of love and respect for Babe Watanabe shocked me. We Nisei women tended to keep our feelings more hidden, especially in the presence of strangers. But Etsuko "Esther" Senzaki was not your average Nisei woman.

"Oh, just to say it out loud is a relief. To have all of my feelings bottled up so long was making me sick. See, Mama, I'm feeling better already."

Mrs. Senzaki was now looking very ill herself. She swiped her hot iron over a shirt, occasionally completely missing the ironing board.

"He never pretended that he was suave and cool like other Nisei boys." In her mind, Esther had transported herself back to the baseball diamond of Gila River. She was eager to engage in such romantic conversation. It didn't seem like she had any peers to confide in. "He would teach me how to improve my throws. He even said that I was probably good enough to play baseball with men."

I understood the power of compliments—real, well-observed ones. Esther felt that Babe saw her—and he probably had, at least on the baseball field.

"I prayed for him regularly when he was in Europe." As Esther continued, I noticed the Buddhist altar in the corner of the room. An orange was placed in front of the altar. "Wrote him, too. And he wrote me back sometimes. But then something happened in early 1945. All letters from him stopped. I knew that he was in trouble."

Esther was regularly corresponding with Babe? I couldn't believe it. "When did you find out that he had returned stateside?" I purposely kept my voice light, as if we were two girlfriends chatting about boys that we liked.

"When my mother began to do laundry for his father. Babe was hospitalized but I knew that he would be all right. I would someday be able to meet him here in Little Tokyo. Seven o'clock every Monday at the San Mark, Mom would deliver the laundry to Mr. Watanabe. And then she mentioned that she had seen Babe there. So I started to deliver the laundry. When I saw him one morning, I could barely speak. I handed him the shirts and practically ran out of the room." Her cheeks became rosy with the memory.

Mrs. Senzaki, who had been intently focused on her daughter's revelation, spoke up. "Et-*chan*, stop it. You don't have to say anything to her."

Esther flatly ignored her mother. "The next week, Mr. Watanabe was still in bed when I arrived. He was by himself. He saw right through me. He made fun of me. Told me that I was too late. That Babe was off to get married to a *hakujin* woman, no less. How Babe was a ne'er-do-well. That he would never amount to anything. That Babe had stolen money. He had discovered the money, gun, and a pillowcase with two cut eyeholes in his room."

Mr. Watanabe knew exactly what his son had done? I was stupefied. And he obviously was not a protective father—quite the opposite.

"On the floor was the gun. I told him to stop talking. But he kept going and going. Babe was a criminal who deserved to go to jail. He was ready to report him to the police, in fact."

Did Mr. Watanabe resent his son so much that he would sell him out?

Esther was now sitting upright, her powerful fists clenched. "How could he talk so harshly about his son? I couldn't let him go on and on." She bared her teeth; her bottom ones were especially crowded together. "I picked up the gun and it went off. I wasn't intending to shoot him. I ran out of there."

"Are you going to tell the police?" Mrs. Senzaki challenged me in Japanese. Her iron was still steaming and I wondered if it could be used as a lethal weapon against me.

"Maybe you should tell them yourself."

Esther's broad shoulders were hunched over. It was as if she was melting right in front of me. "I never had a chance to tell him how much he meant to me. He got me through camp." Esther Senzaki was one of those passionate people whose devotion to a loved one was unyielding.

"Get out, Nakasone!" This time Mrs. Senzaki spoke clearly in English. "Never come here again."

CHAPTER 21

I felt raw after leaving the Senzakis'. Esther had confessed to me, but what was I going to do with that information? Art and I had already compromised ourselves by not coming forward about the shooting of Ox Shannon. We felt that we owed it to Charles to hide the truth for his personal safety, not to mention ours and our loved ones'. Life had been much simpler before the war, when I was a teenager growing up in Tropico. People had had the power to hurt me—not so much physically but emotionally—so I learned to spend time by myself with my loyal dog, Rusty. In Manzanar and Chicago I'd learned that I couldn't survive alone, that I needed trusted people around me. Even though I was hardly aware of it at the time, getting married to Art was the sign that I was leaving my old ways behind me.

Still, a nagging sense of guilt tugged at me. I knew who had killed Mr. Watanabe, yet I wasn't going to report it to the authorities. Art was conflicted about Mr. Watanabe, knowing that he had been such an unsupportive father to his best friend. But I had been there when the senior Watanabe had been at his weakest, at least physically. I needed to talk to someone about my dilemma after my shift at work was over. I wasn't about to talk to a minister. I could, however, go to someone who was the closest thing to it in my life.

Hammer and I sat on some wooden stairs on the back of the hostel. He took out a pack of cigarettes from his shirt pocket. It seemed like all the Nisei men around me were smokers.

As he lit his cigarette with a lighter that I recognized from Chicago, I began to talk:

"You've heard the latest about Haruki Watanabe's killing."

"Sure. Everyone has been saying it was those gangsters in Burbank."

"Only it wasn't."

That captured Hammer's attention. "What do you know?"

"I can't say too much. But I've found out that it's a Nisei. I'm not sure what I should do. I wasn't a witness. If I report it, it will be one person's word against mine."

"What does Art think?"

"I don't know. I'm going to talk with him tonight."

"I'm not a fan of the police."

"I thought that you were going to be a man of the cloth."

"I've had run-ins with them in the past. But that was all my doing. Do you know that I was sent to Boys Town in Nebraska for stealing door latches from camp?"

From my lack of a response, Hammer understood that I'd known.

"Geez, the scuttlebutt in camp is something else," he said.

"I actually heard it in Chicago."

"Great." He blew out smoke and then grinned. "I decided that I'm not going to seminary. I don't have anything in common with those seminary boys. If they hear what I've done—"

"But I thought Jesus hobnobbed with the dregs of society."

"You know your Bible better than you let on." Hammer tapped his cigarette ash onto the stairs.

"I know enough," I said. "Is Haru okay with you not becoming a pastor?"

"Okay? She's elated. The last thing she wants is to be a pastor's wife. Besides, do you know how much money I can make as a gardener? As long as I work day and night, six days a week, I can be pulling in a good sum of money, more than I would make as a minister, for sure. I'm hoping to buy rental property someday."

"Hammer Ishimine, real estate tycoon. I like the sound of it."

Hammer leaned back and laughed. "By the way, Elmer Yamamoto just let me know last night. The court ruled in my favor. Daniel is officially my charge."

"Oh, Hammer." I covered my mouth, which had fallen open in pure joy.

"I think it must have been your letter that did the trick. 'Transported a young girl from the Winona trailer camp and got her medical treatment.' You were the one who actually saved Shiz, Aki. Not me."

"No, I couldn't have done it on my own."

Already Hammer's face had changed shape. It was less angular and tight around his mouth. He was starting to look like a happy person. "We'll be moving out of here into an apartment a couple of blocks away."

"So still near Evergreen."

Hammer nodded. "How about you? You staying in the area?"

I didn't have to think long about my answer. Even with the threat of the gangsters, I wasn't going to let anyone force us out of our home. We had moved too many times already. "We won't be moving," I said. "We'll be staying around Evergreen, too."

When Art came home that night, I told him that we needed to have a meeting in the bedroom. As these early evening convenings were becoming more frequent, I noticed Mom look knowingly at Pop. *It's not that*, I wanted to tell her. *Don't even think about being a grandmother anytime soon.* If she knew that we were discussing matters of crime and punishment, she would be sorely disappointed.

Propping our backs with our pillows on the bed, I told Art the whole story involving Esther Senzaki.

"Should I go to the police, even though the mother will hate me forever?"

"It's just going to be your word against her daughter's."

That was exactly what I was thinking, too.

"It seems like the daughter—what's her name, Esther?— wants to talk, anyway. I bet in due time she'll come forward. In the crime stories that we've been covering, it seems like many times the guilty party wants to be found out."

Esther Senzaki wasn't a typical person, however.

"We probably need to say something at some point," Art said. "We should write all of this down, to keep a historic record, at least."

"Well, you can," I told him. "You're the writer." I only journaled and what I wrote was only for myself.

"You need to, too. What if something happens to me? It will be up to you to tell our story."

"Don't be that way," I told Art. At times, he was too melodramatic. I didn't want to think about one of us outliving the other. "Sometimes you are too over-the-top."

"What's wrong with that?"

"It's a burden, you know. Especially for me."

"Well, then, ignore it."

"I will," I said definitively. But here I am all these years later, putting it all on paper.

CHAPTER 22

My mother surprised me. She said nothing about our missing chinaware. Our busybody neighbor across the street even questioned Mom about the bags of trash that Art and I had left on the curb after our marathon cleaning. Mom told her to mind her own business.

My mother did, however, ask me about the *senninbari*, which Art and I had forgotten underneath one of the patio chairs. While I was at work, Mom had carefully washed it and hung it on the laundry line in the backyard to dry.

"Did someone make this for Art?" she asked, after presenting the fabric belt to me, clean and perfectly folded.

"Ah—" I sat at the dining room table, resting after a hard day's work.

"This is very precious. *Odaijini.*" She emphasized that I needed to take good care of such important gifts.

I didn't want to think anymore about Babe Watanabe. I realized, though, that I had that luxury. My husband, although psychologically affected, was alive and physically well by my side. Gloria Reed couldn't say that about the man she loved.

I wrapped the *senninbari* in one of my mother's crocheted doilies and tied a yellow silk ribbon around it. I left work the next day right at three and took a bus to Pasadena.

I wasn't planning to see Gloria. I was hoping that she had

already left for the day so I could leave my package with a receptionist. But when I arrived at Dr. Sidney Reed's office, there she was, arranging some files. Instead of a tight bun, she wore her hair down, brilliant red streams against her crisp white uniform.

"Oh," I said, feeling terribly self-conscious. "I was going to leave you something."

Her gaze rested on the wrapped *senninbari*. "I'm glad that you are here. Can you stay for a bit?"

We decided to take a stroll in the neighborhood, in the opposite direction of the Colorado Street Bridge. Gloria led us to a pristine paved pathway through a manicured green lawn. The feather-like leaves from expansive pepper trees swept down, grazing our heads.

A part of me felt sisterly toward Gloria, even though she was practically a stranger. But her love for Babe flowed to Art and me by virtue of the men's friendship. "I haven't had anyone really to talk to about Babe," she explained. "My friends were against my romance with Babe from the very start."

I studied our white nursing loafers as we matched each other's stride. My shoes were scuffed and dirty, while hers seemed freshly polished. "Our relationship faced so many obstacles," Gloria said. "I told Babe that it shouldn't be so hard to be together. But every time I tried to pull away, something pulled me back to him. Like our hearts knew that we belonged together."

Her vulnerability was a bit disorienting. I wasn't used to such plainspokenness about feelings, but attempted to adjust.

"My mother is the main person who couldn't accept Babe." Gloria had a strange rhythm in her speech. She spoke the beginning of her sentences slowly but quickened her words as she went along. "She was against him being Japanese and all. I guess I even felt the same when I first met him, too." She fingered a piece of stray hair behind her ear. "You see, my brother, Adam, was captured in the Philippines and forced out of Bataan on foot. He didn't make it."

"I'm so sorry," I said. I felt heartbroken for the Reed family. We Americans had heard about the Bataan Death March, how the Japanese military had brutalized Philippine and American prisoners of war. During this sixty-mile march, these captors would regularly beat men who merely asked for water. I couldn't believe how depraved human beings could be at their lowest points.

"But you know that Babe was American," I said. "He fought to defend our country against the Axis powers in Europe." Our black hair and Asian faces could not be confused with those of her brother's captors.

"Of course. I knew that." Gloria frowned, a line appearing above the bridge of her nose. "And so did my father. It's just that my mother doted on my brother. She couldn't separate the soldiers who brutally abused him from Japanese Americans born here. She thought they were the same."

She wasn't alone. Didn't General John DeWitt declare "a Jap is a Jap," whether we were US citizens or not, before the government locked us up in the ten camps? Even the *L.A. Times* published an editorial in February 1942 that said Nisei were "vipers," claiming that our allegiance was to Japan, a country that many of us had never gone to, over America.

"She refused to get to know Babe." Gloria crossed her arms. "The real man he was. A bit shy around women, but fiercely loyal to his friends. So kind."

I soaked in her devotion to him. I hadn't known Babe in the same way. But I couldn't deny that he was a true-blue friend.

"When he first proposed to me, I said no. I couldn't imagine going against my mother like that. He eventually won me over, though. He wanted to make a new life in Seattle. He said he had some military buddies there. He received a windfall from his father's Arroyo Grande property, did you know that?"

I suppressed an urge to blurt out, *There was no windfall. Babe and his father lost the Arroyo Grande farm. Babe stole the money from mobsters.*

I could not burst Gloria's bubble, her dreams about her future with Babe.

"We had enough money to buy a house in Seattle and make a new life."

I had never been to Seattle but knew of many Issei and Nisei who had lived there. To me, it seemed like the great wilderness, with rivers full of salmon and mountains dotted with cedar trees. That would indeed have been a perfect place for Babe and Gloria to start their new life together.

We looped back to the hospital when the pathway reached a residential area. As we sauntered under the shade of the pepper trees, I noticed clusters of bright pink berries, hidden beneath the protection of the loose-hanging branches. I would not have noticed the presence of those colorful berries if I hadn't bothered to look.

Spending the late afternoon with Gloria made me feel wistful. I missed Rose. I was back home in Los Angeles but the landscape still felt foreign and disjointed. Later that week, when I was running errands in the Model A, I felt a pull to go to our old house in Tropico again. When I arrived, I regretted it.

The house, repainted white, had received a facelift. In the front yard stood the same woman I had seen before, this time watering the baby blue delphiniums and orange ranunculus. As I watched the blooms sway, I started to feel nauseated. This wasn't my home anymore. Before I drove away, that same mangy old dog returned to the property.

"Oh, shoo." The woman aimed her hose at the animal.

He retreated but then attempted to enter the yard from the driveway.

Intrigued, I got out of the car and approached the front fence. "I've seen that dog before," I said to her.

"Yes, he's quite a menace. He keeps coming around here and ruining my flowers. Goes into my backyard, too. Around the neighborhood, we call him our ghost dog."

He was a bit ghostlike. I wasn't sure if his medium-length coat was gray or black, but his muzzle was white. His floppy ears lay uneven on his head.

Mom will kill me, I thought. By the time he proceeded to lick my hand, he had completely won me over. I stuck him in the back seat and as I piled into the driver's seat, the woman with the hose stared in astonishment.

As I drove to Boyle Heights, the dog paced on the back seat. *Oh my goodness, what have I done?* Every time I stopped and turned, he rewarded me with another lick around my neck.

When I reached Evergreen, I spied Art crossing the street with his briefcase. After making a left turn, I slowed beside him and rolled down the window. "Hello!" I called out. "I have a friend with me."

After I stopped the car, Art got in the passenger seat and turned to the back. "Who is this?" The dog was apparently as open to men as women because he promptly began licking Art's hand. In response, Art scratched the dog's chin. He adored animals as much as I did and his greeting further melted my heart.

"Tropico," I said. "His name is Tropico."

When I drove into our driveway, Kilroy as usual jumped on the chain-link fence and made a racket. Art carried Tropico out of the back seat, but our stray got loose and started barking right back at Kilroy, confusing the German shepherd. Kilroy backed off, continuing to bark but from quite a distance.

I opened the fence to our backyard, wondering what story I was going to tell Mom.

I didn't have to wait long. She was standing on the concrete steps leading to the backyard. She laughed, watching Kilroy's reaction to this newcomer. If only to terrorize the Fujitas' dog, Tropico had already won her over.

We only had a few hours to prepare for dinner, a thank-you to the Tonais for hosting my parents. Fortunately we were serving sukiyaki, which required only chopping and slicing. Roy and Chiyo arrived on the dot, and I was surprised but happy to see that Mrs. Tonai had felt up to attending. Her gray hair had become so thin that I could see her scalp in places. Her eyes were as heavy-lidded as a tortoise's. It must have been Mom's sukiyaki that had enticed her to come; she steadily ate the meat, stewed vegetables, tofu, and noodles with deft use of her chopsticks.

After we finished eating, Chiyo joined me in the kitchen to wash the dishes.

The Senzakis' quick departure from Los Angeles was the talk of the Gila River crowd. "I don't know why they left in such a hurry," Chiyo said. Apparently they had not bothered to inform their laundry customers, and had even failed to return some items of clothing to their rightful owners.

I wondered where the mother and daughter had ended up. Their relationship already seemed tenuous, and Esther was certainly on the edge.

Later, when Roy was helping me take out the trash, I had a chance to have a private word with him. "You can't carry everyone on your shoulders, Roy."

"Everyone is depending on me. Like your father."

Pop needs to move on, too, I thought.

"Truthfully, I don't think that we can get Tonai's back. Too much time has passed. It's probably better if I come up with something new."

Kilroy gnashed his teeth at us as we walked toward our metal trash cans with our brown paper bags.

"I'm kind of thinking of international trade," Roy continued. "I've know some MISers who are serving in occupied Japan. They may have some business leads there."

I lifted the trash can lid. "Well, then do it."

Roy stuffed the bags filled with broken eggshells, dirty napkins, and other rubbish into the can. "I'll be starting from scratch."

Welcome to the club, I thought. "By the way, is Mildred Yamato still working for you?"

"No, not you, too. Did Chiyo say anything?"

"Well," I hesitated. I didn't want to tattle.

"We were part of the Japanese Trojan Club together back when I was at USC. She's like my kid sister. Like you."

If only Mildred resembled a regular little sister instead of a Rockette. "It just kind of looks bad," I said to him, making sure I secured the trash can lid.

"You think that I care how I look?"

We returned to the dinner party. I served apple cobbler with vanilla ice cream from Currie's ice cream parlor on Brooklyn. Out of the corner of my eye, I noticed that Roy had brought a chair right over to Pop, who was resting in the easy chair. While their voices never rose, their conversation seemed intense and purposeful. When the Tonais left, I found out that Roy had taken my advice to heart.

"Roy gave up on the produce market," Pop announced. He slumped in his chair, as if he had been shot in the heart. My father obviously also felt abandoned.

I tried to change the subject with some good news that I had heard at the hospital. "The JACL has been talking about getting American citizenship for the Issei."

Mom had heard the same rumors. "So it's true? *Hontou?*"

"Yes, *hontou!*" I replied. Even Dr. Isokane had mentioned that he thought that it could happen, and he wasn't the type to jump on any bandwagon unless there was solid evidence supporting it.

"Aw, fuck them." Pop propped himself up, got to his feet, and stormed into the bedroom, slamming the door behind him.

I was stunned. I had never heard my father use such crass language. I wasn't sure who "them" were. The government, our competitors who hated us, the JACL, or maybe the world in general. Before the war, Pop would have stood at the front of the line to become an American citizen.

After Mom and I washed the dessert bowls, we each retreated into our respective bedrooms.

"I guess Esther Senzaki got away with it," I told Art when I joined him in bed.

Art put aside the book that he was reading and pinched the bridge of his nose. "I don't know if she really got away with it."

"What do you mean? She and her mother are gone to who knows where. And probably with the mob's money, too." I pulled the sheets and blanket up to my chin.

"When something like that happens, you never forget," Art said, and then turned off the light on his nightstand.

CHAPTER 23

Before too long, Art's Chicago family—his parents, younger sister, and widowed aunt—came to visit us. Even though our small Boyle Heights house wasn't meant for so many occupants, there was no money for an extravagance like a hotel. Art and I gave up our bedroom for Mr. and Mrs. Nakasone. We set up a cot in the hallway for Aunt Eunice. Lois slept on the love seat in the living room, while Art and I tried to make do on the floor with a futon that I borrowed from Chiyo and Roy.

Having Lois inches away at night reminded me of sleeping in the same room as Rose. Lois even breathed a little like her, occasionally inhaling deeply and then hiccupping air. I was thankful that she was a heavy sleeper and could not hear Art's nightmare moans. Even though it was difficult for me to rest well, I felt happy, cocooned in the presence of loved ones.

After the Nakasones returned to Chicago, Art and I resumed going to dinners at Far East Café with Nisei journalists. These gatherings had become a regular occurrence, held maybe once every three weeks. We arrived at one in October to find Mary No. 1 already planning what to order.

I sat next to her, hanging my new handbag from a purse hook on the table. "I actually read the Chester Himes novel," I announced.

"You did?"

"It reminded me of a person I used to know. You saw me talking to him, the first time I came to Far East."

"What's this?" Art sat on the other side of me.

"I was telling Mary that I read *If He Hollers Let Him Go*," I told Art.

"Yes, she was working hard on it. Every night for a month."

My face flushed. Sometimes Art's honesty could be flat-out exasperating.

Mary, however, wasn't fazed that I was a slow reader. "What did you think?"

"I could relate to how the protagonist felt that the prejudice in California was as bad as or maybe worse than in the Midwest. And how he was so seething mad sometimes that he couldn't see straight."

"You don't strike me as an angry person," Henry commented on the other side of our round table.

"You haven't seen her when I've purchased the wrong thing at the grocery store." Art attempted to make a joke, but Mary No. 1 and I didn't laugh.

"I've been reading up on escheat cases," I said. The California Supreme Court was, in fact, deliberating on a case right now in Riverside. "And also the details of a new proposition to make alien land laws part of the California constitution. We have to stop it."

Art put his hand on mine, and it wasn't a condescending gesture. He was proud of me and I was proud of myself.

The two killings of the Watanabe men had transformed me—not only personally, but also in a larger way. I realized that fundamental pursuits of happiness—receiving a fair share of the fruits of our labor, living wherever we wanted, and getting married to whomever we loved—could be thwarted and taken away from us at any time. And it was clear that the California judge's decision to take away the KKK's charter wasn't going to stop more cross burnings.

Hisaye arrived late and came with handbills advertising an upcoming dance at a Jewish community center in Boyle Heights. It wasn't like her to promote anything personal, so we knew that this was special. "My brother is going to be playing the horn," she shared, as the dishes of *homyu*, almond duck, chicken chow mein, and sweet-and-sour pork arrived at our table.

"We'll be there," we all chimed in.

When we got home, there was a letter from Chicago waiting for me. I had already heard the news from Chiyo, but it was nice that Louise was letting me know directly. "It's from Louise," I told Art. "The baby's full name is John Ryunosuke Suzuki. Ryunosuke is kind of a mouthful. I wonder where that came from?"

Art, already seated in the easy chair, put down his paper. "I think that may have been Louise's father's name. He was a well-known craftsman in the Pasadena area."

"Really?" Count on my husband to have already surpassed my knowledge about my own native Southern California.

"He died in camp, that much Louise told me that night at the Finale Club."

"Oh, how sad." I had never bothered to find out much about Louise's background. When I'd met her in Chicago, I'd been dealing with the aftermath of my sister's death and later I was consumed by my work at the Henrotin Hospital.

As my parents were already in bed, I brewed some late-night green tea for just the two of us. I carried the cups on a lacquer tray that was originally from my parents' birthplace of Kagoshima.

"Well, here's to Ryunosuke," I said, lifting my cup. I wasn't sure if I was toasting the elder or the newborn, but the name certainly encompassed both.

Art, who had a *neko shita*, a cat's tongue, blew on the surface of the tea to cool it before he joined in the toast. "Yes, Ryunosuke."

I hated to compare my two dogs, but I couldn't help it. We'd had Rusty since he was a puppy; Tropico, however, had been living on the streets for a while, which had definitely affected his ability to obey human owners. Rusty would readily follow our commands, in some cases anticipating our desires and completing tasks before we even asked, while Tropico was completely ill-mannered, pulling on his leash and barking at other nearby dogs.

To help curb Tropico's worst behaviors, Art began to accompany me on evening dog walks. We'd go down Malabar and then zigzag from Evergreen to other residential side streets. I spotted a single red leaf on a sycamore tree in someone's front yard. "Look, Art, fall," I teased him. Art was missing the distinct changing of the seasons in Chicago.

Sometimes we'd walk along the sidewalk bordering Evergreen Cemetery. We wouldn't actually enter because we had Tropico, but we'd look at the gravestones through the wrought-iron gate. On the south side of the property stood a tiny chapel where we'd had a very small and private service for both Watanabes, father and son, with Pastor Nagano presiding. Hammer had helped us with the details. Gloria had brought a nice portrait of Babe in uniform and propped it next to the folded *senninbari*. "To safely transport him into the next world," she whispered in my ear. The Kaneharas had attended; Ken, who had inherited Babe's camera, had hobbled around taking photographs as that was the practice at many Issei funerals before World War II.

One evening after our walk, a strange piece of mail was waiting for me. It was a color postcard mailed from New York City. On one side was an image of a busy Chinatown scene above the printed title, "Greetings from Chinatown, New York." On the other side, my name, and our address, but nothing else. I flipped back and forth a couple of times. I was ready to throw it away when I noticed a sign that was circled in red pen: Chop Suey. And handwriting in small block letters: *THE BEST IN NYC.*

Soto-Michigan Jewish Community Center was one of the newer buildings in Boyle Heights, sleek and blocky with a series of windows open to passersby. The Jewish community leaders hosted intercultural nights for the various ethnic groups of Boyle Heights to gather under one roof. Tonight was the Art Whiting Orchestra with Hisaye's brother, Frank, playing the trumpet.

Everyone was there. I spotted Hisaye and her Black colleagues from the *Los Angeles Tribune* from the door as Art presented our tickets. Once inside, I approached Chole, who was holding on to a man. They were swaying back and forth even though no music had started playing. The man was handsome in an Anthony Quinn kind of way, with wide-set eyes and heavy eyebrows.

"Oh, who's this?" I said, knowing full well who he was.

Chole released her husband, who had recently returned from serving in the occupation of Japan. "Manny, Aki."

"Chole has written so much about you," Manny said. "Thank you for taking care of her."

"She's the one who has been taking care of me, the *guzu-guzu* girl," I replied.

I didn't know if Manny had picked up any colloquial Japanese while stationed in Tokyo, but he laughed whether he understood me or not.

Roy and Chiyo were talking to one of the leaders of the community center. No baby yet, but Chiyo seemed less frantic these days. Perhaps it was because Mildred had moved away to San Francisco and Roy had hired my father to be his new assistant in her stead.

I noted flyers for a community fundraiser on the refreshment table, reminding me that I had left some raffle tickets in the Model A.

"Oh, I forgot something in the car," I whispered in Art's ear before swiftly navigating my way out the door. The night air was crisp, making my body feel electric, and I felt prepared for something unexpected to come my way. I grabbed the envelope from the back seat and headed alongside other younger people to the community center, ablaze in lights.

Boyle Heights was beginning to feel like home. The Tropico I remembered did not exist anymore. Bronzeville was rapidly being reclaimed as Little Tokyo again. The dislocated people were staking new ground. I wondered about that family whose makeshift living quarters I had invaded when my pocketbook had been stolen. Where were they now?

As I reentered the community center, Art was there, standing in his—no, our—circle of friends. "Darling, let's dance," he said, his long fingers outstretched toward me.

I grabbed hold of his hand and together we walked to the dance floor.

AUTHOR'S NOTE

Evergreen is a work of fiction, but real events and even people travel through its scenes.

The *Rafu Shimpo*, my former employer, literally means "Los Angeles Newspaper," and was established in 1903. I've taken the liberty of making up gatherings with real journalists and columnists of the newspaper: Henry Mori, English editor and friend; Hisaye Yamamoto, noted writer of short stories that were published in esteemed magazines like the *Paris Review* and anthologized into a collection, *Seventeen Syllables*; Mary Oyama Mittwer, journalist and social thinker; and Mary Kitano of City News Service, whom I've referred to as Mary Koyano so that fiction should not be confused with fact.

State Attorney Robert Kenny did indeed successfully revoke the California charter of the Ku Klux Klan in 1946. (To serve my narrative, the hearing falls two weeks later in *Evergreen*.) And Mickey Cohen and his underworld cohorts did establish a foothold in Burbank in the 1940s and created a casino in the Dincara Stock Farm. But their involvement in fictionalized crimes in *Evergreen* is only imagined.

The San Mark Hotel was located on North San Pedro Street and a shoot-out with police ignited by a domestic squabble did occur in 1946. Other incidents set at the hotel are totally fictionalized.

My associations over the years with the *Rafu* as well as the Japanese American National Museum, Little Tokyo Historical Society, National Veterans Network, and Japanese American Medical Association have provided me with opportunities to get a fuller sense of what Little Tokyo and the larger community were like immediately after World War II.

Attorney Mia Yamamoto generously shared with me stories about her father, Elmer Yamamoto, a pioneering Hawaii-born Nisei attorney who indeed had his postwar offices in the San Pedro Firm Building. His personality and situation were fictionalized to serve this story.

Brian Niiya, as always, provided a vital list of news items—this time crimes committed by Nisei veterans who, in many cases, struggled with post-traumatic stress disorder or other medical issues after World War II.

My friendship and research work with Gwenn Jensen and Heather Lindquist provide *Evergreen* with its necessary lifeblood. I also thank Steve Nagano for sharing photos and snippets of his father's interview concerning the Nisei Baptist Church. Robert Shoji, the filmmaker behind *The Finale Club*, kindly reviewed the scene set in the historic jazz club in Little Tokyo and offered some helpful tweaks. Others who have helped to clarify and inform historic and cultural details include James Benn, Christine Sato-Yamazaki, Ben Pease, Michael Okamura, Gail Castro, Christilisa Gilmore, Barbara Phillips, Lynell George, Dr. Troy Kaji, Lian Dolan, and Colleen Dunn Bates.

In terms of motivation to get "*oshiri* in chair," I credit my writing sprint partner, Sarah Chen, as well as all the resources provided by Sisters in Crime. Also helpful was my high school classmate, Korie Brown.

Of course, none of this would have happened without the Soho Press crew, which includes my editor, Juliet Grames; publisher, Bronwen Hruska; and many others like Rachel Kowal,

Steven Tran, Paul Oliver, Sheri Cheatwood, Rudy Martinez, Taz Urnov, Yezanira Venecia, and copy editor, Julie McCarroll.

My steadfast agent, Susan Cohen, has been my first reader, cheering on the development of my characters and calling out places where my logic didn't make sense. I'm indebted to her enthusiasm and eagle eye.

For *Evergreen*, my husband, Wes, influenced me in more ways than I am aware of. Thank you for sharing your life with me.

MORE READING
AND RESOURCES

*E*vergreen investigates three various geographies in Southern California—Boyle Heights, Little Tokyo, and Burbank—as well as the return of Japanese Americans to Los Angeles after World War II.

The *Rafu Shimpo*, a Japanese American daily newspaper, restarted publication on January 1, 1946, and its archived issues, available in digital format at various academic institutions and my own Los Angeles Public Library, are absolutely invaluable in piecing together businesses and the transition of Bronzeville back to Little Tokyo. The Japanese American Citizens League's newspaper, *Pacific Citizen*, provides a more national context for community happenings.

Discover Nikkei is also a good online source for history articles. Notable are Greg Robinson's contributions, including a feature on Erna P. Harris, a columnist for the *Los Angeles Tribune* who supported Japanese Americans during their World War II travails.

As a lover of maps, I heavily rely on cartographer Ben Pease's Japantown project (www.japantownatlas.com).

I've mentioned many resources on the "resettlement" of the Japanese American population back to the West Coast in the *Clark and Division* notes section. Helping to add color to the Little Tokyo experience are interviews by Tom Sasaki, a field worker for the War Agency Liquidation Unit in Los Angeles, which can be accessed on Densho.org. Hank Umemoto's memoir, *Manzanar to Mount Whitney: The Life and Times of a Lost Hiker* (Heyday Books, 2013), speaks to life in a Skid Row hotel. Required reading on the topic of postwar Little Tokyo is Scott Kurashige's *The Shifting Grounds of Race: Black and Japanese Americans in the Making of Multiethnic Los Angeles*. Also vital are Hillary Jenks's perspectives in her article, "Bronzeville, Little Tokyo, and the Unstable Geography of Race in Post-World War II Los Angeles," published in the July 2011 issue of *Southern California Quarterly*. For more information about temporary housing like Evergreen Hostel, refer to Jeffrey C. Copeland's "Stay for a Dollar a Day: California's Church Hostels and Support during the Japanese American Eviction and Resettlement, 1942–1947."

Two Arcadia volumes, *Los Angeles's Little Tokyo* (Little Tokyo Historical Society) and *Boyle Heights* (Japanese American National Museum), are good photographic surveys of these two neighborhoods. More haunting are Marion Palfi's photos of children at the Evergreen Hostel and Otto Rothschild's images of a "Little Tokyo clean-up," which capture the families living in Bronzeville in 1944. The *Los Angeles Daily News* archives have the most searing images of the Winona trailer camp.

Lucky for me, George J. Sánchez's *Boyle Heights: How a Los Angeles Neighborhood Became the Future of American Democracy* was released in 2021, while I was writing *Evergreen*. His meticulous work beautifully provides a larger context for the Japanese American resettlement in the 1940s. I highly recommend this work for those seeking to learn more about this Los Angeles neighborhood's legacy and history. The Angels Walk LA guidebook on Boyle Heights, distributed by Metro, also provides great photos and nuggets of information. Boyle

Heights Community Partners sponsors a number of in-person events regarding the history of the area. I was fortunate enough to attend the Boyle Heights Community Public Menorah Lighting and Hanukkah Celebration at the historic Breed Street Shul on Sunday, November 28, 2021.

The significance of Evergreen Cemetery, where many friends and relatives are buried, is well documented, including in books like *Evergreen in the City of Angels: A History of a Los Angeles Cemetery* (Studio for Southern California History).

For a larger picture of Burbank, the Burbank Historical Society has some great exhibits that follow its development and relationship to Disney. For more nefarious stories, see *Mickey Cohen: The Life and Crimes of L.A.'s Notorious Mobster* by Tere Tereba. Various accounts in newspapers like the *Los Angeles Times* and *California Eagle* followed the KKK charter revocation hearing as well as incidents of cross burnings in Southern California.

Regarding life in the Burbank trailer park, see Densho's Winona Trailer Camp entry written by Kristen Hayashi, whose doctoral dissertation is an important contribution to understanding the government's culpability throughout history and specifically during the post–World War II years in disempowering Japanese Americans for both economic and political reasons. Her UC Riverside dissertation is titled, "Making Home Again: Japanese American Resettlement in Post-WWII Los Angeles, 1945–1955."

My former newspaper colleague Takeshi Nakayama, who lived in the Winona trailers with his six siblings, wrote a searing account of his experience in "Trailer Living," in the *Rafu Shimpo* holiday issue published on December 16, 1995.

To learn more of the exploits of the all-Black 92nd Infantry Division, I enjoyed Ivan J. Houston's *Black Warriors: The Buffalo Soldiers of World War II*, co-written with Gordon Cohn.

A very well-reviewed history book, *Half-American: The Epic Story of African Americans Fighting World War II at Home and Abroad* by Matthew F. Delmont was released at the time this manuscript was being finalized. For another side of the 100th/442nd Regimental Combat Team, see Tamotsu Shibutani's *The Derelicts of Company K: A Sociological Study of Demoralization.* On the topic of World War II soldiers and post-traumatic stress disorder, John Huston's documentary *Let There Be Light* is a haunting and earth-shattering account. Thanks to James Benn for directing me to this black-and-white film, which is available on various streaming platforms. And regarding the Pasadena-based McCornack General Hospital, there is the medical facility's newsletter, *Needle.* (I accessed the May 18, 1946 issue.)

There are so many excellent works on the migration of Blacks from the South to metropolitan cities like Los Angeles. To start off, there's Isabel Wilkerson's *The Warmth of Other Suns: The Epic Story of America's Great Migration.* For a more local focus, *Snapshots,* a series of books published by the Community Writers Group of Los Angeles, captures both the flavor of everyday living within Black families as well as extraordinary individuals. (Go to www.cwgla.org to order.) Chuck Haddix's *Bird: The Life and Music of Charlie Parker* contains one of the few descriptions of the Finale Club in Little Tokyo. And, of course, I heartily recommend that readers check out the novels by Chester Himes.

Regarding state legislation, race relations, and Los Angeles city politics, instructive sources are Tom Sitton's *Los Angeles Transformed: Fletcher Bowron's Urban Reform Revival, 1938–1953*; Kevin Allen Leonard's *The Battle for Los Angeles: Racial Ideology and World War II*, Mark Brilliant's *The Color America Has Changed: How Racial Diversity Shaped Civil Rights Reform in California, 1941–1978.*

The Italian American Museum of Los Angeles has a nicely compiled online student's resource on Judge Alfred Paonessa and his landmark decisions to preserve civil rights in California. Frank F. Chuman's *The Bamboo People: The Law and Japanese-Americans* is always a go-to resource.

I have written or co-written nonfiction works that may be of interest and helped provide *Evergreen* with its historic foundation and context:

Green Makers: Japanese American Gardeners in Southern California (2000), Southern California Gardeners' Federation.

An American Son: The Story of George Aratani, Founder of Mikasa and Kenwood (2000), Japanese American National Museum.

Co-authored with Dr. Gwenn M. Jensen, *Silent Scars of Healing Hands: Oral Histories of Japanese American Doctors in World War II Detention Camps* (2004), Japanese American Medical Association.

A Scent of Flowers: The History of the Southern California Flower Market (2004), Midori Books and Southern California Flower Growers, Inc.

Co-authored with Geraldine Knatz, *Terminal Island: Lost Communities of Los Angeles Harbor* (2015), Angel City Press and Port of Los Angeles.

Co-authored with Heather Lindquist, *Life after Manzanar* (2018), Heyday Books and Manzanar History Association.

For Chinese American contributions to the downtown Los

Angeles community, see Tara Fickle's "A History of the Los Angeles City Market: 1930–1950" (*Gum Saan Journal*, Volume 32, No. 1, 2010). The history of the Far East Café in Little Tokyo has been well documented on the website Discover Nikkei. Accounts by a member of the family, Raymond Chong, are especially illuminating.

I mentioned Valerie Matsumoto's delightful book, *City Girls*, in the notes for *Clark and Division*, and it's worth mentioning it again here. Her research on Mary Ogawa Mittwer has been invaluable. Another UCLA professor, King-Kok Cheung, has written extensively on Hisaye Yamamoto, including an article on her *Los Angeles Tribune* experience in "The Dream in Flames: Hisaye Yamamoto, Multiculturalism, and the Los Angeles Uprising," which was published in *Having Our Way: Women Rewriting Tradition in Twentieth-Century America* (Bucknell University Press).

Thelma M. Robinson's *Nisei Cadet Nurse of World War II: Patriotism in Spite of Prejudice* provides details of the vigorous training these health professionals had to undergo. (As a result, I decided that Aki probably couldn't have completed that program.) Also detailed is Rebecca Ann Coffin's "Nursing in Japanese American Incarceration Camps, 1942–1945." And Dr. Troy Kaji, the grandson of a cofounder of the Japanese Hospital, referred me to Susan L. Smith's *Japanese American Midwives: Culture, Community, and Health Politics, 1880–1950*, which provided hints on what the early reopening years of the Japanese Hospital may have been like.

The most knowledgeable academic on medical care within American's World War II detention camps is my friend Gwenn M. Jensen, whom I've dedicated this novel to. My great hope is that a book based on her dissertation research on the health consequences of the Japanese American incarceration will eventually be published.